RECLINING FIGURE

by MARCO PAGE

THE LOCALE OF *Reclining Figure* is California, particularly the exotic home of Lucas Edgerton, arbitrary and capricious eccentric, whose fabulous art collection was begun when Cézannes were a dime a dozen. To sell some paintings for tax purposes he has imported Ellis Blaise, young New York dealer. Thefts from the collection, the sensational forgery of a priceless Renoir and the puzzling murder of Simon Edgerton, Lucas' son, force Blaise into a perilous investigation involving:

Miriam Wayne, curator of Edgerton's collection, shrewd, handsome, with shadowy connections to the murdered man and others.

Cass Edgerton, Lucas' niece, for whose sake Blaise comes on.

Paul Weldon, young painter with more money than he can account for.

Molly Dann, lusty model and Simon Edgerton's ex-mistress.

Victor Grandi, mysterious technician of the collection.

Dr. Wesley Corum, critic and adviser to rich collectors.

Jonas Astorg, an important art dealer.

Hugh Norden, fly-by-night peddler of inconsequential art and occasional erotica.

Marco Page expertly blends characters and action into a fast-moving, literate, completely satisfying novel with an unusually colorful background.

RECLINING FIGURE

Books by Marco Page

FAST COMPANY

THE SHADOWY THIRD

RECLINING FIGURE

By MARCO PAGE

RANDOM HOUSE · NEW YORK

FIRST PRINTING

RECLINING FIGURE

1

Approached from Los Angeles, a level, straight stretch of road allowed the Ocean Inn to loom up gradually so that the arriving guest or passing tourist could study slowly, and in detail, the bewildering network of pointless setbacks and projections that twisted the exterior into a cubist nightmare. The structure had been condemned when three-quarters finished, then that portion had been rebuilt to comply with a slow succession of court orders while the remaining fourth proceeded according to the original plans. The finished product, even in a neighborhood with a restaurant built in the shape of a frying pan, was an outstanding eyesore.

The airport car deposited Ellis Blaise under the soaring porte-cochère and a doorman in an exotic Foreign Legion uniform took his bags into the lobby. This, and the other public rooms, were painted in stark, dramatic green, the color relieved at uncertain intervals by enormous white plaster brackets and ornaments.

Blaise registered at the desk and was taken upstairs by a loutish youth in the uniform of a St. Cyr cadet. The long narrow corridor was surgically bare and all the apartments and rooms had names stemming from the French or Italian Riviera. They passed "Antibes,"

"Juan-le-Pins," "Portofino," and "Nice," and then the boy ushered him into "St. Tropez."

The living room was small and furnished mostly with glass and tubing. It looked as if someone had taken apart a large condenser and been called away to some other duty before it could be assembled again.

The bedroom, being entirely functional, was better. A king-size bed rose barely eight inches off the floor and one wall was a row of built-in cabinets. French doors opened to a balcony directly over the beach. When the bellboy was gone Blaise took off his coat and went out.

It was a bright, clear day, still unmarred by the downtown smog, and the sand looked clean and inviting. The hotel's private beach was deserted, except for a few attendants in the tented bar and adjoining cabanas, but a few early pilgrims were already on the public strand. A battered refreshment stand was still boarded up at this hour, but the projecting counter was being improvised as a ballet bar for two stunning girls who were limbering already lithe and supple bodies.

Blaise watched the girls for a moment, then turned his face up to the early sun. A nearby voice said, "Good morning, Ellis."

Blaise turned left slowly, reluctantly giving up the warm sun. A neat, middle-aged man was watching from the next-door balcony. He recognized Jonas Astorg, an art dealer from New York.

"Lovely girls," said Astorg, waving his heavy hand in the direction of the public beach. "Something in the air, or perhaps the abundance of orange juice, tends to give the Southern California girls uniformly lovely legs, fine bodies and a clear skin." Regretfully, he added, "It also makes them grow too tall for an undersized European like myself."

4

"Tough luck," said Blaise.

Astorg extended a gold cigarette case over the waist-high barrier between the terraces. Blaise took one, then held a match to Astorg's cigarette and his own.

"Lucas Edgerton sent for you?" asked Astorg.

Blaise looked at him speculatively. "You wouldn't say that unless you knew."

Astorg chuckled. "Why be reticent and uncommunicative? What I know I will gladly tell you."

"Tell me."

"Do you know why Edgerton sent for you?"

Blaise shook his head. "He doesn't tell me much."

"He's going to sell some paintings."

"Is that why you followed me out here?" asked Blaise.

Astorg looked pained. "My dear boy. I arrived twenty-four hours before you did. I hardly think that can be called following."

"You know what I mean," said Blaise. "You're here in this hotel, next door. Is that an accident?"

Astorg smiled. "I might say it was if I thought you would believe me. No, Ellis, it is not an accident." He looked wistfully at the open door of Blaise's bedroom. "Could we not talk more comfortably inside?"

"I'm expecting a call."

Astorg nodded. "Very well. Edgerton plans to sell some paintings. He's worried about cash for inheritance taxes. I have some fine customers. Rich, sound collectors. Let's work together." He shrugged and made an artless gesture with his hands. "There—is that so complicated?"

"You say work together," repeated Blaise. "Do we work together for ourselves, or for Edgerton?"

Astorg leaned over his balcony, selected a spot on the beach below and let the cigarette fall. "A man like Lucas Edgerton pays a hundred dollars for a Cézanne. That's fine. It shows early taste, a pioneering instinct, a nice appreciation of obscure, difficult tendencies in art. Let's say that he gets thirty thousand for the painting when he sells it. That's a wonderful profit. He deserves it, mind you . . ."

"Especially if the painting is worth fifty or sixty thousand," said Blaise.

"I doubt if Edgerton has current values at his fingertips," said Astorg smoothly.

"Isn't that why he's hiring me?"

"You talk like a Boy Scout," said Astorg, for the first time betraying any impatience. "This is a chance you may never get again. What do you want to make—ten per cent?"

Blaise laughed. "I might take five." Then he heard the telephone in the bedroom of St. Tropez. "Excuse me, will you, Jonas?"

It took a few rings before Blaise found the telephone, which he located in a closed cupboard beside the bed.

"Mr. Blaise?" It was a girl's voice, cool and pleasant. "This is Miriam Wayne—Mr. Edgerton's secretary."

Blaise knew the name from correspondence. They passed over the amenities of his trip and his comfort in the hotel. Then Miss Wayne said, "Mr. Edgerton would like to see you this morning." Her voice was crisp and efficient now. "Please follow these instructions."

Blaise said, "I'm ready."

"Leave the hotel in just fifteen minutes—that will be at 11:38 exactly. Walk north two blocks on the highway to Emerald Lane. Turn into the Lane, walk slowly to the boulevard. A car will pick you up in the Lane. Is that quite clear?"

Blaise said, "Perfectly." He couldn't resist adding,

"Are we robbing a bank, Miss Wayne, or holding up a gas station?"

Miss Wayne started to say something, but a harsh voice came blaring in. "God damn it, Blaise, follow orders. Do as you're told!" There was a metallic crash as the extension phone was slammed into its cradle, then a moment of silence.

"Is that quite clear, Mr. Blaise?" asked Miss Wayne sweetly.

"I'll be there," Blaise told her, and hung up. He was annoyed with himself for not realizing that the old nut would be listening in. He had known Lucas Edgerton for two years and the relationship had begun and continued in this same furtive, secretive manner, never free from complicated rendezvous and schoolboy codes. He looked at his watch. Just eleven and a half minutes until 11:38. As he put on his coat he was annoyed again to find himself thinking, like Edgerton, in split seconds and fractions.

2

IT HAD BEGUN nearly two years before in Ellis Blaise's tiny second-floor gallery in New York. The holidays were approaching and in the "Main Hall," a cramped 12 x 20, Blaise was showing a variety of French paintings, water colors, drawings, prints and etchings priced at $500 and less in the hope of catching some Yuletide gift business. In his own office, an even smaller room, he was exhibiting eight primitive paintings of city scenes by Harris Little, a Negro clerk in the Department of Sanitation, who was Blaise's own discovery. His one-man show of Little's paintings earlier that year had been the first exhibition of the painter's work, but the reviews were patronizing and the patronage dismal. Blaise was reluctant to take down the show, even when attendance fell off to zero, and the paintings now hung in the office, a vaguely hopeful, mildly defiant gesture.

It was 2:30 now on this cold, raw December afternoon. Some kids prematurely released from school had tracked up the floor in the morning, and lunch time brought the usual assortment of browsers. Blaise was sprawled on the couch in his office with a pile of catalogues when he heard the gallery door open and close. He didn't see anyone at once (the gallery door was out of his line of vision) so he knew the visitor was working his or her way along the right-hand wall. He put down his catalogues, sat up on the couch and lit a cigarette. Then he saw the prospect and at first glance he realized the gallery had rarely sheltered a more unpromising visitor. He saw a man roughly past middle-age whose exact proportions could only be guessed because he was wearing a tight flannel jacket over several sweaters, the bottoms and collars of which made a haphazard fringe at his waist and throat. A gray flannel shirt, the collar askew, was anchored by a brown bow tie apparently knotted with reckless abandon on that or some other morning. The trousers were also gray flannel, but of a different shade, and the shoes, deplorably muddy, were or had been gray suede. The whole effect—reminiscent of a second-class Bowery flophouse—was topped by a thick, wet strand of stubby, wiry gray hair.

The visitor passed his door, continuing on out of sight

along the left-hand wall. Blaise's first impression, that it was a panhandler, he discarded at the succession of snorts that floated back to him as his collection was examined. He got up and went into the doorway. The visitor, with an expression of acute pain, was standing before a small Pascin water color.

"Anything I can do for you?" asked Blaise politely.

The visitor turned. "Yes. You can set fire to all this crap."

Blaise peered uncertainly at the old man.

"This junk," continued the visitor, waving a hand around the four walls, "is what gives modern painting a bad name."

"If you're interested in bad names," said Blaise coldly, "just stick around. I'm warming one up for you." The visitor eyed him curiously, with a partial smile. "What did you expect to find here, one flight up over a chain store—Vermeers?" He turned back into the office. Over his shoulder, he added, "Beat it. Try the Modern Museum—they like eccentrics."

He sat down on the couch again and took another cigarette. He turned to the desk for matches, and when he swung around again the old man was in the doorway peering in. Ignoring Blaise, he came closer to the big Harris Little that hung just inside the door. It was a glaring study of an East River dock, lighted by harsh, naked overhead lamps. It was one of Blaise's favorites.

"What's this?" asked the visitor.

"Rembrandt," said Blaise, puffing at his cigarette. "Very rare. One of the few paintings he did of New York."

The visitor turned to look at him. "You're a snotty boy," he said. "Are you generally this rough on customers?"

"Customer?" repeated Blaise. "What makes you think you're a customer?"

"This." Turning back to the painting the old man lifted it from the hook and down to the floor. Then moving swiftly around the room he did the same with all eight paintings. Blaise watched open-mouthed as he stacked them near the door. When he straightened up from the last move he said briefly. "My name is Lucas Edgerton. How much?"

"Edgerton!" Blaise nodded ruefully. "I suppose I should have guessed."

"How much?" insisted Edgerton.

"They're by Harris Little. He's unknown. This was his first show and . . ."

"What the hell do I care if it was his first show. I don't go by shows. How much?"

"If you take the lot, how about $250 each?" Blaise put this forward tentatively but Edgerton only nodded, took a frayed, folded check from his pants pocket and bent over the desk to fill it in with Blaise's pen. "My office will call to arrange about shipment," he said, while he filled in the check. His voice was formal and distant now. He left the check lying on the desk and straightened up.

Blaise said, "I'm sorry I didn't roll down the red carpet for you, Mr. Edgerton."

"You're doing fine," Edgerton told him. "Don't crowd your luck, son." He went out into the other gallery and paused for one last look around. "What I said still goes," he shouted. "Set fire to this crap."

Blaise was waving the check to dry it. "Yes, sir, Mr. Edgerton. Anything you say, Mr. Edgerton. Thank you, Mr. Edgerton, sir."

The old man looked back with a glare that lightened

suddenly to a smile, then disappeared into the narrow hall.

And that was the start of it. Blaise immediately assembled another group of paintings by Harris Little and wrote to Edgerton asking for some critical comment for the catalogue. The instant reply was an obscene, sulphurous refusal, followed in a day or two by a letter threatening suit if Edgerton's name was so much as mentioned. In the next mail came a glowing eight-page panegyric to be used as an introduction to the catalogue and the respectful suggestion that Blaise release all or part of it to the press before the opening to drum up early interest.

The entire show, twenty paintings and fifteen drawings, was sold on the opening day. Edgerton made an awesome personal appearance, attracting much more attention than either Blaise or the painter, and spent most of the day cursing Blaise for what he considered the inept way the show was hung.

Whatever they thought of Harris Little (and Blaise still found it hard to tell) collectors could not ignore Lucas Edgerton's opinion on anything connected with modern art. His own collection had assumed legendary proportions, even more so because the bulk of it had been acquired when the great names in modern painting were still obscure and unheralded. The exact extent of his hoard was largely a mystery but the few available clues indicated vast quantity and extraordinary quality. He was rumored to have more than a hundred Cézannes, as many Renoirs, great vaults and bins stuffed with masterpieces by Seurat, Degas, Manet, Pissarro, Sisley, and all the Impressionist masters. His accumulation of twentieth-century artists was on the same prodigious scale.

Edgerton never allowed the public to see his treasures, never loaned them to museums, refused information about them to even the most reputable curators, critics and historians. He was, however, the author of several books on modern painting, largely savage attacks on every aspect of taste but his own, and these were illustrated with paintings from the Edgerton Collection. They were stunning examples, and each publication brought a flood of letters from collectors and scholars pleading for a chance to see the paintings. In all but a few cases—chosen unpredictably, as was typical of Edgerton—the supplicant was turned away. If the writer was an obscure person he was let off with a polite refusal written and signed by a secretary, but if it was a well-known collector or critic, or a celebrity in any field, Edgerton himself would write a personal, savagely insulting reply. None but the very most thick-skinned ever wrote twice. His favor, like his rage, was bestowed capriciously, but even his worst enemies grudgingly conceded his knowledge and his taste.

After the second Harris Little exhibition, with the obvious and precious mark of favor contained in Edgerton's preface to the catalogue, Blaise became known as Edgerton's dealer. The relationship had been profitable and rewarding, but also at times so stormy that Blaise found himself thinking wistfully of quieter days in the Army. Under the successive layers of ego, selfishness, arrogance and greed that coated his great client's personality, however, there was a passionate love of art, a real sense of the quality in painting, no matter what name was signed to the canvas. Obscenely, sometimes comically intolerant, Edgerton's venom might be directed at every color and creed in turn or at once, but in art his taste knew no boundary. Also, even at his maniacal, infuriating worst, Edgerton maintained some sixth sense that told him uncannily when he had driven any associate to the quitting point, and he was then capable of rare charm, generosity and consideration.

3

BLAISE made his way along the highway, following orders to the letter, and turned into Emerald Lane on the dot. As he started toward the Boulevard a limousine driven by a chauffeur came in from the other end and slowed tentatively. He stopped and saw the driver lean across to roll down the window.

"Mr. Blaise?" asked the driver, and when Blaise nodded he climbed out to open the door. Blaise settled himself in the back and the car headed swiftly into the ocean highway, turning north toward Santa Barbara. They covered ten or twelve miles in barely as many minutes, then turned off into a narrow road in which there were no signs of life at all. The car slowed and the driver sounded a blast on the horn. Then, on the left, Blaise saw high, spiked iron gates. There was a tanned, husky gateman and a tough-looking unpedigreed dog was yelping around him. The gateman touched his cap respectfully as the car rolled past him, then started closing the barrier.

"Just like Fort Knox," said Blaise.

"Doesn't mean a thing," the driver said over his shoulder. "Mr. Edgerton thinks it scares off tourists. Matter of fact, that's the only part of the place is fenced at all and anybody can walk right on up from the beach. But I guess Mr. Edgerton gets a kick out of seeing the guards and the dogs when he goes in and out."

The house, when it was finally visible around the bend in the driveway, was tremendous. The main building was modified Colonial, with massive columns running to the third floor and a one-story wing at the right was connected by a covered driveway. Some of the detail of of the big house was repeated in the wing, but it was too long and too low to be completely harmonious.

Blaise got out of the car without assistance and saw a girl coming toward him from the covered driveway between the two buildings. She was a handsome girl, about thirty, in a light simple suit.

"I'm Miriam Wayne," she said, extending her hand. "I hope our telephone conversation didn't irritate you."

Blaise smiled. "I've worked for Mr. Edgerton for nearly two years."

"Then you know."

Blaise nodded. "Yes, I know. I wouldn't have been surprised if he wanted me to swim to a buoy and rendezvous with a submarine."

She laughed, but only briefly. A window in the second-floor of the dwelling flew up with a bang, and Lucas Edgerton leaned perilously far out of it. His speech of welcome was characteristic.

"God damn it, Blaise, what the hell do you think I brought you out here for? Stop rubbernecking and come on up here. You, Miriam, wait over in the library."

The window came down with a resounding thump and Edgerton disappeared in the curtained interior. Blaise looked at the secretary. There was a spot of color in her cheeks but she was well under control. "Sweet, isn't he?" she said. "This way, Mr. Blaise." She led him to the massive front door. "Upstairs, on the right."

Blaise went in, then stopped short. Correspondence, photographs, the books and the legends should have prepared him for his first glimpse of Edgerton's pictures in bulk, but the impact was overpowering. The enormous hall was all but plastered with paintings, hung frame to frame and from the floor up. Morever, there was no artistic chronology in the grouping, so that a massive cubist Picasso all but obliterated a delicate Manet; an enormous, vivid Matisse was in shocking contrast to the adjoining canvas, a sunny, precious Seurat. There were other incongruities and as Blaise started up the broad, winding stairs he saw that this area, too, was a jumble of paintings. Here some of the contrasts were even more disconcerting because there were superb classical paintings mixed in with the bold moderns. It was a riot of Bracque, Cézanne, Van Dyck, Roualt, El Greco, Pissarro, Renoir, and, halfway up, hung a good six feet above eye level so that it was almost impossible to see it at all, was a fabulous, tiny Vermeer. Blaise went up a few steps, then leaned back along the rail for a better view of this, and he was so engaged when Edgerton came into the upper hall.

Blaise pushed himself upright hastily. "Sorry," he said. "I resisted everything else, but that little Vermeer got me."

Unpredictably enough, Edgerton smiled. "It gets everybody. Some collection, ain't it?"

"Stunning. Why don't you hang it so it makes some sense?"

"Makes sense to me," said Edgerton, still with his rare, impish grin, "and, frankly, I don't give a hoot about anybody else." He beckoned peremptorily. "Come on. You can take the grand tour later on."

He led the way into his own quarters, a large room with big, curtained windows, monastically furnished with a large, flat table covered with books and papers, a narrow bed against the wall and two modern chairs—one at the table, one for a guest. There were no paintings on the walls, but a few canvases were stacked in a corner, the painted surfaces turned to the wall.

Edgerton closed the door, first putting his head out to look up and down the hall. He sat down at the table and waved Blaise into the chair on the other side. "Nice trip?" he asked grudgingly, as if the amenities hurt him.

"Pretty good," said Blaise. "I'm too big to be really comfortable on an overnight plane trip."

"Wouldn't risk my neck in one for a million a minute," said Edgerton. "God damn things are no good."

Blaise laughed. "That's nice advertising. Don't you still own most of the airline I came out on?"

"Sure thing," said Edgerton readily. "Owning an airline and riding an airplane that's two different things."

There was a pause as if Edgerton was having difficulty bringing the talk around to its point. Blaise knew him well enough to let him simmer until whatever he really wanted to say boiled over. "Everything all right at the hotel?" asked Edgerton.

"Fine. It's kind of an eyesore, though, isn't it?"

"Out here," said Edgerton, "that's a show place. Wait till you know the country. Every fairy with strength enough to lift a bolt of goods is a decorator. Some of them don't know enough about a house to dig a hole for a privy, but they go right on decorating. I've seen places here that cost half a million, with living rooms the size of the Painted Desert"—he chuckled—"wouldn't keep pigs in them." Then his grin faded abruptly. "How's business?"

"Pretty good," said Blaise. "I sold a Van Gogh." As Edgerton peered up at him suddenly, he added, "An early one. Dutch."

"Junk," was Edgerton's comment.

"And a Cézanne," Blaise added, unruffled by the interruption. "The still life from the Haller collection."

"Haller let it go, eh? Fatheaded ignoramus. Only decent painting he had." As Blaise smiled, he roared hotly, "What the hell are you laughing at? You made a few dollars peddling Haller's picture and now you think he's Jesus Christ Almighty! Hell, if it wasn't for me you wouldn't even be allowed in Haller's house. You'd still be peddling calendars."

"Very true," said Blaise. "And it's kind of you to remind me from time to time. Keeps me from getting a swelled head."

There was another pause, longer this time, and Blaise sensed that his patron was about to divulge the nature of his assignment. He was thinking back to Jonas Astorg, wondering how he knew Edgerton's decision and whether or not to precipitate a howling rage by divulging the leak, when Edgerton suddenly blurted it all out. "I want to sell some paintings. If you can handle an important job without falling over your feet, speak up and say so."

"Sure," said Blaise. "Why not?"

"It doesn't seem to mean a hell of a lot to you," said Edgerton irritably.

"I've learned to control my emotions," Blaise told him. "Makes me a better salesman, as a matter of fact." As Edgerton got up and walked toward the window, he added, "What's wrong?"

Edgerton turned to face him. "Nothing. Nothing special, that is. For all I know I may live to be a hundred, but I'm well past sixty and too much of my estate is tied

17

up in paintings. Some idiot from Washington might come down here, put a ridiculous value on everything and then where do I stand?"

"You might duck some taxes. Ever think about leaving part of the collection to a museum?"

"No numbskull tourists come gawking at my collection when I'm alive and they won't come after I'm dead." This declaration gave Edgerton at least a fleeting pleasure, and he returned to the table. "No, sir. Not a bloody single painting to any museums, schools, libraries or phony foundations."

Blaise laughed. "Public spirited as always, eh?"

"Public spirit, my eye!" exclaimed Edgerton. "What the hell did the public ever do for painting, or for any art? Show me where the public ever rushed around to help a painter with a new idea?—or a musician?—or a writer? Where was the public when a man like Franz Schubert was freezing and starving? Or when Van Gogh was going mad with neglect? Then in fifty or a hundred years, when their ignorant eyes are opened by people with taste, that's when the public whines that art should be a public trust, part of the national heritage, it belongs to the people. Well, anybody that doesn't know yet what I think of the people can read my will and find out."

"I could argue with you," said Blaise, "but it's your blood pressure and they're your paintings. Where do I start?"

"Go talk to Miriam," said Edgerton, as he sat down. "She'll give you a list of what I want to sell."

Blaise stood up. "I'll get busy."

"Don't get busy. Take it easy. If word gets out that I'm selling a lot of paintings you'll scare the hell out of the market and bring prices down. Play it smart. Take one at a time and pick a spot."

"I thought of loading them on a pushcart and hawking them up and down 57th Street," said Blaise.

"And don't be funny," said Edgerton wearily. "Go on. Get over to the library and start to work."

Blaise entered the library from the driveway door and found himself in a long, low room, a third of which was the library, with tall stacks of books reaching to the flat ceiling, the remainder a gallery for more of the Edgerton collection. A row of index and filing cabinets, chest-high, separated the two sections. As Blaise came in he heard an anxious, angry voice from the larger area:

"I know there's a sale coming. I've got to know what the old man is planning to let go. Don't get coy with me now, Miriam. I've got to know." Then Miriam Wayne's cool, easy voice, saying, "Ask your father. Or ask the run-down floozy who takes so much of your time. Or just go on sweating. You won't find out . . ."

By this time Blaise was at the row of cabinets. He rapped on the nearest one. "Anybody minding the store?"

Miriam Wayne had already moved a few steps away from her companion, a tall, handsome young man in a linen shirt and trousers. She looked at Blaise curiously. "This is Ellis Blaise, Simon," she said, and to Blaise, she added, "This is Simon Edgerton."

Blaise put out his hand and young Edgerton shook it firmly. "Glad to meet you," he said, and after a moment added, "Dad told me you were coming."

Aside from the incongruity of hearing Lucas Edgerton called Dad, Blaise's first reaction was that he had told Simon no such thing. Then Simon mentioned a date on the beach and left with more composure than Blaise would have expected from the agitated man whose voice he had heard. When he was gone, Miriam Wayne moved to a desk in the library end of the room and Blaise followed her.

"The son and heir?" he asked.

"Himself."

"I didn't frighten him, did I?"

"The Edgertons," she said sourly, "are a high-strung, sensitive clan." She unlocked a section of one file, a card-index, and started through the wads of cards with deft, practiced fingers, occasionally flipping one card aside. In his first chance to study her, Blaise saw that she was truly a handsome girl. She had a high, narrow forehead, keen blue eyes and a fine nose a shade too long to be really beautiful. She wore no discernible makeup but lipstick, and her black hair was pulled back in a tight knot that set off her clear, white skin. There was something oddly prim about her looks, personality and dress, and Blaise felt that she could be drab or beautiful, depending on her own mood and that of the beholder. Right now she was somewhere in-between. She reminded him of what he used to call the curator type—earnest, intelligent students who haunt the museums and libraries during holidays from school, winding up in the art departments of slick magazines or on the junior faculty in progressive schools.

While she flipped through the cards and the little stack to one side mounted, Blaise asked, "How long have you worked for Edgerton?"

"This is my third year," she told him, turning momentarily from the files. "I started just a few months before you met him in New York."

"Rugged kind of a job?"

"We get along." She turned again. "You manage with him, don't you?"

"The three thousand miles between us helps a lot. I'm not sure I could take it on a day-to-day basis."

"He's a bully," said Miriam. She was locking the cabinets from which she had extracted a stack of cards perhaps an inch thick. "Like all bullies, his bark is worse than his bite."

"You're right," said Blaise. "The only thing is, his bark is so bad I don't think I'd even notice it when he bit me."

She smiled. "I promise you, you would." She put the cards on the desk before him. "These are the paintings Mr. Edgerton wants to sell. Some of them are in the house, a few are here in the gallery, most of them are in the vaults. When you're ready, I can assemble them all in here. Now do you want to browse or talk?"

"For now," said Blaise, "I'll browse."

"All right. I'll do some chores and see about renting you a car. I've left word at the house for your lunch to be served in here. Cigarettes are in the boxes and that's the bar over there." She took one key from the carved gold ring. "This is for the files. Mr. Edgerton said you were to have it. I made the catalogue of the collection and you're the only person aside from Mr. Edgerton and myself who has ever seen it."

"Thanks," said Blaise, and picked up the key. "I'll try to prove myself worthy of the honor."

She smiled again. "It's Mr. Edgerton's secret, not mine."

The rest of the morning and the early afternoon flew by as Blaise began to absorb the extent and scope of the Edgerton collection. Starting in 1908, when Impressionist painting was still a drug on the market, the old man had steadily and shrewdly amassed great examples at prices, as now recorded in these files, that bordered on the ridiculous. Then, with great taste and foresight, as each trend in painting manifested itself, Edgerton's instincts stayed abreast or ahead, his purchases now reflecting the whole roster of the founders of modern art. When the depression loomed, he applied himself to the great classical masters, concentrating on dealers and collectors with money problems in this trying time. In this last orgy of buying, naturally, a bargain was only that relatively speaking, but Edgerton was amply equipped with courage, money and taste. Glancing over the prices paid for paintings by Vermeer, Giorgone, Rembrandt and El Greco it was easy to see why the old man was now worried about inheritance taxes.

At two o'clock a neat, elderly houseman brought his lunch. Blaise stopped working to eat it, and afterwards wandered around the gallery.

He was in the far, shadowy end of the gallery, where most of the light came from the soft glow of reflectors fitted to each painting, when he noticed that the door was open. A girl in white shorts and a sleeveless shirt was watching him. She had a highball glass in one hand and smoke curled up from a cigarette in the other. She came inside, leaving the door open, resting her elbows on the dividing bank of cabinets. Blonde hair hung down to her shoulders and deep, green eyes leveled on him candidly as he approached.

"I'm Cass Edgerton," she said, "and I know who you are, mister. You're from the wicked East, a New York sharper out to trim us Edgertons of our rightful inheritance. The object of my visit," she continued with great dignity, "is to inform you that we have papers ready, proving that Uncle Lucas is incompetent and can't dispose of a thing."

"I want to be around," said Blaise, "when he hears about that."

The girl shuddered. "I don't." Then she smiled suddenly. "The whole Edgerton family was on hand to get a look at you at lunch. Where were you?"

"I ate in here," Blaise told her. "Miss Wayne arranged it."

"I'll bet she did," she said emphatically.

Blaise let it pass. "I'm sorry I missed the whole Edgerton family at lunch. Sorrier, now that I know what I missed."

Her smile widened. "Charming. A pretty speech. You have a way with you, a smooth manner that has probably enabled you to victimize hundreds of rich young girls before me."

Blaise moved around to her side of the cabinets. "Are you a rich young girl?"

"Can you imagine Lucas Edgerton with a poor niece?" She followed him to the desk, bringing her glass, and sat facing him on the edge. Her warm, sunny smile seemed to give the huge library a new and friendly charm. Rich or poor, thought Blaise, a stunning girl.

"How many Edgertons, all told, did I miss at lunch?" he asked.

"Just a few. It's quite exclusive, you know. Very difficult to get into the clan Edgerton, and," she added thoughtfully, "darn near impossible to get out. But to get on with the inventory, you've met Uncle Lucas, of course." Blaise nodded respectfully, and she went on. "Uncle Lucas is my guardian, counselor, friend—more a father than an uncle. Then there's my cousin, Simon, not just a cousin but a true pal; and then there's me, Cassy, a creature of silk and flame, elusive as the wind."

23

"You're quite a talker."

"I can kick it around," she said, "but I didn't come here for small talk. I came in to pump you."

"Pump away."

"Well, first off, how much of the Edgerton treasure are you peddling, to whom and for how much?"

"Shouldn't you ask your uncle that?"

She laughed, with an edge of bitterness. "What? And be cut off without a shilling? In the summer of 1935, when I was nine years old, I asked him a question and I still treasure the grunt with which he replied. It's upstairs, in my grunt box."

Blaise leaned forward and gently took the glass from her hand. "You don't want to say all that. I'm just one of the hired hands. You'll hate yourself in the morning."

She didn't seem to resent this at all, but took a cigarette from the box on the desk and Blaise struck a match. "I pictured you in black broadcloth," she said, "with a neat Vandyke and eyeglasses on a black silk ribbon." She looked him up and down searchingly. "Art expert, my eye! With those shoulders?"

"It's mostly padding."

"And you're handsome, in a mean, secretive sort of way. I expected to find a frustrated, elderly man I could wind around my little finger."

"Stay with it," urged Blaise. "I've been wound around some little fingers that couldn't compare with yours."

She started to smile, then Blaise saw that she was looking past him to the door. He turned as Simon Edgerton came in. Cass waved to him gaily. "Come in, Simon. This is Ellis Blaise right here in the chair and he's just about to become putty in my hands."

Simon came in so warily that Blaise could feel his guard up. "Has she been drinking?" he asked Blaise.

Cass answered first. "Not me. Not with old Carrie Nation Blaise on hand to snatch it away. I am already a better and finer woman for having known him."

"Don't mind Cassy." Simon ran his hand lightly over her hair. "She gets wound up on one highball and then she just has to run down her own way." He put his hands on her waist and lifted her easily from the desk. "Come on. This man has to work. I'll walk you up and down till you sober up."

Then Lucas Edgerton's rasping voice cut in on them. "Simon!"

He was standing in the doorway with a small, wiry dark man in work clothes. Edgerton came over to the desk with short, funny little steps as if he were literally hopping mad. The other man stayed in the open doorway, watching impassively.

Edgerton confronted his son. The boy squirmed uneasily. "Simon, I told you never to set foot in here. Did you understand me?"

"Yes, sir," said Simon hastily. "It was just that I came in to pick up Cassy. We were just leaving, weren't we, Mr. Blaise?" He was heavily relieved when Blaise nodded.

Edgerton didn't look to Blaise for confirmation or denial. He walked to the gallery end of the room and as he passed his son he said quietly, "Get out."

The other man stepped out of the doorway to let Simon pass. He betrayed no reaction at all to the ugly little scene between father and son and the others quite plainly took his presence for granted.

Cass stood by the desk until Edgerton turned back at the sound of the closing door. She faced him defiantly.

"I've got some work to do, Cassy," said Edgerton. The rage was all out of his voice now, leaving it with a hollow, exhausted tone. He beckoned to the man in the doorway. "Come on in, Victor."

"The nice part about living here," Cass said to Blaise, "is that you don't have to leave home to go to the fights."

Edgerton moved down the gallery and as Cass went out he pressed a switch that turned on the overhead lights. In the glare of these he looked old and haggard. He reached out to make a minute adjustment in the position of a canvas and Blaise saw that his hand was trembling. The man he called Victor came up beside him and studied the painting, a fine Degas nude.

"It requires only to be stretched, Mr. Edgerton," he said. His voice was soft with a vague and undefinable Latin accent. "The canvas is in good condition. I have already examined it. It is a trifle loose."

Edgerton nodded. "This is Victor Grandi, Blaise." He waited for Blaise to join them. Grandi extended a small, remarkably tough and muscular hand. "Mr. Edgerton has told me about you," he said, in the same soft voice, oddly suited to his stained and shabby clothes.

"Victor does all my restoring, cleaning, sees to the framing—damn good technician."

"Handyman," said Grandi, showing even little teeth in an apologetic smile.

"When you've had a chance to examine the paintings I want to sell," continued Edgerton, "you should go over them with Victor, make sure everything is absolutely presentable."

Blaise nodded. "Good idea."

"You are a dealer, Mr. Blaise," said Grandi. "You know that very often a dirty canvas hurts a fine painting. A bad frame, too."

"He knows. He's been around," said Edgerton impatiently. "All right, Victor."

Grandi showed no resentment or surprise at the abrupt dismissal. He lifted the Degas from the wall, tucked it carefully under his arm. "I am at your service, Mr. Blaise. My little shop is right here on the grounds. I hope you will come to see it."

When Grandi had gone, Edgerton started groping in the bulging pockets of his corduroy coat. "Came over to give you a lead on that Degas. About a year ago the Museum down here wrote me about it. Seems some benefactor wanted to buy it for them. Your kind of a public-spirited boob," he said, the familiar mockery back in his voice. "You'll hit it off fine." He fished out a folded paper. "Here's the letter."

Blaise took it. "Thanks. I'll check on it."

Edgerton was already leaving as Blaise unfolded the letter. It was a polite inquiry made by the museum on behalf of Andrew Kullman, a motion-picture tycoon whom Blaise knew by reputation alone. It was a good introduction to Kullman, whether or not he was still interested in the Degas.

Blaise picked up Cass Edgerton's discarded highball, to return the glass to the bar, then stopped with the glass in hand. The little stack of index cards was gone. He made a quick search of the desk, the drawers and the nearby furniture. He was down on his hands and knees for a better view of the carpeted floor when Miriam Wayne came in. Blaise got up, dusted his palms and looked at her sheepishly. It was not, he decided, a time for beating around the bush. "You picked yourself one hell of a custodian for your precious files," he told her. Her eyes narrowed as Blaise walked past her to the bar. "The Edgertons dropped in. There was assorted badinage, then harsh words and when the smoke cleared away, egg all over my face. The cards you selected for me

27

vanished into thin air." He raised the highball. "To Blaise of Scotland Yard."

"Was it Simon?" asked the girl.

"The company included the squire himself, young Cassy, Simon and a handyman called Grandi. You pick one."

"Simon, I suppose," she said reluctantly. "He was tearing down the road as I drove up."

"What accounts for his personal furore?" asked Blaise.

"Guess," said Miriam wearily. She poured a drink for herself. "Did Mr. Edgerton find Simon here?"

Blaise nodded. "That set off the harsh words. By the way, can you assemble another set of the cards?"

"Oh, yes. That's no problem."

"So all that's happened," said Blaise philosophically, "is that the boy now knows what his father plans to sell. How much of what he's stolen is represented there, by the way?"

Miriam flushed. "I don't know." She turned the glass restlessly in her hands. "He's in trouble, Mr. Blaise. Can you help him?"

"How?" asked Blaise.

"I don't care about Simon," she said, not altogether convincingly. "I'm worried about Mr. Edgerton. I don't know if he can stand another of these shocks."

"Another?"

She ignored his comment. "Will you?"

"It's not my line of work," said Blaise.

"No, I suppose not." She put down her glass. "You're staying for dinner?" When Blaise nodded, she started out. "I'll make sure they know up at the house."

Blaise waited until she was at the door. "Where do you suppose Simon was headed in such a hurry, Miss Wayne?"

She hesitated. "I think you're right to want to stay out of a family quarrel."

"Okay," said Blaise. "See you at dinner."

4

"I AM WORRIED," said Jonas Astorg, "and when I worry I hate to worry alone. I share my problems with my associates. It makes me feel a lot better and it is an indication of my complete trust." He laughed a little, shaking the ice in his highball.

Kenneth Lurie was standing by the table, idly turning the drawings in a large folio laid open there. Lurie was a big man, well over six feet, and his dinner jacket, though extremely well-cut, seemed to be poured over him. His skin was dark, but it didn't look tanned, and the hairline came down to give him only a short forehead for a man of his size. He was attractive, in a crude way, and his manner had confidence. "It's a lot too soon to worry. A little precaution is all the situation calls for."

"I'll be interested to hear your prescription," said Astorg.

Lurie walked to the open doors leading to the balcony and stepped out, turning to face the interior. He looked left to Blaise's room. "Not home yet?"

"He's not the answer," said Astorg.

Lurie came back into the room. "He's more or less got to be."

Astorg put his glass down with an impatient gesture. "You'll think I'm joking—Blaise is honest."

Lurie seemed to dismiss this. "Everybody's honest. I'm honest, too. There are points of departure."

"Well, if he's got one," said Astorg irritably, "his is somewhere off in space. You vegetate out here. You should keep in touch with people. I know Blaise a long time. He had a good job at VanGrand before the war. He was fired for telling a customer quite candidly what he thought of a Corot that VanGrand himself was selling."

"Did he stand to make anything on the Corot?" demanded Lurie.

Astorg laughed. "Naturally. The customer was one Blaise brought in. That's why he felt a responsibility."

Lurie went out again, looked at the dark windows of the bedroom, and closed the balcony doors when he came back. "Which way do you think Edgerton would turn if Blaise wasn't available?"

"What kind of a question is that?" asked Astorg.

Lurie was pouring himself a drink. "Suppose Blaise got a better job, or didn't care for this one? What the hell—a dynamic fellow like that, anything might happen."

"He used to do business with Ford Manson," said Astorg slowly. "He might again. The quarrel was trifling."

"And have you done business with Manson?"

Astorg smiled. "Ford Manson is an art dealer after my own heart."

Lurie touched his glass lightly with his own. "So in the last analysis, we're worrying about nothing."

The phone rang and Astorg picked it up. "Wait a minute," he said into the phone, and buried the mouthpiece in his lap. "Simon Edgerton. He wants to come up." As Lurie slammed his glass down on the table,

Astorg said, "I told him not to come here. He sounds agitated."

"Let him come up," said Lurie, and while Astorg repeated these instructions he moved to the windows, drawing the heavy curtains. Astorg went to the door, and held it open a bit. In a moment there were footsteps in the hall and Astorg was ushering in Simon Edgerton. He looked bright-eyed, flushed with excitement.

Lurie said, "Hello, Simon."

Simon was already explaining. "I know you told me to stay away, Mr. Astorg, but this is important." His voice held a suppressed triumph. "I've got the list of what's to be sold. Here." He thumped the cards on the table, and added, "I took a chance, but it was worth it. By now I guess Blaise knows, but by now I don't care." He started to laugh and Astorg looked up sharply at Lurie who was thumbing rapidly through the cards.

"Not one," said Lurie, in an awed voice. "Not a single, solitary God-damned thing!"

Simon leaned against the bar, weakly happy as though the Governor had just handed him a reprieve. "That's right. Not one of our paintings."

Astorg nodded. "Our paintings," he repeated, "is a felicitous phrase, Simon. Help yourself to a drink, my boy."

Simon poured one, quickly and heavily. "Luck," he said.

Astorg nodded and raised his glass. "That seems to be assured."

Simon drained the glass in feverish gulps. Lurie snapped the rubber band back around the cards and handed them to Simon. "Can you get into the gallery tonight?"

"Later on—after midnight. There's a window on the ocean side I can manipulate."

"What about the alarms?" asked Astorg.

The boy laughed. "There's a window I can manipulate."

"Return the cards," said Lurie insistently, as Simon gave him a puzzled look. "Drop them down between two pieces of furniture, or back of something—a spot where they might have been overlooked."

"It won't work," said Simon. "He must know it was me or Cassy."

"How the hell do you know if he's even missed them yet?" demanded Lurie.

Young Edgerton shrugged. "Suppose he's already told my father?"

"I doubt it," said Astorg. "I know Blaise. He's a snooper. Besides, he'll want to spare your father any unnecessary pain."

"And if he says anything," added Lurie, "he's admitting that he pulled a boner."

Simon smiled again. "Maybe. It's worth a try." He put his glass down. "God! I feel better."

"We are all much relieved, Simon," said Astorg pleasantly.

Lurie took him to the door. "Go out at the side. No use bumping into Blaise if he's on the way in." The boy nodded and Lurie closed and bolted the door after him. "Want a drink?" he asked Astorg.

"No." Astorg pointed to the chair opposite his own. "Sit down, Lurie. I want to tell you something."

Lurie sat down. "What's so sinister?" he asked, lighting a cigarette. "We're in the clear."

"Maybe." Astorg leaned back in the chair. His voice

was casual. "I haven't told you this, Lurie, because I wanted first of all to find out where we stand on what Edgerton is going to sell right away. Nathan Ordmann came into my gallery a couple of weeks ago." At Lurie's sudden, questioning look he repeated, "Yes, Nathan Ordmann. He told me of a rare honor he'd had. It seems the curator of the San Francisco Museum brought Lucas Edgerton to his home to see his paintings."

Lurie said, "Jesus!"

Astorg nodded. "Something like that flashed through my mind."

"What happened?" Lurie ground out his cigarette. His voice rose. "Jonas, what happened?"

Astorg leaned forward. "Edgerton walked right past the Renoir. His only comment was that it was too early for his own taste."

Lurie looked at him for a moment in wide-eyed surprise, then laughed out loud. "Remember what I told you. Edgerton never knew just what the hell he had in those vaults."

Astorg shook his head. "I've dealt with him. Besides, nobody forgets a painting like that. Ordmann paid me sixty thousand dollars and thanked me for giving him a bargain."

Lurie seemed to be groping for an answer. "Edgerton is getting old. He draws blanks now and then. He's always been a little nutty."

"About some things," agreed Astorg. "Not about paintings." He stood up slowly, looking down at Lurie. "It's rare. Priceless. Granted that Edgerton has a lot of paintings, even a lot of Renoirs. How does he walk by this—his own. Even comments on it. It doesn't make sense."

"Maybe the comment is the answer. He doesn't like the early paintings. He's had this forty years and forgotten about it."

"I don't know," said Astorg slowly. "It bothers me."

"Serves you right," said Lurie bitterly. "Our deal was that you would hold the paintings, or get them to Europe, but you finally decided that since Edgerton was such an old man and since he never looked at other collections it was worth taking a chance. You knew there might be trouble."

"I've paid out nearly a hundred thousand dollars," said Astorg. "I had a chance to get back a little. Certainly I knew it was risky but the worst thing that could possibly happen did happen. And still there's been no trouble."

"And that worries you?" said Lurie.

Astorg nodded. His stare held Lurie's gaze as in a vise. "Yes, my friend. That worries me very much."

5

BLAISE was in the sun room of the main house, a spacious glassed-in loggia where drinks were customarily served before the evening meal. There was a vivid, blazing sunset at this hour, thanks to Daylight Saving Time, and Blaise admired this perfunctorily. Then he started for a stack of magazines on a table at the far end of the room and at this moment he saw Victor Grandi tramping along the beach down near the water's edge. After some fumbling, Blaise found the catch on the sliding door, and as he stepped out into the bricked patio Grandi saw him and raised his cane in greeting. When Blaise came closer he saw that the other man was still in his stained, rumpled clothes.

In a matter-of-fact tone Grandi said, "I do not dine with the family, Mr. Blaise. I have a kitchen in my shop, and in the village there is a superb Super Market." He moved on slowly, taking it for granted that Blaise was falling in by his side. "You are familiar with the local Super Markets, Mr. Blaise?"

"I've passed by," said Blaise.

Grandi's small, fine hands made a gesture as if he were a gourmet just tasting a masterpiece. "Astonishing! Every conceivable thing under one faked Spanish roof. Caviar! Kleenex! Automobile tires! Endive is flown in daily by giant planes. I believe one can also purchase spare parts for the planes."

"Just so they don't sell modern paintings," said Blaise.

"It will come," said Grandi. "Someone in this great country will become impatient of the laborious methods by which artists produce paintings one by one. There will be an assembly line. Think of it, Mr. Blaise. A Cézanne will block out the canvas, arrange the composition; a moving belt will carry the painting to the next easel where a Manet will fill in the background; then a Renoir to do the figures and on to a Redon to paint in some flowers."

"Who signs it?" asked Blaise.

Grandi shrugged. "General Motors." He turned to look back at the house. "We can walk a little yet, if you like."

"Do you know the paintings I'm supposed to sell?" asked Blaise.

"In a general way," said Grandi, after a barely dis-

35

cernible pause. "I would like to see them, of course, as you select them for exhibition or sale."

"You will," promised Blaise. He turned to look back at the house, but there were no signs of life in the sun room. He glanced at Victor Grandi, who seemed to be drinking in the beauty of nature through every pore, reacting spontaneously to everything, and he remembered his first impression, only a few hours ago, of a stolid, impassive man. He quickly selected and discarded various ways of bringing up what he wanted to discuss, but once again, with his singular omniscience, Grandi beat him to the punch. They were about two hundred yards up the beach, the light was going fast, and after a glance at the house, Grandi turned to walk back. "It is useless to concern yourself with extraneous matters, Mr. Blaise. Under that heading I would certainly include the relationship between Mr. Edgerton and his son."

"Why?" asked Blaise.

"You can expedite the eruption of an infected area by lancing it," said Grandi, "but you cannot otherwise arrest it. Matters have gone too far. There is a morbid area, but it will, of its own accord, come to a head."

"And cure of its own accord?"

"Kill or cure," said Grandi. "I believe that is the common phrase." He looked up at the house and then said, "Good night, Mr. Blaise. I think the family is waiting for you."

"Good night," said Blaise. He watched as the other man tramped down the beach, then turned thoughtfully back into the house.

Edgerton was waiting for him with a tall, white-haired man. When Edgerton introduced him, he learned that this was Dr. Corum, a critic who, like Edgerton, had been a passionate and early advocate of modern painting, one of the few authorities Edgerton ever cited in conversation and writings without blistering and libelous contempt. Wesley Corum was in a dinner jacket and even Edgerton had made some concession to the dark by wearing a reasonably well-preserved blue suit. With it, however, he wore a hideous brown flannel shirt and an electric blue tie so far askew that it was in danger of sliding under his ear like a hangman's knot.

Edgerton was in a good mood now, as if he customarily bounded from pole to pole in the emotional scale, taking Corum's comments on his clothes with great good humor. "Trouble with Corum," he explained while he made a drink for Blaise, "is that he's been on so God-damn many lecture platforms that now he has to change into a tuxedo every night at seven o'clock. It's a conditioned reflex, like one of Dr. Pavlov's dogs."

Corum smiled amiably, then rose to greet Miriam Wayne. He briefed her on the conversation while Edgerton busied himself again at the bar. "Lucas is of the opinion that I'm a creature of habit now and that this apparel"—he smoothed his pleated shirt— "is a uniform, like a fireman's. Actually, I like dressing for dinner. I think women, too, like men to dress for dinner."

"Probably so does he," said Miriam, as Edgerton gave her a glass. "And probably that's why he doesn't do it."

"Even the help talks back to me," grinned Edgerton. "After I've spent a lifetime building up the toughest personality on the West Coast. Sad, ain't it, Blaise?"

"Who knows?" ventured Blaise. "You may still turn into one of those gruff, lovable old characters."

He got to his feet, as did the others, to greet Cass Edgerton. She was in a black linen dinner dress which left her shoulders bare, and the long, lustrous blonde hair was coiled in a knot. The change gave her a poised, cool beauty. She greeted Dr. Corum and Blaise and re-plied politely to Miriam Wayne's murmured respects, after which the secretary withdrew to the far end of the loggia and the magazines.

Edgerton looked at his watch impatiently. "Simon coming down, Cassy?"

"I believe he's gone into town," she replied. Miriam Wayne, Blaise noticed, was looking over the top of her fashion book.

Edgerton looked annoyed. "Town? What's in town?"

Cass shrugged her smooth bare shoulders. "Maybe freedom from fear."

The old man winced as if reacting to a sudden pain and Blaise saw instant regret in the girl's expression. She reached out, as if to touch his hand. Then the houseman announced dinner. Edgerton, Dr. Corum and Miriam Wayne went in together, Blaise and Cassy following.

"Just like one of the family, aren't you?" she asked. "You may call me 'Uncle Ellis.' "

"I think I've got all the relatives I can handle right now," she said, smiling, "but I'll pencil you in for something."

She seated the little party with an experienced host-ess's ease. Blaise found himself on her right at the foot of the huge table.

Edgerton, naturally, dominated the conversation. He teed off with an outburst against art schools, expressing the opinion that a man with guts enough to dynamite them all would ultimately be celebrated as the greatest patron of art since Lorenzo de' Medici. This tirade lasted through the soup, after which he switched to the incompetents who ran the state and federal governments, nominating them as the most desirable targets for any left-over dynamite.

"You're old-fashioned, Lucas," said Corum, with his customary good humor. "Actually, I think you mean well, and care about people."

"What people?" demanded Cass.

Corum turned to her, as if to say something, but Edgerton cut him off. "Hell, Cassy's right. I don't care a hoot about people." He leaned toward her, but without anger. "Only mistake you make, Cassy, is in calling me a reactionary for it. I'm a liberal, a real liberal. I say let people do as they damn please. Ain't that being liberal?" he asked Blaise.

"Depends on what the people want to do," said Blaise.

"Strike, for instance," said Corum.

"Then let 'em strike," said Edgerton promptly. "If that's what they want to do, fine. And if what I want to do is to bring in a few carloads of scabs, let that be fine, too." He chuckled happily, "There, that's liberal."

"You wouldn't think he'd ever read a book, would you?" said Cass wearily. "Unfortunately, it was printed a couple of hundred years ago."

The argument ended as abruptly and arbitrarily as it had begun. Edgerton started a long, involved discussion of his print and book collection with Corum and Miriam Wayne, and they were soon deep in technicalities of editions, state of proofs, bindings and other fine points. They were still immersed in these technicalities when dinner ended and Edgerton led them back into the library. Cassy went into the sun room, where a television screen was glowing with animated cereal boxes. Blaise tagged along to the library, but Edgerton dismissed him after fixing an appointment for the next afternoon. He came back into the loggia, but Cass was nowhere in sight, and on the television screen something like crudely materialized ectoplasm was bubbling inanely. He poured himself some brandy, took a few minutes to drink it then wandered into the main hall for another look at the paintings. He was on the lower stairs, absorbing what was visible of the dizzying jumble of art, when the house-man, Jennings, came through on his way to the gallery with a fresh bucket of ice.

Blaise made up his mind suddenly. "Oh, Jennings."

The butler turned. "Yes, Mr. Blaise?"

"I gave Mr. Simon a book this afternoon. He promised to leave it in his room for me."

Jennings turned to a side table to deposit his tray. "If you'll tell me the title, sir, I'll be glad to get it for you."

"I'll get it. Which is his room?"

"To the left," said Jennings. "At the far end of the hall."

Blaise said, "Thanks," and continued up the stairs. He examined the paintings until Jennings came through again with the empty tray, then moved up to the hall and down to the far left end.

Simon's room was a comfortable combination bed-room and study, one end paneled in light wood that made a nice background for the flat English desk. There were a large bed, two chairs and a tall chest, all the furniture being arranged to give the room a spacious and uncluttered look. It was a school of decorating of which Blaise generally approved, now more than ever since it all but eliminated hiding places. He made a thorough search of the room and its furnishings without learning more than that Simon Edgerton was an ex-tremely well-dressed man. Dozens of shirts were laid out neatly in the drawers of the chest and rows of suits hung in the deep closets. Blaise frisked these quickly, still with no luck in his search for the vanished cards, then had one last look around in the room itself. Finally he moved back to the door, turned out the lights and stepped out into the hall. He heard a rustling sound then and turned to find Cass Edgerton watching him. She had been against the inside wall, out of sight when he emerged.

"You are indeed becoming one of the family," she said. "That used to be Simon's room."

Blaise considered the situation. "I was searching it," he told her. "I had no right to do any such thing. You want to whistle for your uncle or for the police?"

"I don't know you," said Cass, "but I do know Simon. I don't think I want to whistle for anybody."

Blaise took her arm. "Let's go outside."

"I know just the spot," said Cass, and led the way. She picked up a shawl in a closet downstairs and steered him out, away from the house to the bare frame of a cabana near the water's edge. There was a stack of beach pillows and pads. Blaise knocked some off the top and carried them to a clean, dry hard spot. She sank down on one of the pads. "If this was just a ruse to get me out here, it's not a bad idea at all."

Blaise sat down on one of the pillows. "It's a great idea. I'm sorry I didn't have it."

"You don't find me irresistible here in the scented dark?" asked Cass politely.

Blaise laughed. "You're jumping a couple of chapters, Cassy. This one is about Simon."

"So it is. I caught you red-handed. I nearly forgot." As Blaise fished out some cigarettes she reached out to him. "Give me one."

He gave her the cigarette, then a light. "Is Simon in any trouble, Cassy?"

"Would you be searching his room if he wasn't?"

"You're fond of him, aren't you?"

"Yes, of course." Thoughtfully, she added, "More

than that, I guess. The two of us have always been a sort of a united front . . ." She let the sentence trail off aimlessly.

"Against his father?"

"Not exactly. It sounds like that, doesn't it? Actually, to keep from being trampled." Her voice took on a faraway quality of recollection. "You know the Laird of Edgerton Manor pretty well—how would you like to be his son?"

"Aside from the prospects," said Blaise promptly, "not at all."

"I've lived here since I was a little girl," said Cassy. "In many ways Uncle Lucas has been kind and generous. It didn't matter so much to me that he liked children less than paintings of children. But it mattered a lot to Simon. I doubt if he thinks about it now, but when we were kids it mattered a great deal. Now, of course, he's weak and sullen. It seems silly to say that he didn't have any advantages—the son of Lucas Edgerton—but it's true."

"I think I know what you mean," said Blaise. "I'm not a trouble maker. I was searching Simon's room because I'd like not to make any trouble." He told her about the cards, recalling Simon's anxiety about what was to be sold. When he was finished, Cass ground her cigarette carefully in the sand as if she wanted to be occupied with something that would keep her eyes averted.

"What do you think he's done?" she asked.

"Probably stolen some paintings." It was too dark to see her face in more than shadowy outline, but he didn't think that she looked surprised. "It's only in recent months that there has been any kind of a catalogue of the collection. Before that, apparently, it was just lying around in heaps. My guess is that Simon helped himself to a few paintings. With any luck it might have been years before they were missed. If he took things that weren't too rare or notable, the chances are his father wouldn't remember them at all. But now, with the sale coming up, I think Simon is rattled." He waited for some comment and when she didn't make it, he said, "How does that sound to you?"

"Awful," said Cass. "Mostly because I suppose it's true."

"Maybe I'm all wrong. I haven't a shred of evidence, you know," he admitted. "Aren't you accepting a harsh judgment of Simon rather too readily?"

"It's happened before," said Cass. "I'm not surprised, except at his being such a fathead. About two years ago," she continued, "a collector brought a Van Gogh drawing to Dr. Corum. It happened to be one he remembered from the collection—I don't know how, there must be thousands of drawings by everybody—and not knowing much of the home life of the Edgertons at the time, he made a beeline here." She shook her head as if to clear it of the painful memory. "It was Simon, of course. He'd sold it to some fly-by-night dealer."

"Remember his name?"

"Norden. Hugh Norden. Why?"

"If he's been at it again," said Blaise, "a dealer must be helping him. He couldn't do it alone. Is Norden still around?"

Cass shrugged. "If he is, I doubt if he has any nerve left. He's a jittery type. He wasn't prosecuted, but when Uncle Lucas finally finished with him he could barely walk out of the house."

"Does Simon have any other contacts with dealers or collectors?"

Cass shook her head. "He doesn't take much interest

in art." Ruefully, she added, "Except in the way you've indicated."

He tried a shot in the dark. "Ever hear him mention Jonas Astorg?"

"Not that I can remember."

"If I knew exactly what he sold, and to whom, I might be able to do something."

Cass was quiet for a moment. Then she said, "Why don't you ask Miriam Wayne?"

"Is that feminine intuition?"

"More or less," she admitted. "I don't like her, but I wouldn't go by that alone."

"What else?" asked Blaise.

"Just that she knows every little squiggle of a drawing in the collection and she's got most of it under lock and key—her lock and her key."

"It may have happened before she came to work."

"Then why would he be burning up for a look at her damn catalogue cards?" demanded Cass. "If the paintings were gone before the catalogue was made he'd know the cards didn't matter."

"True," said Blaise thoughtfully. He stood up, then reached down to give Cass his hands. He pulled her up and for a moment she stood close to him. "You're a smart girl, Cassy."

"You know," she said, "I think that's the first time anybody ever took me out to the beach at night to tell me that."

He smiled down at her. "Are you tempting me or teasing me?"

"Which do you think would be the most fun?"

Blaise took her arm and started back to the house. "Are you always so candid, Cassy?"

"Am I being spurned?" she asked, as they pushed through the heavy sand.

"Just until I figure out whether you're interested in me, or in what happens to Simon. I'd like to help him, Cassy, but the fact remains that I'm working for his father."

"What possible difference can it make if the Edgerton collection contains a few square feet more or less of canvas? It stopped being a collection years ago. Now it's a mania. He doesn't even own it any more. It owns him, and all of us. Many's the night I've longed for nerve enough to get a bucket of kerosene and a box of matches and go to work on it."

"It would make quite a bonfire," said Blaise, "and it would undoubtedly solve Simon's problems." He took her arm. "Hold your fire, Cassy—I'll think of a tidier way out."

"Will you?" They were in the dark shadow of the gallery now and she stopped to look up at him searchingly.

"It just means shifting my loyalty a few degrees. It's all in the family."

"Softy," murmured Cass. "A little moonlight and your moral fiber cracks wide open."

"Just as well," said Blaise. "It was getting too tight for me."

He bent his head, but before their lips could meet a cold voice cut in between them. "I beg your pardon," said Miriam Wayne. "Here are the keys for your car, Mr. Blaise."

Cass stepped back and Blaise took the keys the other girl extended. "Just what I wanted," he said sheepishly.

"You might have waited, Miriam," said Cass. "It took

me hours to get him worked up to that point. Now I'll probably have to start from scratch."

"I'm sure you'll manage very nicely," said Miriam. "Good night."

"Good night, dear," said Cass, as the other girl walked swiftly away. Blaise looked after her until she was lost in the shadows, then he heard a door slam viciously. "Miss Wayne is steaming," Cass said cheerfully. "I can tell from the well-manicured sound of that voice."

"Does that give you so much pleasure?" asked Blaise.

Cass took his arm. "Wait till you've been around this haunted house a while. It's a hotbed of feuds and intrigue. I hope you didn't come here for rest and quiet."

"If I had any such idea," sighed Blaise, "it's long since evaporated." He stayed behind, letting her go up one step. "I ought to have a talk with Simon. Off the premises, I think."

"He's got a girl," said Cass, "and a lot of the time they go to the Lido—that's a night club on Sunset Boulevard."

"I'll give it a try."

"Want me to come along?" asked Cass, and when Blaise shook his head, she ventured, "Are you angry at me?"

"I did have an impulse," Blaise told her, "to turn you over and smack you until some of that hard-boiled veneer peels off, but that's evaporated, too."

Standing on the step above, her eyes were level with his. She stared at him for a moment, then shifted her gaze uncomfortably. "I know," she said awkwardly. "I'm sorry." Then she turned to look at him again. Her eyes were misty. "This is a lousy place," she said huskily. "You're a fool to stay."

Blaise put his hand out to her, but she turned, went quickly up the last two steps and into the house.

Paul Weldon was sprawled on the couch in his darkened studio. There was some light from the street lamps in the quiet Hollywood street high up in the hills above the city and he could hear his model, Molly Dann, humming in the studio bathroom which was her dressing room. His eyes ached from the strain of a hard day's work, but he rose from the couch, turned on a light, then moved to the easel. He snapped on the two glaring worklights, focused them on the fresh canvas and stepped back to study his work. The painting was a seated nude, the tones of flesh and background airy and delicate, the body glowing with the translucent quality he worked so hard to achieve. The drawing, however, was foreshortened and grotesque as if he were trying to impart not grace but power; the beauty of flesh and something unbearably ugly that was joined to it in his mind. His model, Molly Dann, came in from the studio bathroom, dressed now except for the jacket of her suit which she was just buttoning over her brassiere. She was a strikingly handsome girl with a stunning figure. Her features, like Molly herself, were big, and her short black hair and olive skin gave her a barbaric beauty which would probably be coarse and unattractive in another ten years. Now, however, it was undeniably effective.

Molly stood back of the artist, studying the painting

while he braced himself for her reaction. "Is that how I look to you?" she said. "Christ! Why do I even take off my clothes?"

"Maybe it's force of habit," said Weldon waspishly.

Molly grinned. "That burns you, too, doesn't it?" She turned back to the canvas. "I was telling a friend of mine about your painting. All that lovely flesh you spend hours and hours sweating over—and the hideous way you make the body come out in the end." Quietly, almost daintily, she added, "My friend said that was pure fag."

Weldon whirled on her, his fists clenched.

"If you touch me," said Molly, "I'll put my foot right through that canvas."

Weldon glared at her, then backed away to the mantel over the fireplace where he groped for a pack of cigarettes and matches.

"Why do you needle me?" he muttered. "Why can't you leave me alone?"

"Who calls who?" demanded Molly. "Who has hysterics when I pose for other painters? Why don't you try leaving me alone?" She picked up her purse, a pair of black gloves and a short loose coat. She paused for another look at the canvas. "My friend—the same one —also said that a man named Pascin did this kind of work so well it was foolish for anybody to come along and imitate him."

Weldon flushed, but he ignored the extra insult. "Where are you going, Molly?"

"I've got a date. I'm meeting Simon Edgerton at the Lido."

He blocked her path. "Why, Molly?" he pleaded.

"Because you give me a pain." She stepped around him to the door. "Want me to pose tomorrow?"

He nodded unhappily. "Yes, I suppose so."

"Make up your mind," said Molly sharply.

"Yes," said Weldon angrily. "Yes."

Molly smiled. "I'll see if I can make it. Depends on what time I get home tonight." She gave him a big smile and went out. Weldon heard her heels clicking on the steps, then the sound of the front door closing. He stood by the window, watching as Molly moved gracefully down toward the intersection and then turned right to the road that wound down to Hollywood Boulevard. He let the curtain fall back and stepped to the easel to turn off the work lights. He sat in the still, dark room for a few minutes, then jumped up suddenly, took his hat and started swiftly down the stairs. He followed the same route to Hollywood Boulevard and when he was a block away he saw Molly just getting into a cab. He called to her, but she ignored it or didn't hear him. His steps slowed down as the cab drove off.

The Lido was situated in that part of Los Angeles known as the County Strip, usually just "the Strip." It was a winding section of Sunset Boulevard between Hollywood and Beverly Hills but belonging to neither and dependent on the County for all municipal services. It was the accepted location for all of Hollywood's theatrical agencies, decorators' establishments and smart little dress shops. It was also the center of the night life in the community, the whole length of the Strip being dotted with places that ranged from smart spots like Ciro's and Mocambo to dreary little clip-joints in which strip-tease acts and modified B-girls hustled servicemen for drinks and tips.

The Lido was in the first category, full of subdued glamor. There was a bar near the entrance, and beyond this, roped off from the cheaper patrons, an overdecorated, gaudy room with low-keyed lighting. There was a smooth band and a fair-sized dance floor.

Blaise had returned to the Ocean Inn at ten o'clock and telephoned the Lido from his room. Simon Edgerton had not yet arrived, nor was there a reservation in his name, but the manner in which the headwaiter asked for a message indicated that Cassy was right and that Simon was indeed a habitué. He changed his clothes and drove to the Lido in the excellent car hired for him by Miriam Wayne, and now he was at the circular bar, having taken a seat as far from the front door as possible, but one that gave him a good view of the bar and the entrance to the main room. There was a fairly steady procession of arriving supper guests, and of the dinner crowd, since this was Southern California; those lucky enough to be working were going home to rest for early calls. Among the men, the outstanding characteristic was a harassed, worried look. The women shared a lacquered, consistent beauty so much alike in details of makeup, hairdo and dress as to seem to be the product of one great cookie cutter. There were also the standard variety of eccentrics: a turbaned Sikh, complete with ceremonial jewels and, as Blaise could hear in his conversation with the headwaiter, a distinct New York accent. There was a cowboy star, in white buckskin, who wore his ten-gallon hat into the dining room, and a party of drunken oilmen, each of whom, in some accustomed ceremony, pushed a dollar bill into the strapless decolletage of the checkroom girl. She squealed rewardingly, regarding them with blank hatred as they moved uproariously into the other room and fishing uncomfortably for the currency in her bosom.

At just about eleven o'clock, Simon Edgerton arrived with Molly Dann. He was a welcome and familiar

50

guest. As they waited briefly in the doorway, Blaise heard the headwaiter say, "Couple of calls for you earlier, Mr. Edgerton."

That left one call unaccounted for, thought Blaise, as he settled his bill and followed them.

Simon looked up as Blaise approached the table. He seemed unruffled by any care, absolutely sure of himself. "Hello, there," he said warmly. "Alone?"

Blaise said, "I'm a stranger in these parts." He didn't have to fish for an invitation. Simon summoned a waiter who swiftly brought another chair. There was a bottle of whiskey on the table, ice, soda and water. There were also, he noticed, three glasses.

"This is Molly Dann," said Simon, and introduced Blaise. "Art expert," added Simon. "Great pal of my father's. Molly's in the racket, too," he told Blaise. "She's a model."

"Just for laughs," said Molly.

"She gets more whistles than laughs," Simon assured him. He smiled his friendliest smile for Blaise. "Looking for me?"

"As a matter of fact," said Blaise, "yes." He returned Simon's frank stare. "Expecting me?" he asked.

"You boys want to spar in private?" asked Molly.

"Maybe you ought to go powder your nose or something," said Simon.

"Sure," said Molly amiably. She pushed back her chair and both men rose with her. "Don't fight, boys —play nice."

Simon looked after her tall, undulating figure for a moment and so did a number of the other men in the room. Even the cowboy star, from an adjacent table, violated the austere code of his calling by frank interest in her sexy walk.

"Hell of a nice girl," said Simon. "Regular. No beating around the bush with Molly."

"Or with me," said Blaise. He marveled at the change in Simon, the great assurance he now exuded. "Miriam Wayne gave me some cards from your father's catalogue —the paintings he wanted to sell. I had them on the desk in the gallery. They vanished."

"Too bad," said Simon. "Makes you seem kind of a mug, doesn't it?"

"It does that. I don't enjoy the prospect of telling your father I lost them."

"Can't say I blame you," said Simon. "I've heard he has a lousy temper."

Blaise laughed. "After all, we did wind up beating around the bush, didn't we?"

Simon managed to look boyish and incredulous. "Look here, old man, do you think I took your cards?" His smile opened into a grin. "But why?"

"You bloody little fool!" said Blaise harshly. He saw Simon's expression change to instant apprehension. "How long do you expect to get away with this? The first time your father takes an inventory, or remembers some pet piece you've already sold, he'll light rockets under you. Now don't give me any more lofty poise and wisecracks. If you want me to, I'll help you. If you want to go to hell in your own wheelbarrow, I'll give you a push."

"You've been talking to Cassy," said Simon.

"What if I have?"

"Nothing. I know she means well. You do too, probably."

"She is worried."

"Is that why you're here?" asked Simon, and when Blaise offered no reply, he went on: "You probably won't

52

believe this, but as it happens, I've done nothing."

"What do you mean by that?"

"Work it out," urged Simon. "In time, perhaps I'll tell you."

Molly Dann was slinking back to the table. "Everything all right, boys?" she asked cheerfully.

Blaise was standing. "I'm just leaving."

"You just got here. Stick around," Molly urged.

Simon didn't add anything to the invitation. "Be sure and tell Cassy not to worry."

Blaise nodded, and said good night to Molly, who was already pouring herself a drink, and went out through the bar to the side entrance and the parking lot. The attendant was just bringing up a smart Cadillac. A man and woman went off in this and before Blaise could give his check to the attendant a small convertible pulled in from the street, the tires squealing as they scraped on the dividing curb between the exit and entrance driveways. A tall, loose-boned man climbed out of the little car, stooping to duck the top. As the attendant scribbled a number on a check for him, Blaise heard him ask for Mr. Edgerton.

"Yeah, he's here," said the attendant, and the new arrival took the check and went past Blaise into the club. He wore thick glasses and had a concentrated, anxious look about him. He wore a dark suit which needed pressing. Blaise looked after him, then turned back to the driveway as the attendant asked for his check.

"I'll take a walk," said Blaise. "I'll come back for the car."

The attendant nodded and sank wearily down on the steps, turning up the volume on a little portable radio tucked into a niche in the wall. Blaise walked up Sunset Boulevard, west to the first intersection, then turned into a street that fell away in a perilously steep grade. He found an alley halfway down this dark residential thoroughfare, and as he moved along the lane he could hear the music of the Lido band. He came into the parking lot of the club with ease, since it was railed off by only a heavy chain suspended from iron posts. The little gray convertible was parked handily near the chain and because its owner was apparently a law-abiding man, an envelope was strapped to the steering wheel, with an isinglass window making the license visible to Blaise. He struck a match and leaned in to read the typewritten details of the registration. The car was registered to Hugh Norden, 772 Pickett Lane, Hollywood.

He saw the glare of headlights and ducked back into the alley, retracing his steps to the Lido entrance. He redeemed his own car, and after driving out, a U-turn enabled him to park on the opposite side of the street, headed for Hollywood. He stretched himself comfortably across the seat, lit a cigarette and turned on the radio. The air was full of the standard nightly hosannahs sung to the used-car dealers of the community; a group of frantic specialists who miraculously suspended all economic law in order to buy any used car at a handsome premium while simultaneously selling similar vehicles for a fraction of their worth. There was also a program of authentic New Orleans jazz sponsored by an institution which guaranteed to wean friends and loved ones from the evil of alcoholism, and a dolorous string ensemble sawed at standard classics under the auspices of the most conveniently situated burial park in all Los Angeles. Meanwhile, a sound truck patroled the boulevard on behalf of the Rev. J. J. "Fighting Jack" Linnit, "the little evangelist with the big message" and a hideous purple neon sign at the far end of the street urged the wayfarer to refresh himself with nutburgers, cheese-burgers and SkiHi Malts.

Blaise had been sampling the sights and sounds of Southern California for only about twenty minutes when he saw the gray convertible come up the Lido driveway, heading east into the boulevard. Blaise pulled away from the curb and in the flow of traffic following the car ahead was easy.

The trail was brief, involving only one turn—into a canyon below the Strip—and then a climb of two or three blocks to a circle. An arrow lettered "Pickett Lane" marked one spoke of the shaded wheel of streets inter-secting here. With this to guide him, Blaise was content to let Norden's car go ahead. He saw the gray convertible parked at the dead end of the street and stopped halfway down. Number 772 was a small house of two duplex units. He pushed Norden's bell and the door instantly clicked open. There was a flight of steps with a landing, the second section of staircase doubling back so that until he reached the landing he would not be seen from the apartment door.

He hesitated in the hall, then heard a door opening above. A high-pitched, questioning voice asked, "Yes?"

Blaise stopped on the steps. He made no reply and he heard the voice again. "Simon? Is that you, Simon?"

Blaise went up to the landing. The man he had fol-lowed was standing in the open doorway. "Mr. Norden?" asked Blaise politely. He got a worried, sullen stare. "I'm a friend of Simon Edgerton," he said. "I'd like to talk with you."

Norden watched him come up the last few steps, but he didn't move aside or make any gesture that might be construed as an invitation. He had furtive, darting eyes behind the thick glasses and they flickered over

Blaise uncertainly. "Did Simon send you?" he asked.

"His father sent me," said Blaise, and for a moment thought that Norden would yelp in pained surprise. Then he stepped up quickly, in time to get his shoulder against the door that was instantly slammed in his face. Norden was frail and it wasn't hard, despite his panting efforts, to push inside. He found himself in a small, crowded living room in which books seemed to overflow from the rows of shelves to the floor and over each article of furniture. Norden backed away, coming to rest against the shelves that lined the far wall. Facing Blaise, he stretched his long thin arm to fumble behind some old volumes, and as Blaise took a step forward Norden was ominously waving him back with a gun.

Blaise obediently retreated. Norden was not handling the revolver with much conviction, but he was a nervous man and under the circumstances it seemed wise to oblige him.

"What do you want?" demanded Norden.

"It's not a holdup. And I'm not from the police. My name is Ellis Blaise. I'm an art dealer. Right now I'm working for Lucas Edgerton."

Norden considered this and Blaise was glad to see that he found it reassuring. "Put the gun away," he urged. "It's a silly damn thing to be waving at visitors."

"How am I to know?" Norden let the hand with the gun in it sink down. "You come pushing in here. And this damn neighborhood, with prowlers around." He pushed the gun back into its niche behind the books. "What's old man Edgerton want with me?" He was fumbling in his pockets for cigarettes and he lit one with hands that trembled slightly. "He probably thinks you're leading his son into paths of evil," said Blaise. "And by the way, are you?"

Norden puffed nervously at his cigarette. "No. That was years ago. I told the old man all about it. I haven't had anything to do with Simon in . . ."

"Before you get too far into that," Blaise told him, "I followed you here from the Lido." While Norden digested this, he added, "And you were expecting him when I rang your bell?"

"Personal matter," Norden muttered. "Anyway, what the hell business is it of yours?"

"I told you. I'm working for Edgerton."

Norden rubbed his cigarette out in a dish on one of the shelves. "Tonight was just a personal thing. We're friends, but I haven't touched anything from the Edgerton collection since we had all that trouble."

"How is it Edgerton didn't prosecute you?" asked Blaise.

"Ask him," snapped Norden.

"I will."

"You're getting it all wrong," Norden insisted. "I'm a dealer. I've got a big following. Lots of important movie people buy from me. This boy came along with some drawings—nothing sensational—just fair Impressionist drawings. After all, he's Simon Edgerton. And these drawings, they could be something his father gave him for Christmas, or a birthday. I sold them openly, nothing undercover about it . . ."

"Did you tell your customers they were from the Edgerton collection?"

"Strictly speaking," said Norden, "they weren't. It would be a misrepresentation," he added virtuously. "At the time I thought Simon needed some money and was selling some of his personal things." As Blaise looked at him skeptically he went on with some heat. "You say you're a dealer. All right, put yourself in my position. A man like Simon Edgerton comes in—no bum, mind you—and offers a few drawings. What would you do—call the police?"

"What's your business with Simon now?"

"I'll tell you," said Norden hesitantly. "I let Simon use this place once in a while. He's kind of a ladies' man, and it's handy for him to have a place in town." At the frank look of amusement Blaise gave him he stopped abruptly. "Well, then get the hell out! You asked me and I'm telling you."

"Thin," said Blaise sadly. Norden shook another cigarette out of his pack. "I'd like to be around," continued Blaise, "when you tell Lucas Edgerton that story. Or when the police get to it."

"You're dumb," said Norden. "Dumb as they come. Do you think I'm chump enough to get mixed up with that fire-eating old bastard again?"

"I'm puzzled," admitted Blaise. "It would be a sucker trick, wouldn't it?"

"Yes, it would." Norden's initial terror seemed to have given way to a confident exhilaration. There was a feeling of power and command now, as recognizable as the pure panic with which he had greeted Blaise. He was certainly terrified of something or somebody, but Blaise was forced to admit that he himself did not inspire this. "If Edgerton sent you," Norden was saying, "tell the swashbuckling old hellion that I'm in the clear. Whoever sent you, tell him that." He held the door open, jerking his thumb to the hall. "That's all."

"I can just picture you in the clear," said Blaise. "What you mean is, you think you've covered your tracks."

Norden leaned against the door in an easy, arrogant pose. "Haven't I?"

Blaise laughed. "This room and everything in it look hot to me. And the hottest thing in it, my friend, is you."

"I'm in a different line now," protested Norden mildly. "In a way, I'm a consultant." He closed the door, gently but firmly, easing Blaise into the small, dark hall, and then there was the rattle of a bolt and chain.

Traffic was thinned out now and he had an easy drive to the beach. The night clerk at the Ocean Inn gave him three messages, all from Cass Edgerton, all within the last hour and he heard his phone ringing as he opened the door of the suite. He stumbled to the phone in the dark. It was Cass again.

"I've been calling you," she said. "Have you been ignoring me?"

"You know better than that," he told her. "I just got in."

"Well, so much for my outraged vanity. Did you talk to Simon?"

"At some length, Cassy. Say, that's quite a girl he's got. Built like . . ."

She interrupted him sternly. "That was not your mission. There is such a thing as being too observant. What about Simon?"

"I think he's in the clear," said Blaise. "I've only got his word for it, but I don't think he's been dipping into the family treasure. I'll tell you all about it in the morning."

"And you're not mad at me?" asked Cassy.

"No. If you had waited another minute I would have told you so. Then you could have gone peacefully to sleep."

"Think you're smart, don't you?"

"Yes," said Blaise. "Good night, Cassy."

She laughed. It was clear and friendly. "Good night, Ellis."

Blaise put down the phone. He undressed swiftly and was asleep within a few minutes. The night before had been spent in the plane and he was grateful for the deep, wide soft bed provided by the Ocean Inn. The hammering on his door, when it began, had no effect at all, but it penetrated slowly, merging with some unremembered dream, so that even when he opened his eyes it took a while to convince him that it was real. It was still dark in the windows facing west and with no recollection of where the switches were located he stumbled to the door in the other room. "Coming," he growled in transit, then cursed vividly as his bare foot banged into the edge of a chair.

He opened the door. The night clerk was in the hall with two men. "Sorry, Mr. Blaise," said the clerk. "I had to wake you. It's the police."

"County Homicide Bureau," said one of the other two men in a soft, unhurried voice. "My name is Ives. Lieutenant Ives. This is Sergeant Bonner." Ives turned to the clerk. "All right. Thanks." As Blaise moved back both men came in, Sergeant Bonner closing the door. By that time Blaise had groped his way to a switch and turned on the lights. Sergeant Bonner stood by the door, as if on guard.

"Simon Edgerton was killed up at the house this morning," said Lieutenant Ives.

Blaise sat down abruptly, looking up at the detective.

"Surprised?" asked Lieutenant Ives.

"What the hell do you think?" replied Blaise.

"Do you own a gun, Mr. Blaise?" asked Ives, and when Blaise shook his head, he motioned to Sergeant Bonner. "Mind if the Sergeant has a look around?"

Blaise shook his head again and Ives motioned his aide into the bedroom. Then the Lieutenant sat down in a chair near Blaise and hunched it forward so that he was in an attentive pose. "You were searching Simon Edgerton's room last night. Later on you were with him in a night club." Having said this, he leaned back as if he was positive that a flood of information would be released. When Blaise didn't instantly speak up, he leaned forward again and in a friendly tone, asked "Ever have much to do with the police?"

"Not much," said Blaise.

"I have," said Lieutenant Ives, all but twinkling in his geniality. "One thing I learned from being around the police so much: in a murder you've got to tell what you know. That's how it's got to be."

"I know," said Blaise reluctantly. "The thing is, I work for Lucas Edgerton."

"You're a picture dealer," said Ives, "not a priest or a lawyer." He looked up past Blaise as Sergeant Bonner came from the bedroom. The sergeant said nothing but shook his head and Ives said, "Wait a minute."

As Bonner took up his post at the door again, the Lieutenant said, "What about it, Mr. Blaise?"

Blaise nodded. "Sure. I guess that's how it's got to be."

"Wait in the car, Bonner," the Lieutenant told him.

"Have you talked to Cass Edgerton?" asked Blaise.

"Some. Not a lot."

"Didn't she tell you about my searching Simon's room?"

"No," said Ives. "We found your fingerprints in the library, then on every drawer in the boy's room."

"It doesn't matter," said Blaise. He told Ives the nature of his assignment to sell some paintings and about Simon's anxiety earlier that day. Then about the loss of

61

the cards and what he knew of Simon's previous escapades. "That's why I went to the Lido to talk to him. The odd part," he said thoughtfully, "is that he told me he wasn't in any trouble and I believed him. Then, as I was on my way out, Hugh Norden was going in." He described the simple maneuver that revealed Norden's identity and Norden's conduct with the gun when he pushed his way into the dwelling.

"What time did you leave Norden?" asked Ives.

"Between twelve-thirty and one—say twelve forty-five."

"Simon Edgerton was shot at about three," said Ives. "We sent a car to pick up Norden at four-thirty. He was gone—packed in a hurry, and gone."

"I had the damnedest feeling about him last night," said Blaise. "He was scared to the trembling point when I came in, but when I told him I thought he and Simon had been selling stolen paintings he seemed relieved. He wasn't frightened any more, but actually patronizing, as if he knew something big and private."

"He didn't get around to any details?" asked Lieutenant Ives wistfully.

"No. But I felt the same thing in Simon. He was a jittery wreck earlier in the day but in the Lido last night it was as if he had the upper hand and knew it."

"The gatekeeper," said Ives, "tells me he passed Simon's car in a few minutes before three. Apparently, he then went up to the house. A few minutes after three, the gateman thought he saw a light on the beach. While he was investigating he heard a shot somewhere on the grounds and found Simon's body outside the gallery, under an open window. He'd been shot by someone standing right beside him, at point-blank range. It was a mess." The Lieutenant looked out at the gray dawn that was starting to stretch over the ocean. "Been a long night," he muttered and yawned heavily. "How were things at the house? All one big, happy family?"

"I just got here," said Blaise pointedly.

Ives nodded, accepting this. "The old man's secretary —Miriam Wayne—she was hit hard. An emotional type, would you say?"

"I would if I could."

"Anything special going on there?"

"I wouldn't know."

Lieutenant Ives stood up wearily. "Sorry I broke up your sleep. Thanks."

Blaise took him to the door. It was after six now. He dressed quickly and fortified himself with some coffee at an all-night fisherman's stand, then drove to the Edgerton estate. There was a police car in the driveway, just inside the gates, and a trooper was standing by the gatekeeper. The Edgerton man identified him, the gates were opened and Blaise drove up to the house.

Lucas Edgerton was standing in the driveway between the house and the gallery. He wore a black, belted raincoat against the morning fog and he watched with dull, somber eyes as Blaise parked the car.

"I'm sorry," said Blaise. "The police woke me up and I thought I'd drive out and see if I could help with anything."

Edgerton beckoned him into the gallery. "Come on in."

Blaise followed him in. One lamp was lighted on the desk and Miriam Wayne was seated there now. A pot of coffee was on a typewriter table and she had a cup in front of her.

Edgerton said, "Show him the cards, Miriam."

She lifted the blotter on the desk, first moving the

coffee to one side, and handed him the small, flat package of cards. "They were on the floor, between those two cabinets," she said, pointing to the nearest section of the index.

"Did you look there when you missed them?" demanded Edgerton.

"Yes, I did."

"Positive?"

"I made a point of looking under the desk, back of the files—everywhere."

"The damn fool," blurted Edgerton suddenly. "The poor damn fool boy," he said again, and then he turned his back abruptly. Miriam Wayne looked at him, shook her head sadly and swung her chair around to the desk. Blaise stood there awkwardly, caught in the tableau. After a moment, still with his back turned, Edgerton said, "I want an inventory taken right away."

Miriam nodded. "That won't be difficult. I'll start on it at once."

Edgerton faced them again. In the lined and tired face his eyes were burning. "We'll do it together," he said fiercely.

"I see." She faced him steadily, her voice, as always, perfectly controlled. "Very well, then. Whenever you're ready." She picked up her purse, dangling on the back of the chair, and started out. "I'll be in my room," she said, not addressing Edgerton in particular.

Edgerton was already pacing up and down between the desk and the door. Blaise lit a cigarette, idly riffling the retrieved cards in his fingers.

"Blaise!" snapped Edgerton.

"Sir?"

"What kind of trouble was he in?"

Blaise found it hard to meet the old man's eyes. "I

don't know that he was in any trouble at all." He felt called upon to expalin his own role in last night's activity. "Cassy—your niece—was worried, and I wanted to have a talk with him about the cards I lost."

"Well?"

"I talked to Simon, and then I talked to Hugh Norden. They had some sort of a racket going," he said candidly, "but my own idea is that it had nothing to do with your paintings. That's my own idea," he finished lamely. "I'm not sure that it's a very good one."

"I'd like to think it was true," said Edgerton. "I'd like to be sure it was true."

"The police will sift it all now. Last night, when it was still all serene, at least on the surface, I thought I might be able to throw a scare into Simon—or into Norden. That was based on the notion that something had been stolen, and probably sold, out of your collection. I honestly believe that was wrong. They laughed at me."

"What could it have been?"

Blaise shrugged. "It's wide open." Confronted with Edgerton's staring, hopeless expression, he added reluctantly, "If I come on anything, I'll follow it up. Mostly, though, it's for the police."

"All right." The old man walked to the window, cranked it open and shook his head as if to clear it of the weariness and anxiety written on him. "I'm an old man, Blaise," he said dully. "I was past forty when the boy was born. Not a good age to be a father. Not if you're busy with a bank, factories, real estate, airlines and an art collection. I was hardly aware of my son until he was in trouble."

"What the hell," said Blaise uncomfortably. "You probably did the best you could."

"Maybe. I doubt it. I didn't want to be a heavy father, but I didn't know what else to be. I'm not cut out for heart-to-heart talks. I thought that if I kept raising his allowance that would solve everything. But I didn't turn him away," he said anxiously. "Not ever. I just never knew how to do the things I should have done. And to lose him this way—this ugly, violent way—and not to know even what caused it . . ." He looked at Blaise for a moment, or rather Blaise had the feeling that he was looking at some point beyond him. "Stay on for a few days," said Edgerton, in a matter-of-fact tone. "We'll get back to business when I feel better."

"Anything you say," Blaise promised. He watched the old man go, then moved to the desk and put his hand on the coffeepot deserted by Miriam Wayne. There still some warmth in it and he poured a cup of the black, dull brew. He was drinking it when Cass came in and, behind her, Jennings with fresh coffee and some rolls.

"Miriam told me you were here," she said, as Jennings put down the tray and removed the old service.

"How do you feel, Cassy?"

"Tired," she said, pouring the coffee. "But I guess that's the rock-bottom minimum emotion under the circumstances. And I'm not being hard-boiled." She handed him a fresh cup of coffee. "I've been imagining and dreading so many terrible things for so long that now that this nightmare is really among us I just can't work up any of the conventional flow of tears and maidenly grief. I just feel so sorry for him."

"For Simon?" asked Blaise.

"Of course. Whom did you have in mind?"

"Just asking."

"You're really an all-out, hundred-per-cent employee, aren't you?"

"The old man's been hit hard," said Blaise. "He's full of guilt about what he thinks is his own share in the tragedy. He left here a moment before you came in. He wasn't the high and mighty Edgerton of Edgerton— just an old man with a load of pain strapped to his back. He could use a kind word."

"Him?" Cass was frankly incredulous.

"Failing that," said Blaise, "in your case, what about some common, garden-variety gratitude?"

She studied him. "You've got that feeling again, haven't you? About smacking me?"

"Unless you're a good girl," said Blaise, "I won't. Anyway, you'll be all right. You've got good instincts."

Cass pushed back her chair. "Excuse me."

"Where are you going?"

"I'm going up to the house to talk to Uncle Lucas," she said defiantly. "What's wrong with that?"

"Not a thing," said Blaise, smiling. He walked with her to the door of the gallery. "I'm going into town, but I'll be back later on in the day. I'll take you for a ride. Get the roses back in those cheeks."

"I'll go," said Cass, "but only because it's good for me. I'm not sure I like you any more. I find myself doing what you think I ought to do. That's a hell of a way to start a friendship."

"Don't swear," said Blaise. "It's not ladylike."

He walked back to the desk, picked up the little wad of cards and fanned them thoughtfully. He was only vaguely aware of the names, titles and prices flashing by. Undoubtedly the brief possession of these cards had given Simon Edgerton that precious sense of security so evident in their last interview, but Blaise could form no intelligent reason for it. He stacked them in a neat 3 x 5 pack, looped the rubber band twice around and dropped them into his coat pocket. Then he went out to his car and started down toward the gate, but at the bend in the driveway he noticed for the first time a small, neat brick-and-stucco building screened by large eucalyptus trees. It was about a hundred feet from the driveway, with a little flagstone walk that started between the trees. Blaise remembered Victor Grandi's shop on the premises, and the other man's invitation to visit him. He eased the car onto the graveled shoulder of the driveway and went up the walk to the house. He heard the whir of a small motor and smelled a vague, not unpleasant aroma of mingled paint and oil. He wielded the heavy brass knocker on the front door and the motor stopped. Then the door was opened by Victor Grandi, who instantly threw it wide, beckoning Blaise inside.

"I heard the shop noises," said Blaise. "Kick me out if I'm disturbing you."

"I was carving a frame," said Grandi. "That is like whittling toy boats—an occupation to be set aside on any pretext." He took a small section of frame from a vise on his work-table, carried it to the window where an abstract Bracque was propped on a chair and placed the piece of wood carefully on the upper edge of the un-framed canvas. Then he stepped back to stand beside Blaise.

"You see what I am trying to do?"

Blaise nodded. "Something like the pattern of the painting repeated in the frame, isn't it?"

"Splendid!" said Grandi, in the manner of a school-master complimenting a pupil.

"It's beautiful work," said Blaise, moving closer to it.

"It requires only patience and some rudimentary skill. A few centuries ago a man like myself would have found employment in a monastery, perhaps illuminating manuscripts. In that time the Church was a refuge for craftsmen; today it is men like Lucas Edgerton."

"You make it sound like a complete retreat from the world," said Blaise. "Is it?"

"I live in California," said Grandi simply, "and I do not own a car. That can only be described as vegetating." He drew Blaise into the next room and closed the door. This was a bed-sitting-room, with a fireplace. A large studio couch was covered with a burgundy spread and a Regency desk stood between the two windows. There were some paintings on the walls, including a Sisley landscape, a Corot painting and the little Degas nude that had been taken from the gallery the night before.

"The paintings," said Grandi promptly, "are on loan." He poured a small glass of cognac which he offered first to Blaise, who refused it. "I understand," said Grandi. "However, it seems like much later in the day to me. The police woke me at three-thirty." He sipped the brandy slowly. "Have you seen Mr. Edgerton?" he asked.

"Yes. He seems quite shattered."

Grandi nodded. "Of course. It is a matter of ego." Hastily, he added, "You understand, I do not underestimate a father's natural feelings. Poor Edgerton was never able to understand how a man like himself could have a son who was anything short of the perfect successor."

"Do you think Simon was stealing paintings from the collection?"

Grandi's gesture seemed to dismiss the question as unimportant. "Perhaps."

"Did he need money?"

"The police asked that question. I told them, quite truthfully, by the way, that I had no means of knowing whether he did or not. To you, however, I will enlarge on my answer." In the same odd, professorial manner which lacked only a pointer and slides to be completely academic, Grandi said, "Consider a young man like Simon Edgerton. He is brought up by a succession of governesses, tutors and private schools—all admirable people and institutions but all substitutes for a father who is completely submerged in a peculiar collection of paintings which the boy does not even remotely understand. Wouldn't you hate the collection?"

"Yes," said Blaise.

"Simon loathed it. His feelings were for a long time outweighed by his fear of his father, but little by little the scales began to tip the other way."

"That makes sense," conceded Blaise. "Who helped him?"

"I don't know," said Grandi promptly. "I don't know when the thefts began or when they stopped."

"Do you know a girl named Molly Dann? A model?"

Grandi smiled quietly. "I know there is such a girl."

"How did Simon meet her?"

Grandi's smile widened. "Very sensible, Mr. Blaise. An excellent place to begin. The police will search for enemies and motives and clues. Simon's artistic connections will prove much more rewarding." He drained the last of the brandy in the little glass. "Now I must return to my whittling."

Blaise walked back into the shop with him. Grandi picked up the section of frame and locked it into the vise, then turned to study the painting for which it was intended. He picked up the electric drill, holding it as delicately as a painter might hold his finest, thinnest brush. He snapped the switch and the hum of the motor began, whining up the scale to a shrill crescendo. Then he bent over his work in absolute concentration. His expression was blank and serene. Blaise watched him for a moment, then went out quietly.

7

Molly Dann lived in a tiny bungalow in a new development of similar houses near Culver City. She came to the door stretching and yawning from sleep, but she asked Blaise in quite cordially and sat him in a window-seat while she moved in and out of a miniature kitchen, answering his questions easily and with apparent candor. She was wearing a soft, flannel robe, only loosely tied. She seemed utterly unconscious of her superb body and the revealing flashes her sweeping movements occasioned. She settled herself at last on a low hassock, the coffee and rolls on a little table. So far her ready, instinctive responses gave Blaise the impression that she was fond of Simon Edgerton, but not much more than that. He was good for laughs and presents; they went out a lot to night clubs to dance, and once in a while to Laguna, Coronado, Palm Springs or Las Vegas for the week-end, depending on the climate or the mood.

"He was a nice guy," said Molly, summing it up. "What I liked was he was tolerant. He liked what I wore, didn't try to correct my grammar or my manners and if we went out and I got stewed he'd look after me without any high and mighty nonsense. Some guys," she went on wrathfully, "in a restaurant or at a party they're on pins and needles for fear you might say 'ain't' or show your legs when you sit down. Then they get you

71

home and you find out all of a sudden that they're not so proper. Damn peculiar, some of them." She eyed Blaise speculatively. "You look like a regular guy. Tell me what happened. So far, with the cops pumping me, I haven't found out a thing."

"I don't know much," said Blaise. "What happened after I left the Lido?"

"That Norden came in a couple of minutes later. I think Simon was expecting him. Anyway, I got fobbed off to dance with some fellow we knew in another party, and after a couple of turns I came back to the table and they were just sitting there."

"How was Simon? I mean, what kind of a mood was he in?"

"Like a kid with a new baseball mitt. Honest, he was grinning like an ad for some pep medicine. If I didn't know him better I'd have thought he had a shot in the arm while I was dancing. I was surprised at the way he was acting and Norden was, too, I think. He left in a few minutes. First he whispered something to Simon. I couldn't hear what it was, but it didn't bother Simon a bit. When Norden was gone, he sent away the bottle of whiskey on the table and ordered champagne—a magnum. Then he wanted to dance. He lifted me out of my chair and swung me around—he was that chipper. On the floor, he seemed to be chuckling about something, and once he laughed right out loud. I kept on asking him to let me in on the joke, but he'd just give me a little pat and say he'd tell me later. About one in the morning he paid the tab and then he brought me home. He was in such a good mood I thought he'd want to—well, you know—sort of stick around here, but he said he had to do something important. He just kissed me good night," she finished sadly, "and off he went."

"You never got any idea of what was making him so happy?" asked Blaise.

"Not a glimmer. I wish I did. Anyway, if a guy has to go, Simon certainly went out laughing. But he was mostly that kind of a fellow. I've seen him drop five thousand in a dice game, then borrow a hundred from a dealer and buy drinks for the house with it."

"Where did you meet Simon?" asked Blaise.

"At a gallery here, about a year ago. I pose a lot for a painter named Weldon, and . . ."

"Paul Weldon?" asked Blaise, interrupting.

"Yeah. Do you know him?"

"I know who he is. Pretty good painter."

"He is?" Molly looked surprised. "I guess he is at that. His stuff gets shown and people must buy it. Anyway, the Kenneth Lurie gallery gave him a show and they opened it with a snazzy cocktail party. Weldon took me to it . . ." She giggled suddenly. "Remember what I told you that Simon was tolerant. I'd been working in a movie, just in a bit, but I wore an evening gown. It was in two pieces, with nothing here." She stroked her robe, at the midriff. "And not a hell of a lot anywhere. It had some white fur tacked on, too. It must have been ghastly," she added candidly. "Even I know that now. Weldon turned all colors when he saw it and for a minute I thought he was going to leave me home. He didn't, but when we got to the gallery he parked me in a corner and didn't come near me for hours. Simon was the only person in the place who was pleasant to me. We left the party—it was full of creeps—and went dancing."

"Did that amuse Paul Weldon?" asked Blaise mildly.

"Him?" Molly laughed. "He's the kind of a guy that doesn't want a girl—he just wants the torch. With fellows like that a girl is just an excuse for crying jags. He was

73

always burned up when I went out with Simon, though —more than when I went with other men. Some special grudge, maybe because he was Simon Edgerton. I posed for him yesterday. He was doing one of those creepy nudes. I'm sure he paints them because it's his way of hitting back at women. Anyway, when I was dressed and leaving he found out I had a date with Simon and he hit the ceiling." As Blaise looked at her sharply, she added, "Oh, I told the cops. They can check on him but it's a thousand to one he just stayed home with a bottle, then cried in his pillow."

"Sounds charming," murmured Blaise. "How did Simon get to that first party? Was he a particular friend of Lurie?"

"Nothing special. We went there one other time, to another party, but if Simon had anything to do with him aside from that he didn't tell me."

"Did he see much of any other dealers or artists?"

"None at all, as far as I know. Maybe Norden, but I doubt it. Whatever Norden was bothering him about didn't date back more than a couple of days."

"You know that Simon and Hugh Norden were in some trouble a while ago, don't you, Molly?"

"I know."

"Do you think Norden could have been blackmailing him about that—or about anything?"

"Would that have made him so happy?" asked Molly.

Blaise nodded his agreement. "Just testing. You're right, of course. I'm sorry I crashed into your nap."

"It's all right. I was glad to talk to somebody who didn't have a badge on his chest." She rose gracefully from her cross-legged pose on the hassock, and as Blaise got up from the window-seat she stopped him. "No.

Wait. Are you a dealer? Is that on the level, or are you some kind of cop?"

"Dealer," said Blaise. "If you call that being on the level."

"Simon left something with me," said Molly. "I didn't tell the police"—she hesitated—"well, you'll know why when I show it to you." She took a cardboard tube, open at both ends, from a table near the door, and with two fingers carefully drew out a sheet of drawing paper protected by sheets of tissue. She spread this and held it flat on the table for Blaise to examine. It was a study in pencil and charcoal, a reclining figure, half-nude. It was unsigned but the master hand of Auguste Renoir was in every stroke that formed the luxurious beauty of the face and figure. Even in the harsh black and white medium it glowed with the artist's warm and tender style.

"It's a Renoir, isn't it?" asked Molly.

"One of the best. An early one, probably 1880 or thereabouts."

"I think Norden brought it to the Lido last night. Anyway, Simon had it when we were leaving. He asked me to keep it for him. He said it was worth a lot of money and he didn't want to ride around with it. I didn't tell the police because I thought maybe it was hot."

Blaise had taken the drawing, was holding it to the light. "It was things like this one that Simon and Norden handled the time before."

"I know," said Molly. "Will you take it?" He turned to look at her. "Do whatever has to be done with it."

"It may not be hot. Simon may have meant it as a present for you. It's worth a couple of thousand dollars. Maybe as much as three."

"I'll trust you with it," the girl said simply. "If it's

75

mine you can sell it for me. I just wouldn't want to kick up any scandal for his family."

Blaise rolled up the drawing in its protective tissues then fitted it into the tube. "All right, Molly. It's very decent of you."

She laughed wearily. "Be sure and stick a gold star on my report card."

8

THE KENNETH LURIE GALLERY was housed in what had once been one of the downtown area's finest mansions. It was an enormous English brick house, set well back from the street. There was a circular driveway surrounding a fine, clipped lawn. A bronze marker was the only external clue to the commercial nature of the establishment.

The paneled oval drawing room was the main exhibition hall, but the spacious foyer and the dining room opposite were also used for this purpose. Beyond these was the large library, and this, because it was Kenneth Lurie's private office, was kept as it had been in the old days of the establishment, when early settlers who had cleaned up in oil, railroads and real estate frolicked on the premises.

Jonas Astorg was seated in an enormous, high-backed leather chair in the library, almost lost in its vast proportions, while Kenneth Lurie sat at the large flat desk, his chair tilted back, his feet up on a revolving bookstand at his right.

76

"Of course I'm sorry about the boy," said Lurie irritably. "What do you suggest I do? Close the gallery for thirty days? Fly a flag at half-mast? Or I'll tell you what," he drawled sarcastically. "Let's make up a purse and present it to his poor deserving father." He swung his feet down from the bookstand and turned the chair to face Astorg directly. "You can be as sanctimonious as you like, Jonas. From my point of view, Hugh Norden did us a hell of a big favor." His heavy features relaxed into a broad smile. "Now if the police will only arrest and execute him in a hurry, that will be perfect."

"Will that take the load off your mind?" asked Astorg.

"What do you mean?"

"Why should Norden have wanted to kill him?"

"Why? How the hell should I know why? Maybe he was holding Simon up for money and the boy got tough. Maybe he was out to steal some pictures on his own and Simon caught him. Maybe they were sweethearts. I can think of a million reasons."

There was silence for a moment, then Astorg shifted himself so that he sat on the edge of the chair. "I'm thinking of buying back the Renoir," he said quietly.

Lurie's head came up slowly. He fixed the other man with a pained, puzzled look. "This is some new nonsense, isn't it?"

"I'm not happy with the deal. It's too complicated."

"Then buy it back. I doubt if Ordmann will sell it to you. He's very proud of the painting."

"I may give him a small profit. We ought to do it together. You've had nearly a hundred thousand dollars from me, and . . ."

"I've had!" Lurie repeated it incredulously. "I've had! How do you think I got the paintings, Jonas? My own share, so far, has been insignificant."

"Nevertheless," insisted Astorg, "we are partners and we should act in this as if . . ." He stopped at the sound of a buzzer and turned to the door as it was opened by Lurie's clerk.

"Yes, Casper," said Lurie irritably. "What is it?"

"A Mr. Blaise to see you," said the clerk.

"Ellis Blaise?" asked Lurie.

"Yes, sir," answered the clerk. "He has a gallery in New York," he added, while Lurie and Astorg exchanged glances. Then Astorg nodded, sinking back into his chair, and Lurie said, "Show him in, Casper."

The clerk backed out, leaving the door open. Astorg rose from the chair and was facing the open door when Blaise came in. He was carrying the tube in which the Renoir drawing was rolled and shifted it to his left hand as Astorg stepped up, his own hand extended.

"Ellis! What a pleasant surprise. I told Lurie he ought to meet you while you were here. I didn't expect the pleasure of introducing you." He drew Ellis to the desk.

"It's an honor, Mr. Blaise," said Lurie, while they shook hands. "You're as close as I've ever come to the Edgerton collection." He opened a cupboard behind the desk. "What about a drink?"

"Small whiskey," said Blaise. He put the tube in his pocket, though it projected uncomfortably, and sat down in one of the chairs Lurie indicated near his desk.

"Terrible thing, that business with the Edgerton boy," murmured Astorg.

Blaise nodded. Lurie handed him a glass and Blaise said, "You knew him, didn't you, Mr. Lurie?"

"Slightly. I used to ask him to parties here." He smiled sadly. "Frankly, because I thought that through him I might get to meet his father. But I don't think he had much influence there."

Astorg took a little glass of brandy handed him by Lurie. "Well, here's luck, Ellis."

"Luck," repeated Blaise, and Lurie chimed in with, "And may all my customers strike oil."

Blaise put down the empty glass. "How's business?"

"It's not a good town," said Lurie. "I'm not saying that to keep you from opening a branch, if that's what you've got in mind. The movie crowd buys a little but the few that spend really big money like to do it in New York or Paris. The rest of the well-to-do citizens, the merchants and bankers, they're still gushing over Rosa Bonheur and genuine hand-painted Corot copies."

"Don't let him cry too much, Ellis," put in Astorg. "Lurie has a fine business."

"Oh, I do all right, but most of it is business I've built up in Texas, Oklahoma, and the oil states. Thank God for Texas! Anything with a frame around it brings a price down there. They stamp out millionaires overnight. I got to Dallas once with a car full of paintings and made my first stop in the suburbs to see a struggling young lawyer who had asked me to look for a cheap Modigliani drawing he wanted. The night before I arrived, a tremendous oil strike was made on a tract next door to some land he owned. That's as far as I got that trip. He bought everything in the car and I gave him the drawing for a present. That's Texas."

"Speaking of drawings." Blaise took the tube from his pocket and passed it to Lurie. "Have a look at that. I just got it today."

Lurie carefully drew out the enclosure and Astorg came around behind the desk to examine it with him. Lurie pressed the drawing down flat on his desk and snapped on the light.

"Say, you've got something!"

"Beautiful," murmured Astorg. He looked across the desk to Blaise, who was lighting a cigarette. "You say you bought this here?"

"I haven't bought it," said Blaise. "I've got it on a sort of consignment basis. It's worth about three thousand, I should think."

"Sure." Lurie took his hands off the corners of the paper, letting it roll up loosely. "Who owns it?"

"Private party. Wants to stay that way," said Blaise affably.

"I've got a customer for it," said Lurie. "I'd like to have it."

"Perhaps later on," said Blaise. "I haven't quite made up my mind about the price."

"I'd like to please this particular customer. He bought a Renoir here, but he couldn't afford this period in an oil. I promised him a fine drawing and he's been riding me about it. It's an accommodation, actually, and it's important to me for the good will, so I'll tell you what I'll do: I'm sure I can get the three thousand. You can have it all. A deal?"

"It's fair enough," said Blaise. "More than fair. I'll wait on it, though. Give me twenty-four hours."

"No hurry," said Lurie, and carefully rolled up the drawing, slipping it back into the tube. He handed it across to Blaise who put it back in his pocket.

"Let's forget about the drawing," urged Astorg, "and talk about some real money. I was right, was I not, Ellis? Edgerton is going to sell some paintings, isn't he?"

"Right. By the way, Jonas, how did you learn that?"

"Private party," said Astorg, smiling. "Wants to stay that way. How many paintings are for sale, Ellis?"

"Forty canvases," answered Blaise promptly. "All Impressionist paintings."

Lurie whistled. "Jesus! Forty paintings from the Edgerton Collection." He looked wistfully at Blaise. "Texas, the Lone Star State, welcomes you, Brother Blaise."

"I'd say the lot is worth about a million and a half," continued Blaise. "I'm working for Edgerton and my prices are net to him."

"Send in the list," urged Astorg. "I'm sure we can do business. I've got some fine customers, Lurie has his Texas plutocrats; between us, we might handle the whole sale."

Blaise agreed to furnish the list, turned down another drink and shook hands all around. Then he left the Lurie gallery with the Renoir drawing under his arm.

Astorg seated himself again in the big armchair. He watched silently as Lurie poured himself a large straight whiskey and tossed it off like a man who needed it. Then he said, "Lurie, who is your customer who is so crazy about early Renoir drawings?"

"Nobody you know," was the curt reply.

"It's odd," mused Astorg. "I'm worrying myself to death about the early Renoir painting and in comes Ellis Blaise with an early drawing. It's barely worth the three thousand, you know," he went on gently. "You'd be making nothing, maybe taking a loss."

"Not likely," said Lurie. He sat down at the desk and his strong fingers drummed heavily on the polished surface. "Jonas, I've got some business uptown. A client I promised to call on today."

"I'll go," said Astorg promptly, rising from the chair. "Is it the client who is so anxious to have an early Renoir?"

"God damn it!" Lurie's fists were clenched and his

mouth tightened into a hard line. "Why are you nagging at me? Just what the hell is it you want?"

"I want the truth about those paintings," said Astorg calmly. "It's very important to me."

Lurie was livid with barely suppressed rage. "Is that why you went to see Simon Edgerton last night?" Astorg had taken a few steps toward the desk, but now he backed away. "Did he tell you?" demanded Lurie. "Did you like what he told you, or did you lose your fine Continental calm?"

Astorg's face was gray and beads of perspiration had sprung up on his veined forehead. "You were there," he said thickly.

"Correction, please," sneered Lurie. "We were there."

As if to himself, Astorg mumbled. "You knew he was going to put the cards back in the gallery. It was your idea. You knew just where he'd be and at what time."

Lurie smiled. "Sure. Go tell the police. They'll thank you for it." Astorg shook his head and sank down into the big chair. Lurie stood over him. "They have a new gas chamber upstate. Exquisite, functional modern. I can't tell you what it's like inside, but maybe you can find out for yourself." He started to the door. "Help yourself to a drink, Jonas—you look awful."

On the way uptown Blaise bought the afternoon papers from a boy hawking them in the main stream of traffic. Then he headed west again and turned off at a drive-in, deserted at this in-between hour. A pretty girl in perilously tight slacks and a distracting halter top brought him a sandwich and cup of very good coffee. By using the steering wheel as a reading-rack he could manage the papers and the sandwich together.

The Edgerton murder was all over the front page, and in inside spreads there were pictures of the house, Lucas Edgerton, Cassy, and one of Lieutenant Ives standing by the open gallery window where Simon's body had been found. The text indicated that Hugh Norden was much in demand and that the Western states had been alerted in the man-hunt. Each of the papers had a last-minute news bulletin on the search, one stating that Norden had bought gas in San Diego that morning, the other that he had been seen at about the same hour in Reno, some six hundred miles to the north.

Blaise let the girl take away the papers with the tray, then started west again. Near the U.C.L.A. campus he found a large art-supply shop, and after careful examination of the stock, he bought some drawing paper in blocks.

It was early afternoon when he returned to the Edgerton estate, passed the gateman and the uniformed trooper still on duty at the entrance, and drove up to the house. A plain-clothes man and a uniformed policeman were photographing the exterior of the gallery and another technician was on his hands and knees in the shrubbery beside the window, busy with some other apparatus. The gallery doors were locked and the detective told him that Miss Wayne was in the house. He found her in Lucas Edgerton's combined bed-workroom, lunching there with Edgerton and Dr. Wesley Corum. The critic was once again faultlessly dressed, everything tasteful and somber, ideal for visiting bereaved friends. Miriam and Edgerton had been working and the table was covered with sections of the index. There were also dozens of notebooks, apparently Edgerton's own original catalogue of his hoard.

Blaise shook the Renoir drawing loose from its holder and laid it flat on the table, anchoring it with two paperweights.

"Anybody recognize it?" he asked.

Edgerton looked annoyed. "I know what it is," he said, "if that's what you mean."

"Of course," said Miriam Wayne. "Renoir."

"Early," said Dr. Corum. "Damn fine, too."

"Simon gave it to a girl last night," said Blaise.

Miriam gave him a puzzled stare and Edgerton bent over the drawing, examining it now carefully. "It's not mine," said the old man and looked to Miriam for confirmation.

The girl said, "No. I'd know at once if that was from the collection."

"Want to look at it again, Dr. Corum?" invited Blaise.

The critic obediently bent over the paper for a second examination. Then he straightened up. "What is it you want me to say, Blaise?"

"Yes, damn it, Blaise. Speak up," said Edgerton impatiently.

"It's not a Renoir," said Blaise quietly.

Corum turned instantly to the drawing. He bent the pliant neck of a desk lamp so that the paper was caught in its bright glare. Edgerton, however, barely gave the drawing a glance.

"You're crazy," he said to Blaise.

Corum straightened up, switching off the lamp. "You're wrong, my boy," he said indulgently. "It is certainly Renoir."

Blaise turned to Miriam Wayne. "What's your guess?"

"I don't know enough," she replied, "but Dr. Corum does and certainly Mr. Edgerton's word . . ."

"Maybe you're in the wrong business," said Edgerton.

"It's not Renoir," insisted Blaise. "It can't be."

"Don't keep babbling it's not Renoir," shouted Edgerton. "Why the hell isn't it?"

"Because," said Blaise, "it's on modern paper, made right here in Los Angeles." Edgerton stared at him, then turned to look at the drawing again. Corum's cheerful bedside-manner expression was gone. He looked tense and worried. "I'll be damned," muttered Edgerton softly. "I'll be double damned." He glanced at Corum. "Hell of a pair of experts, aren't we?"

"I don't believe it," said Corum. His voice was stubborn and petulant.

"I don't blame you," said Blaise. "Everything about it is absolutely genuine. I would have bought it and sold it unquestioningly except for the feel of the paper." He laughed. "Hold it to the light—you'll see the water-mark."

"What's the meaning of it?" asked Edgerton. "Where did Simon get it?"

"Apparently from Hugh Norden."

Dr. Corum was standing over the paper again, shaking his head slowly, as if he couldn't quite assimilate the shock. Blaise had unwrapped the blocks of drawing paper purchased on the way out. He tore off a few sheets and laid them with the drawing. "I know how you feel," he said to Dr. Corum. "The idea was driving me crazy, too. However, unless you're willing to believe that Renoir bought his drawing paper in West Los Angeles within the year, that's a forgery."

"I've never seen anything like it," said Dr. Corum.

"Never," he repeated. "I've seen forgeries, hundreds—and lots of them made to look like Renoir—but this—this is so free, so natural. It's perfect."

"But on modern paper, with a modern water-mark," said Miriam Wayne. "Surely a great forgery like this would be more skillfully prepared."

"This was done for practice," said Blaise. "Dr. Corum commented on the freedom and natural execution of the drawing, and that was achieved by relentless practice. This drawing, and maybe hundreds like it were dry runs, practice rounds made and destroyed so that finally the artist would have achieved the natural hand of the man he was imitating. You can enlarge it by a thousand diameters—I doubt if you'll find a cramped movement, or a line that looks any more labored. And the object of so much care and effort could not have been to sell a few drawings. Remember Han van Meegeren, Dr. Corum?"

Corum nodded slowly. "Yes, of course."

"He painted Vermeers," said Blaise to the others. "Sold at least six, and each of them was authenticated by the greatest experts in Europe. They were subjected to X-rays and shadowgraphs, magnified under electric microscopes—pure Vermeer was the verdict. He sold one to Herman Goering for a million dollars, and when Holland was liberated the Dutch tried him as a collaborator. His defense was that the paintings were forgeries and that he had actually cheated Goering out of the million. The experts came again, the equipment was brought into court and the whole process started again. The paintings could not possibly be forgeries. They even chipped off bits of paint and chemical analysis proved that these dated back to the time of Vermeer. Van Meegeren's defense, this time, was quite simple. He asked for an adjournment, brought some supplies from his home and painted another Vermeer—just as genuine —in his cell, under the constant supervision of the guards. That settled it."

Blaise rolled up the drawing, and put it back into the tube. "Don't buy any Renoirs until you hear from me," he said to Edgerton.

"What does it mean?" asked the old man. "Was Simon involved?"

"I think so," said Blaise, "but I don't know just how. It may account for some puzzling gaps in what the police know so far, and if it does . . ."

Corum interrupted him. "You're going to the police with that?"

"Of course." Blaise looked at him curiously. The critic had recovered some of his composure. Blaise waited for Corum's response, one which was apparently to be carefully framed.

"I was thinking of the effect on the market for paintings—any paintings—if a forgery of this caliber is publicized. It is always distressing, and now, when some things from the collection are to be sold . . ."

"I'll be damned!" said Edgerton. "Do you suppose my mind is on how much a painting brings today?"

Corum looked pained. "Naturally, I don't mean that, but a thing like this"—he looked back at the drawing on the desk—"has unpredictable effects."

"Thanks," said Edgerton coldly. He picked up the drawing and handed it to Blaise. "Get going. Do whatever has to be done. I've got a hundred Renoirs and I'd sooner see them sold for wrapping paper than stand in the way of getting at the truth." Then he turned on Corum again. "Have you handed down an expert opinion on a Renoir lately? Is that what's bothering you, Wesley?"

Corum looked at him reproachfully, then turned away in silence.

"I'm on my way," said Blaise. "Any surprises in the inventory?"

"Not so far," said Miriam. "We've only checked about half the catalogue."

Blaise went downstairs to the sun room and telephoned to Lieutenant Ives. He told the detective he had some information and Ives promised to come to the Ocean Inn at once.

He was on his way to the car when Cass came out of the kitchen door. She had a sandwich in one hand, a glass of milk in the other. She was pale and seemed to be sagging with fatigue. He looked at her critically. "Cassy, you must be all done in. Why don't you get some sleep?"

"It's on the agenda," she said. "I was just taking this upstairs"—she extended the sandwich and milk—"and I saw you tearing out. I just wanted to thank you for giving me hell. I had a good cry on Uncle Lucas's shoulder and I think we both feel better."

"Don't mention it," said Blaise. "Any time."

She stepped down into the driveway. "Coming back?"

"I promised to take you for a ride, didn't I? Do you think my word is idly given?"

She followed him down to the car. "Am I missing something? You're dashing up and down the beach like a man of much mystery."

"I'm a bloodhound," Blaise told her. "The rare short-eared variety. Only a few of us left in captivity." He leaned out of the car. "How old are you, Cassy?"

"Twenty-five," she replied. "Why?"

"Better get some sleep," he said gently. "You look like an old hag of twenty-six."

He took his foot off the brake and the car started down the drive. He caught a glimpse of Cass in the rear-vision mirror just before he turned the bend. She was waving and he waved back.

At the hotel he picked up his key and a letter from his office. He glanced at this in the elevator as he went down the hall to the suite.

He jammed the letter into his coat pocket while he fumbled with the key, then opened the door and stepped in. The shutters were closed, as they had been that morning, and the room was in semi-darkness. As he closed the door he was suddenly conscious of a movement behind him, but in the instant of his wish to turn, something heavy crashed down on him and the darkness exploded into light. He felt himself falling and was aware of being caught before he hit the floor. Then the darkness closed in again.

10

PAUL WELDON had another of the maddening alibis that were beginning to make Lieutenant Ives feel like a shadow boxer. It was simple and straightforward; Weldon could not substantiate it and Ives could not topple it, though he bombarded it skillfully at various levels for an hour.

Weldon readily admitted his jealousy of Simon Edgerton's success with Molly Dann, but in his waspish, biting way he pointed out that to be consistent he would have had to murder every man she slept with, thus competing with mass production experts like Landru and the Butcher of Dusseldorf.

After watching Molly drive off in the cab, he told Lieutenant Ives, he stayed in the outside world only long enough to buy two bottles of whiskey in a store on Hollywood Boulevard. He then returned to the studio, locked himself in, and suffered silently and alone until Lieutenant Ives came with the news.

Weldon showed only perfunctory interest in Sergeant Bonner's deft and thorough search of the studio while Ives questioned him, exhibiting no relief or triumph when Bonner silently indicated his lack of success and was sent to wait in the car below. Ives followed him in a few minutes and the painter remained inert and drooping in his own chair until he heard the cars departing. Then he got up heavily and in the first release of tension kicked out savagely at some books on the floor. He threw up all the windows in the workroom, and started to pace up and down as a man might try to walk off the effects of a drug.

Later, when his nerves quieted, he started to work, but it went badly and the broken brushes on the floor around the easel were the result of his jittery impatience. He made repeated telephone calls to Molly Dann, but there was no reply. At noon he poured himself the first drink of the day. The bottle was nearly full and he laid out a rationing scheme that would give him just enough to keep his nerves under control for working. He went back to pacing the floor, read last week's magazines and stared out the window until the middle of the afternoon. He had given himself one extra drink by that time and was about to abandon his self-imposed discipline and kill the bottle quickly when Molly arrived.

Some sleep had restored her fresh, dark beauty, but she was listless and apathetic.

"I didn't think you'd come today, Molly," said Weldon tentatively, as if the subject frightened him.

"Neither did I." She glanced at the bottle, then at the broken brushes on the floor. "Are you getting boiled?"

"I was upset. The police were here."

"I know." After a moment she said, "I'm sorry. I don't even remember how your name came up. That cop—Ives—he's smart. He's so damn polite and easy-going. I hope it didn't make any trouble."

"Oh, no," said Weldon quickly. "I don't mind." As she slipped out of her coat he moved up to take it and stood close to her. "Thanks for coming in today, Molly. Thanks a lot."

"I got jumpy, too," said Molly uncomfortably. She stepped away from him. Weldon looked crushed for an instant, then moved to the closet with her coat.

"Feel like working?" the girl asked listlessly.

"Might as well."

She nodded and kicked off her shoes. Then she sat down on the couch and lit a cigarette. Pulling her dress up, she groped for the garter fastenings, then slid the stockings down on each leg. "I'd like to go away," she said, in a reflective tone, as if it were more a thought than a statement. "I'd like to go away," she repeated. "That's all I seem to be able to think of today." She reached up and behind her to pull the zipper of the dress. "I had a funny sort of reaction to this business about Simon. It knocked the wind out of me somehow. I'm not sure how or why."

Weldon had been shaking tubes of paint out of a cardboard box. "Were you in love with him, Molly?" he asked.

"We had a lot of laughs," she said simply. "Maybe I was in love with him and wouldn't let myself think it because he certainly wasn't in love with me. But we did have a lot of laughs. I liked him a lot."

"I know you did," said Weldon. As Molly started to the bedroom in her slip, carrying the dress and shoes in both hands, he reached out and caught her bare arm. "Come away with me, Molly. I've got money. I've got quite a lot—more than you think. I'll take you to Mexico, or to Europe—anywhere you say."

"Thanks, Paul. We'll talk about it."

"I mean it, Molly. You can trust me—I'll take good care of you."

"I know. We'll talk about it."

Then the doorbell rang in sharp, jagged bursts, as if someone was jabbing at it fretfully.

"Who's that?" asked Molly.

"I don't know," said Weldon. He pushed the release button for the lock on the door below. He waited until Molly was in the bedroom and the door was closed, then opened the studio door.

There were heavy footsteps on the stairs and he backed away as Kenneth Lurie filled the low doorway, scowling angrily at the painter. Weldon gestured nervously to the open bedroom door just as Molly appeared in one of his own terrycloth robes.

"I was just starting to work," explained Weldon.

"Beat it," said Lurie to the girl, and at her angry stare he turned to Weldon. "Get rid of her. I've got to talk to you."

"Who the hell are you to give orders?" demanded Molly. She took a step into the room.

"Couldn't we go somewhere?" asked Weldon uneasily. "Molly just got here, and . . ."

"I told you to get her out of here," said Lurie, and with that he turned his back, elaborately examining the books on the built-in shelves at the front of the room. Weldon turned back to Molly with a pained, unhappy smile. "I'm sorry," he said uncomfortably.

"The Lord and Master, eh?" Molly looked at him contemptuously.

"It's business," pleaded Weldon. "It's about a show." He started toward the bedroom, but Molly backed away and slammed the bathroom door in his face.

Weldon sat down near the easel and stared at the floor. Lurie continued to examine the books until Molly emerged, fully dressed. Weldon didn't look up, nor did Lurie turn around.

"What is it?" asked Molly curiously. "A lovers' quarrel?" She stopped near Lurie at the door. "A big boy like you," she added reproachfully.

Lurie lifted his heavy black shoe. "That caboose makes quite a target, Molly. Want me to help you down the stairs?"

"Want to try?" she asked defiantly.

Weldon stepped between them quickly. "Please, Molly!" As she opened the door, he said, "I'll call you later."

"Do that," said Molly cordially, and smacked his face with her open hand. Then she went quickly down the stairs.

Lurie closed the door and Weldon, who was rubbing his cheek, heard the click of the lock. He looked up hastily. "What's the matter?"

"She's a bright girl in some ways," said Lurie thoughtfully. "Full of good ideas." His right fist flashed up, landing heavily on Weldon's jaw, knocking him over backwards. The painter skittered across the floor, the easel and the fresh canvas crashing down with him. Before he could move, Lurie was over him. His big hand gripped Weldon by the collar, yanking him to his feet. He let go of his collar then, and Weldon, his hands crossed over his face, staggered back with Lurie stalking him step by step. Weldon came up against a chair and Lurie pushed him down into it savagely. As the painter looked up at him fearfully, Lurie waggled his fist. "Now, you cheap crook, either you come clean with me or I'll break everything on you that's worth breaking."

"I don't know what you're talking about," stuttered Weldon. "What is it?"

"Ellis Blaise showed me a drawing today. One of yours. Where did he get it?"

"Who?" This was almost a scream and its high-pitched sincerity seemed to register on the other man. "I don't know anybody by that name. I didn't give anybody any drawings. I burned them all." Lurie stepped away, as if for a better look at him and Weldon continued pleadingly, "I haven't made any drawings. Not any real ones. I did a lot for practice. I had to do those all the time when I was working out the compositions but they were all on cheap paper. I couldn't sell them that way. I burned them all."

The dealer's taut facial muscles relaxed. He brought the bottle of whiskey and a glass, then poured a drink for Weldon and handed it to him.

"Thanks," muttered Weldon. He gulped down the whiskey, and as Lurie offered him the bottle he shook his head. "I'm all right now."

"Good. Now listen carefully. I know you had to make a lot of practice drawings. Did anyone—anyone at all—

ever see you doing them?" When the artist shook his head, he said, "Now, did you keep count of how many you made?"

"That's crazy. I must have done thousands."

"I mean, each time that you worked at it?"

Weldon shook his head. "I'd keep them all together while I worked, then burn them."

"But if you were called out, or went out for a drink or a meal, or answered the phone?"

"I kept some," said Weldon automatically, and at the darkening glower on the dealer's face, he added shrilly, "For Christ's sake! I had to! That's how I worked out the composition. I had to work from something. I couldn't use a model."

"I understand," said Lurie mildly, though it cost him an effort. "Do you remember one in pencil and charcoal, a reclining figure, half nude?"

Weldon shrugged. "I did hundreds of them. Not many that were half-nudes, though," he added, in a troubled tone. "I did a few of those because I had to practice the drape and hang of the material."

"Do you remember when you did those?"

"Not at any special time. Off and on for perhaps a few months." He got up unsteadily, shaking his head as if to clear it, and reached for the bottle again. Lurie waited patiently until he poured himself a drink and tossed it off.

"The drawings you kept to work from—were they locked up?"

"I'm not a fool," said Weldon.

"Show me," said Lurie.

Weldon went into the bedroom, Lurie at his heels. This was a pine-paneled room with a wide, low bed. Beside the bed stood a circular night table with a heavy, metal lamp. The table was patterned after a revolving bookstand with shelves about twelve inches deep. Weldon lifted the lamp and put it on the floor. Then he reached into the top shelf and the apparently solid table-top opened, revealing a deep, hollow cylinder.

"I made this myself," said Weldon sullenly. "Nobody ever knew it was there."

Lurie bent over the table, peering into the opening. There were tubes and pots of paint and jars of liquid that gave off a slight order of varnish or something similar. When the dealer straightened up, Weldon snapped the top shut and replaced the lamp.

"Who is the fellow you said had one of the drawings?" asked Weldon, following the dealer into the studio again.

"Ellis Blaise. He's a dealer in New York. He works for Lucas Edgerton."

"Any idea how he got it?"

Lurie shrugged. "A woman—someone out here—gave it to him to sell."

Weldon giggled, but at the other's sharp look his nervous mirth broke off abruptly. "I was only thinking," he said apologetically, "you should have bought it."

"I tried to," said Lurie irritably. "How easy will it be to detect the quality of the paper?"

"Maybe right away—maybe never. It's quite a bit heavier than old paper. Lighter in tone, too. Depends on what you're looking for when you examine it."

"I only saw it for a couple of minutes," Lurie told him. "It seemed fine."

"The drawing is perfect," said Weldon smugly. "The giveaway is in the paper. Hell, if he holds it to the light he'll see a water-mark."

"If it comes to that," said Lurie grimly, "I'll put a water-mark on you." The painter began to whine some protest, and Lurie snapped, "Shut up. This one drawing may ruin me." His cold, menacing glare held Weldon's gaze. "You sniveling, blubber-headed drunk. You probably passed out here and left the room plastered with drawings. Suppose somebody wandered in from the street?" He seemed to be pondering this distasteful eventuality, then briskly, he said, "All right. There may be some snooping set off now. Maybe the police, maybe this man Blaise. Be careful."

Weldon nodded. "Want me to get rid of all the paints and chemicals?"

"No," said Lurie. "I think they're safe where they are. I may have a job for you."

He went out and down the stairs to the street. He quickly walked the two blocks to the Boulevard, where his car was discreetly parked in a public lot. He drove to the beginning of the Strip and turned off into a narrow street. He went into a seedy bar, kept dark by day and night for the maximum pleasure of watching the television set high in one corner. Lurie bought a drink at the bar and, after a quick look around, borrowed an afternoon paper from the bartender and carried that and his drink to the last booth. After ten or fifteen minutes there was a new arrival, a compact heavy-set man about forty. A broken nose and spots of scar tissue on his face made him singularly ugly, but he carried his weight with an athlete's grace.

Lurie leaned out of the booth and the newcomer quickened his steps. Lurie pointed to the opposite seat. "Sit down, Sully."

Sully glanced back over his shoulder, then shook his head. "Move over, Boss. Let's watch the door."

Lurie obediently slid over in the booth and Sully sat down beside him. He unbuttoned his tight brown double-breasted jacket and gave Lurie a glimpse of the paper tube jammed down in the waistband of his trousers. He smiled at Lurie's manifest delight. "It was easy," he said, in a flat, matter-of-fact voice. With a cautious glance at the front of the room, he fished out the tube and passed it to Lurie. "It's a lousy picture," he said. "The broad ain't even all bare. Sure it was worth the trouble?"

"Positive," said Lurie happily. "Have a drink, Sully."

11

"THIS MORNING," said Lieutenant Ives, "I thought you were a pleasant sort of a chap, with sense enough to mind his own business. Now this cockeyed story convinces me I was wrong. You had no right to start nosing around, and the girl had no right to hold the drawing out on me to turn it over to you."

"You must have a badge for a heart," said Blaise irritably. The doctor had given him some pills, but his head still ached. "She didn't give it to you because she thought maybe her boy friend had stolen it. She didn't want to cash in on it; she just wanted to spare his family any extra scandal if it was hot. Personally, I think that makes her a pretty nice girl." He sat up and reached for the cigarettes. "As for me, it's true that I picked up a piece of information, but I didn't go into business for myself with it. I called you as soon as I knew what it was. Suppose Molly had given you the drawing? Would you have known it was a forgery?"

"In time," said Ives.

"Sure. Maybe three weeks from now."

"Maybe six weeks, maybe a year. But we'd still have it."

Blaise leaned back against the cushions. "Touché," he murmured.

"Did Simon say why he was leaving it with the girl?" asked Ives.

"He said it was too valuable to be lugged around. Want to hear a hypothetical case?"

"Sure," said Ives. "Does it make any sense at all?"

"We'll see." Blaise sat up and swung his feet off the bed. The pills were working now and only a dull, vague ache remained. "The first thing you've got to realize, Lieutenant, is that faking great art is a big business. It's been going on ever since paintings and sculptures became valuable, and that's been quite a time now."

"I'm a cop," said Ives impatiently. "You don't have to start back in the Renaissance. Get to it."

"Coming. Painters learn a lot by copying. That's not important because you can't sell copies, but every once in a while a student or a painter realizes a technical affinity with the artist he's copying. A little practice and he finds he can turn out a very creditable imitation. For the next step, maybe he studies the composition of the master and makes one up along the same lines. Painters are human beings, with families, responsibilities and a natural desire to have a little tucked away in the bank. The style becomes grooved and the subjects standardized in whatever form the dealers and the public like the most. It's not just commercial art—it's usually an extension of some subject the artist is really passionate about. Utrillo's streets of Paris; Degas' ballet girls; Pissarro's landscapes; Daumier's courtrooms, laborers and riff-raff. Well, take an imitator with a strong technical talent, who's probably an intelligent painter in his own right, he can usually turn out a first-class forgery."

"Sure. But there must be ways of spotting them."

"Right. Usually, the terrific strain of imitating another painter's style is a dead giveaway. The eye alone spots the labored, tedious application of the paint. If it can't, the X-ray and the microscope show it up at once. But you know the criminal mind, Lieutenant. How soon after someone invents a burglar-proof safe does a thief go a step further and by-pass it?"

"Pretty soon," said Ives. "They get better all the time."

"Then add the ego of an artist to the natural crooked competitive streak in such a character and you'll get a refinement of the type that sets out to beat the burglar-proof safe. The first thing the modern expert looks for in any forgery is to see if this specimen is in the natural hand of the supposed author or artist. Some great fakers have beaten that test by simple patience and practice, endless repetition of subjects in the assumed style until their forgeries are entirely natural.

"The next step is the canvas and the paint itself," continued Blaise. "Both are actually simple. The canvas is usually an obscure painting of the same period, stripped down to the original material. The paints are mixed by hand from materials used in the original artist's time, in exactly the same proportions. Chemical analysis won't show a speck of difference between the artist's mixture and the forger's."

"How do you tell the real thing?" asked Ives skeptically.

"Luckily, that kind of forgery is rare. But it happens, and when it does, it can be very rough on the experts. The best guarantee, of course, is the history of the painting. The happy hunting ground for the forger is the collector looking for a bargain who is romantic enough to swallow a yarn about a masterpiece that languished in some eccentric's attic for decades. That's when all the tedious and expensive preparation pays off."

"Very interesting," said Ives, "but if this doesn't tie up with the death of Simon Edgerton, I'd just as soon you told it to the Bunko squad. It's a little out of my line."

"That's next," Blaise assured him. "Simon Edgerton needed money. His father's collection must have seemed like buried treasure to a poor man with a shovel, and it has some great advantages for a dishonest dealer or collector. First, all the paintings were bought years ago and dropped out of sight at once. The old man has never exhibited them or allowed them to be reproduced. Second, until very recently there was nothing like a catalogue of the collection; just scattered notes and the old man's memory. Third, Edgerton is getting old, doesn't get around much, hardly ever looks at any paintings but his own. Even at his nerviest, all Simon had the guts to steal were a few cheap drawings—in my hypothetical case he doesn't steal a thing but collects exactly as much as if he did. All profit, no risk."

Ives was now listening intently. "So the dealer is double-crossed—is that it?"

"Exactly. Simon gives him forged Renoirs—early examples, worth a fortune—supposedly lifted from his father's collection. That's the best guarantee of authenticity in the world today. The dealer either hands over cash and waits it out with the paintings, or, if he can invent a good enough background, quite conceivably can dispose of them at once. I can tell you this much, Lieutenant: if the drawing is a fair sample of the work, and the paintings were of the same quality, a million dollars might be hauled in painlessly and with a minimum of risk."

"That much, eh?" Ives expressed no special surprise. "I imagine a piece of that would look good to a man like Hugh Norden, eh?"

"A rainbow," said Blaise, "complete with pot of gold. Armed with that fake drawing, Norden was in the driver's seat. He could prove the existence of these incredible forgeries and wreck the market for them. Simon may have bought the drawing from Norden, or" —he shrugged—"maybe he put up a fight."

"Norden was on the beach last night," said Ives thoughtfully. At the quick look of surprise Blaise gave him, he added, "He parked his car in an empty driveway a block from the Edgerton place."

"Congratulations," said Blaise. "Now all you have to do is catch him."

"And prove it."

"How did Simon go in and out of the gallery so readily after hours?" asked Blaise. "I understood the place was wired like a television studio."

"It was worked from inside," Ives told him. "Simple, too. One of the windows was fixed so that the alarm switch held even if the window flew up and down all night."

"Enterprising boy. I didn't think he would be that much inclined mechanically."

Ives stood up to go. "That's an interesting yarn about the forgeries. Without the drawing, though, it isn't much to go on."

"I can make some inquiries," said Blaise. "I think I know the kind of paintings they're likely to be. If any have changed hands recently, that might lead to something."

"All right," said Ives reluctantly, and as Blaise smiled, he went on firmly. "I'm not swearing you in as a deputy. This isn't a permit to strap on your Buck Rogers pistol and play games. Understand?"

"Suppose I catch up to the guy that slugged me?" asked Blaise.

Ives gave him a pitying look. "The next time, he'll probably kill you. Stay home and keep your door locked."

12

THE SCENE in the Edgerton library, when Blaise arrived the next day, resembled a council of war. Records and files were spread on the big desk and grouped around it were Edgerton himself, Wesley Corum, Miriam Wayne and Lieutenant Ives. Victor Grandi, as if aware that his lowly status did not entitle him to a seat, leaned against the index cabinets, watching the group with what seemed to be only thinly veiled amusement. Ives, whose seat was directly under a shocking black and yellow Juan Gris abstraction, looked uncomfortably out of place.

"Come in, Blaise," snapped Edgerton in greeting. "Close the door," he yelled, as Blaise started in. He, at least, seemed very much his old self.

As Blaise approached, Miriam rose as if to give him her chair but he waved her down and pulled up another.

"Well, we counted the stock," said Edgerton grimly. He didn't say any more and none of the others wanted to add anything.

"Bad?" asked Blaise.

There was another moment of silence. Then Miriam Wayne said, "Nine paintings are missing."

"Including a Turner," put in Corum.

Blaise whistled, openly taken aback by this information.

"The Turner," went on Corum, "was a particularly fine example, one that I personally . . ."

Edgerton interrupted him brutally. "Shut up, Wesley. Damn it, man, don't start out with your lecture-slides and your pointer."

"What made you so sure," asked Lieutenant Ives carefully, "that no paintings had been stolen?"

Blaise returned his look uncomfortably. "I wish I knew. I told you what was in my mind, Lieutenant."

"Yes," sneered Ives, "you told me."

"Stop bickering," said Edgerton. "Ives, you're supposed to know your own business. If you're shaky enough to listen to outsiders, that's your fault."

Under his lean, tanned face, Ives flushed hotly. "Thanks, Mr. Edgerton, I'll bear it in mind." Then, in his accustomed, mild manner, he asked, "Were all the paintings insured?"

"Doesn't matter," said Edgerton. "I'm not going to file a claim and have the insurance company tell me the paintings were stolen by my son."

Another spell of silence fell over the group at the table, this one broken by Victor Grandi. Very quietly, almost in a whisper, he said, "The Turner was reproduced." He smiled as Blaise whirled around in his chair. "I see that Mr. Blaise knows what I mean by that."

"Yes, I do."

"In other words," said Grandi softly, "it is a pointless, witless, unprofitable theft. It cannot conceivably be sold."

"Why not?" asked Ives.

"Because the painting was known to be in this collection. No dealer or collector would touch it," said Blaise.

"Exactly." Grandi nodded his approval. "All the others, as well as most of our paintings, are unknown to the world at large. They might readily be sold by an influential dealer. The Turner, however, would lead to the immediate arrest of anyone who offered it for sale."

"That's true," said Edgerton. He seemed puzzled by this development. "Silly damn thing to steal—it doesn't make any sense."

"Perhaps in Europe," ventured Corum. "Stolen paintings frequently find some market there. Traders anxious to convert black market or illicit currency."

"Even there," said Grandi gently, "a painting known to be in the Edgerton collection would hardly be a desirable asset."

"That's true," said Edgerton.

Ives pushed back his chair and Miriam handed him a sheet of paper. The strain of recent days, it seemed to Blaise, had told on her. Her naturally pale complexion seemed to have acquired a taut opalescent quality and her eyes were bright and alert.

"This the missing lot?" asked Ives, and when she nodded, he folded the paper and put it away. Edgerton followed him out silently and Grandi waited in the doorway as if to allow them a good start. Then, as he went out, Blaise walked with him.

Grandi seemed to take his company for granted,

circling the library to the beach. "I understand, Mr. Blaise," he said, with what was almost a roguish, sidelong glance, "that you had an interesting and fruitful day. I'm glad I didn't underestimate you."

"I was lucky. Then I got careless. All told, I didn't cover myself with glory. At least, it doesn't smell like glory."

At the driveway, Grandi picked up a branch with which he made absent doodlings in the gravel. "I am a technician," he said. "The component parts of paint itself, the age and quality of canvas, the subtle difference between two parts of the same canvas that may have been executed by master and pupil—those elements of painting are my specialty. I have worked in museums and for distinguished collectors. In my time, the most unerring instinct for the true and false in painting belongs to Lucas Edgerton."

"True enough. But yesterday he accepted as genuine a Renoir drawing that was certainly a forgery."

"Fascinating, isn't it?" murmured Grandi. "What a pity that you no longer have the drawing!"

"There isn't very much I can prove without it," said Blaise. Grandi paused in the path leading to his own shack and faced him with the encouraging smile of a teacher urging a backward pupil on with his lesson.

"You know that this is basically an affair of forgery," said Grandi lightly. "Then you know a great deal."

"It seems to be now an affair of robbery."

"Of murder, too," said Grandi promptly. "But the robbery, and the murder, are incidental. They are other voices in the fugue, but the main theme is one of forgery and everything will be resolved in that ending."

"You say that with great conviction," said Blaise. "Why?"

"Because I am an arbitrary and opinionated man,"

said Grandi promptly. "Because Lucas Edgerton has a crushing effect on every ego but his own and I am glad of the chance to give mine an airing." He turned and started up the walk. "Drop in whenever you're in the mood for a lecture, Mr. Blaise."

Blaise went slowly back up the driveway, his eyes down on the road, so deep in thought that he walked into Cass Edgerton, who was planted in the middle of the drive watching his somnambulistic approach.

"This is California," she said reprovingly. "Very rough on pedestrians. You ought to watch where you're going."

"If I knew whether I was coming or going," said Blaise, "I would."

She fell into step with him. "I had a lamp burning in the window for you last night. Remember your promise as you sailed away to seek your fortune in the new world?"

"I met a man with a hammer. Seems he was making a survey of the thickness of skulls prevailing among Eastern art dealers. The results won't be published for quite a while yet but I think I'm out in front by inches." Walking slowly to the house he related the events leading up to the blackout. "And as if having my skull creased wasn't enough in itself, it also turns out that my bright, brave theory about Simon was the work of a congenital idiot, none other than your present correspondent."

"I know," said Cassy soothingly. "Uncle Lucas told me about the paintings. He knew that Simon confided in me, but this time, I'm sorry to say, he didn't." She stopped in the driveway to look squarely at Blaise. "The night he died, when I called you, what made you so certain that Simon wasn't in any trouble?"

"That's becoming my favorite question," sighed

Blaise. "In a nutshell, Cassy—which is one of the better ways of describing my head—I didn't think he had stolen any paintings. Shows you how smart I am," he added reflectively.

"You said you'd been talking to him. Was it something he said?"

"Something he said, or implied, or his attitude—I'm damned, Cassy, if I know now what it was. But I said it and I'm stuck with it. I got that feeling from Simon, and then, when I talked to Hugh Norden, it was intensified. I wouldn't have told you he was in the clear that night if I didn't believe it to the hilt. You know that."

"Yes, I know."

Approaching the house, Blaise led her away from the library toward the beach front. "Were you here all day yesterday, Cassy?"

"Yes."

"Last night, too?"

"Waiting and waiting and waiting."

"Was Miriam here all the time?"

"As far as I knew, never left the premises. They couldn't go on with the inventory until this morning because the police were all over the gallery and the grounds. She spent all the time in her room, but she came down for dinner."

"Did Simon have any money of his own?" asked Blaise.

"Just his allowance. He got ten thousand a year and some extra at Christmas and on his birthday. Thirteen or fourteen thousand all told."

"Seems ample," said Blaise. "Why did he need money so badly, Cassy?"

"He didn't really need it," she explained carefully. "You have to understand about Simon, and his relationship with Uncle Lucas, and all sorts of psychological mixups. Simon didn't need money; he needed a sense of power. Gambling for very high stakes was one way of achieving it. Poor Simon, he was quite bad at it," she finished sadly.

"Where did he gamble?" asked Blaise.

"Just about everywhere. On trips to Mexico and Nevada, here in town with some of the big shots in the oil and picture business."

"You've got money of your own, haven't you, Cassy?"

"Some." Gravely, she added, "You'll probably be given the details when you ask for my hand."

Blaise laughed. "I was thinking of you as a possible source of income for Simon."

"Oh, that. I'm a soft touch. Anyway, I didn't need it."

"You don't feel the lack of a sense of power?" asked Blaise.

"I have my moments," said Cassy loftily.

"How much did Simon borrow?"

"All told, quite a bit. We called my money 'The Fresh-Air Fund for Needy Edgertons.' The last couple of years Simon got most of it, so it must amount to quite a sum. He kept track of it, though. He'd even compute the interest once in a while and announce the total."

"Did he ever repay any?"

"Simon?" Her eyebrows went up expressively. "I'm sure he meant well and some day, of course, he would have been in a position to give back the whole bundle. It didn't matter. I was always glad to let him have it. If only to avoid the hair-raising scenes that went on with his father."

"To shield Simon, or his father?"

She stopped again, her voice was troubled. "Until today I thought I knew. Remember, I told you that more than being fond of Simon we were a sort of united front?" Blaise nodded, and she went on. "That was true. We were children together in an atmosphere that didn't have much time for us. I defended Simon and hated those who were hostile to him, not because what he did or what he thought was admirable. He conditioned me to believe in his excuses, or to invent fresh ones for him. If he liked something, I made myself like it. If he developed a hatred or a phobia, I pumped away until I had one just as strong. I raged at Uncle Lucas because of what he was doing to Simon." Sadly, as if she was trying to recall something now dimly remembered, she finished with, "I never dreamed of raging at Simon. As I grew up, I think I knew the truth but I wouldn't let it emerge."

"Did you tell him today?" asked Blaise.

"He knew," said Cassy. "He's a smart old man." She brightened now, as they came into the driveway. "Just you be as smart when you're his age."

"I hope I have as pretty a niece."

"You did get hit on the head!" marveled Cassy.

"It's a good head, and none the worse for a few dents and grooves. It's packed with interesting thoughts."

"About me?"

"You come boiling to the surface now and then," Blaise admitted. "There's quite a cast of characters churning around up there, but you've got a compartment all to yourself. How much money did you say you had of your own, Cassy?"

"I didn't say. It's quite a chunk. You'll never have to work again."

"That's what you think," he said, looking off toward the library. Miriam Wayne was standing in the driveway between the two buildings. Walking from the house to the gallery she stopped at the sight of Blaise and the girl, and now she seemed to be waiting for him.

"I'm going to work right now. Read an improving book for a spell, Cassy. When I've earned my pay I'll seek you out." He went up to the driveway, and as Miriam saw him coming alone, she walked through the library door, leaving it open for him.

Blaise followed her in and closed the door. The curtains were drawn at all the windows in the gallery end of the huge room and the resultant gloom was faintly relieved by the one lighted lamp on Miriam Wayne's desk. She stood against the row of cabinets, the pallor of her face set like a cameo in the dark, shadowy area that reached beyond.

"Very dramatic setting," said Blaise.

"I've a headache," was the low reply. "Do you mind a little less light?"

"We can share our headaches." He sat down near the desk in the little pool of light. "Mine dates back a bit. I acquired it yesterday afternoon, shortly after I left here, as the result of a rude encounter with a person or persons unknown." He could feel rather than see the reaction to this. "I went into this business," he continued, "because it seemed like such a genteel, sedentary life. It's a topsy-turvy world, isn't it?"

"You were attacked?" asked Miriam Wayne slowly. "Are you joking, Mr. Blaise?"

"I thought you knew. It seemed to be common knowledge on the estate. I took it for granted that Lieutenant Ives must have conducted some inquiry."

"I didn't know."

"I'll see that you get on our mailing list," Blaise promised. "As a matter of fact, the next time I'm knocked cold you can have an exclusive."

"Do you know why?"

"Someone wanted that drawing—the beautiful forgery I showed you—and didn't care whose head was in the way." Irrelevantly, he added, "Make me a drink, will you, Miriam?"

She started across the room to the cupboard that served as bar. "The problem," mused Blaise, "is that quite a few people knew I had the drawing, and, of course, anyone here could have telephoned to a confederate on the outside. The drawing was all the proof I had. Without it, my theory of a great forgery ring goes all to pieces." He waited for some comment from Miriam.

"Ice?" she asked from the bar, in her constantly even voice.

Blaise laughed. "Yes, thank you."

When she brought him the drink he looked up, then tilted the lamp so that it threw more light on her. "You're a very beautiful girl, Miriam."

"Please, Mr. Blaise."

"I'm rather more forward today. Cassy thinks it did me good to get hit on the head. So for the record, put down that I think you're a very beautiful girl."

"Thank you."

"Now, can I ask one question, perhaps a touchy, delicate question?"

She faced him proudly. "If you like."

"Here goes." He reached out for her hand and drew her unresistingly close to his chair. "What's your racket, Miriam?"

Her eyes betrayed only momentary surprise. Then she gently took away her hand. "My, you are aggressive."

"My theory," said Blaise mildly, "is that if I'm going to be slugged like a private eye; well, then, why not act like one? You're the first chance I've had. I repeat, what's your racket, Miriam?"

"I presume," she said thoughtfully, "that you're not merely being rude, that you have some reason for talking to me this way."

"Nothing that would make any sense," he admitted. "A lot of people covered up for Simon Edgerton, you among them."

"What if I did?" she asked calmly.

"Did you?" When she didn't answer, he went on gently. "I think you did. I don't see how Simon could have stolen any paintings without your help—at least, without being able to count on you."

She laughed indulgently. "You came in late. When we discovered the loss Mr. Edgerton did not want to notify the police. It was I who insisted that Lieutenant Ives be called in. That was to expose myself, naturally."

"Quite candidly," said Blaise, "that puzzles me. Perhaps I'm stupid."

"Let's say," she suggested delicately, "that you're out on a limb."

"Very charitable of you. But what I said still goes. If Simon stole those paintings, he must have been able to count on you somehow—I don't care if you urge the old man to notify the Sûreté and Scotland Yard."

"A few hours ago," she reminded him with perfect aplomb, "you were quite positive that Simon hadn't stolen any paintings. Now, you're just as certain that he did, and furthermore, that I helped him."

"Bear in mind," said Blaise humbly, "that I was hit on the head. Hard, too. You may feel my bump, if that intrigues you."

"I work here," she said. "I'm responsible to Mr.

Edgerton for anything I've done or failed to do. You should certainly tell him what you suspect at once."

"I would," Blaise assured her amiably, "except that it sounds so dopey." Wistfully, he added, "I was hoping you'd confess."

"Another time, if you don't mind."

"You'll feel better for it," Blaise urged. He finished his drink and stood up, stretching wearily. "You won't? Well, then, short of the third-degree, not that it might not be fun, I don't see what I can do about it." He studied the girl. For all the mockery and by-play, she had the intent, concentrated air of a fencer ready to parry attack in any position.

"If Simon stole those paintings before you came to work here, Miriam, your catalogue wouldn't show them at all. After that, even if he could manage to lift them by himself, any check you or his father made would instantly show the theft. As indeed it did today. Simon wasn't equipped for that kind of a strain; just plain lacked the nerve. Nerve is what counts in these coups. Some have it; others have not. You've got it," he finished bluntly, "and to spare. I admire you very much."

"I see that you do," she murmured. "It's comforting to know that, Mr. Blaise. I'll certainly keep it in mind."

"Do that," said Blaise warmly. She started out past him, erect and dignified. He was silent until she was at the door. Then he said quietly, "A source of much concern to the police is how Simon managed to open that window"—he pointed to one of the curtained spaces—"without touching off the alarm. It indicates intimate knowledge of the premises. When they know that he was forbidden ever to be here they will be even more concerned."

She simply nodded, as if he had given her the most casual, everyday information, and went out.

"Thanks for listening," said Blaise.

13

CASS was reading a magazine in the sun room of the house. She looked up as Blaise slid back the door to the beach and she got up at once when he beckoned to her.

"Want to break a law, Cassy?"

"In broad daylight?" was her astonished reply.

"Just a law," said Blaise, "not a commandment." She followed him to the driveway between the gallery and the residence, then behind the house to the row of garages.

"Which is Miss Wayne's car?" he asked, and when she pointed to a neat blue sedan in one of the center stalls, he added, "Keep an eye peeled for intruders."

"I'll whistle the last movement of Beethoven's Ninth Symphony," she promised. "That only takes about eighteen minutes."

"Plenty of warning," said Blaise, as he disappeared into the garage. He looked quickly into the interior of the car, picking up the seats and replacing them, then took the keys from the ignition lock and opened the trunk. There were only the usual tools and a spare tire. He lowered the trunk lid, locked it and replaced the keys. Then he took Cass to a spot on the beach that gave him a view of the house and gallery and the driveway to the street.

"Any questions?" he asked, grinning.

"Don't look so smug. I'm seething with curiosity, and you know it."

"So am I, Cassy. But a bright, observant girl like you can gratify most of mine. Were Miss Wayne and Simon kicking it around?"

"In your delicate fashion, I suppose you mean was there a romance?" She went on at once. "Yes, I think so, and almost from the day she got here. It bowled me over because if ever I saw a deep-freeze dish it's Miss Miriam Wayne."

"I happen to know the possibilities of the quiet, brooding types," said Blaise, "because I'm one myself."

"When you stop talking," said Cassy.

"Who jilted who?"

"I think it finally got too intellectual for poor Simon. And then Molly Dann came along to take the pressure off his brain. Simon and Molly were made for each other, just as Simon and Miriam definitely were not."

"How did Miriam react to the heave-ho?"

"How does she react to anything? As far as I know, she didn't bat an eye."

"I think she did," said Blaise thoughtfully. "I think she batted both eyes, and maybe more. By the way, does she live here?"

"There's a room in the house for her. She also has a flat in Santa Monica—I don't know just where."

"Were you around when the inventory was being taken today, Cassy?"

"In and out. I saw Miriam and Uncle Lucas and Dr. Corum in the house once or twice, but not after they disappeared into the gallery."

"Do you know why Dr. Corum was in on the inventory?"

"I imagine," she answered thoughtfully, "because he understands a lot of the original records—the notebooks Uncle Lucas kept before he had a catalogue." She looked at him curiously. "This isn't just a tailspin, is it? What fascinates you so about the inventory?"

"Here's a list of the missing paintings," said Blaise. "Look it over. Read the names."

She read them aloud: "Whistler, Renoir, Van Gogh, Sisley, Turner, Redon, Pissarro."

"Excellent," said Blaise. "You read very well. Do the names mean anything to you?"

She looked at the list again. "What is it—a code?"

"Don't they all have something in common?"

She handed him the paper. "I don't know how you got so bright suddenly, but it's obviously not contagious."

"The catalogue," said Blaise, "like catalogues the world over, is in alphabetical order. When I got here with the fake Renoir drawing about half the catalogue had been checked and nothing was missing. Then I laid down the evidence of the forgery and went away. The inventory went on into the second half of the catalogue, and now look at this list again. What these names have in common, Cassy, is that they're all from the second half of the catalogue. No Degas, Cézanne, Manet, Corot, Lautrec—or any other painting that would have been in what had already been checked."

The girl nodded slowly. "I think I know what you mean."

"A smoke-screen," said Blaise, "to distract your uncle and the police from investigation of the forgery. I don't believe Simon stole those paintings, or any others." He stood up. "I'm going to find out how the inventory was taken now, and while I do that, I want you to watch the gallery and give me a whistle if Miss Wayne leaves the premises."

"All right. The Ninth Symphony again?"

"Sure. If you need an encore, try 'Love in Bloom.' "

14

DR. CORUM was an obliging, straightforward witness and seemed to accept Blaise as an investigator, asking no questions about the propriety of the examination. He confirmed what Cass had said, that he was asked to participate in the inventory because many of the original records of the collection were his own. The procedure followed, though complex, was thorough and efficient. He himself had checked the catalogue cards against the old, scattered records; then the cards were checked against the actual canvases. All of the missing paintings were from the vault; most were unframed, though all were mounted on stretchers for preservation.

He remembered clearly and firmly that when Blaise arrived with the Renoir drawing, "the unreasonable facsimile," he called it wryly, the index had been checked through the letter "M" and he also verified Cassy's recollection that the police activities in the gallery prevented any resumption that day. He himself had spent the night in town, returning for duty with the inventory squad at 9 A.M.

"Was anyone in the gallery when you arrived?" asked Blaise.

"Oh, no. It had been locked up after the police

finished. Lucas had the keys and we waited for him." At
the quick, searching look Blaise darted at him, he added,
"Lucas thought it best, for security, that he alone should
have the keys until the inventory was quite finished. At
any rate, we waited until Lucas came down at about
nine-thirty and finished the inventory. Then Grandi was
called in to make sure that none of the missing paintings
was in the shop."

"Was there much talk about the drawing I showed
you?" asked Blaise.

"Oh, yes. We were all stunned. I wish," sighed Dr.
Corum, "that I might have had another look at it. I was
jolted hard by what you told me. It rather paralyzed
my optic nerve, I'm afraid."

"I flashed it on you rather unfairly," said Blaise
placatingly. "Under normal circumstances, I'm sure
you would have spotted it."

"I'm an expert," said Corum sadly. "I'm supposed to
be one thousand per cent correct all the time. The
trouble is," he added plaintively, "the forgers keep
getting better all the time. And it's most awkward when
something you're certain is genuine turns out to be a
fake, and the one you're positive is a fake turns out to be
genuine. I was sued once, because a painting I certified
as a Cézanne was eventually proved to have been painted
by Maurice de Vlaminck."

Blaise grinned. "Well, it was a real Vlaminck, at any
rate."

"Yes," said Corum, "and worth a thousand dollars.
As a Cézanne, it sold for twenty-six thousand. Luckily, I
got out of that dilemma with a whole skin. The Cézanne
signature was genuine. Someone had brought him the
painting late in life and he claimed it as his own and
added his signature. Since it fooled Cézanne, it wasn't

so disastrous that it also fooled me. I saw a spread on Utrillo recently. He was posed with a row of paintings, presumably his own. Some were forged, some were real. He himself was unable to do more than guess at which was which."

Blaise laughed. "He drinks quite a bit."

"I'll be taken to it myself," said Dr. Corum, "if these critical setbacks continue. To think that there should be a forger with sufficient skill and talent to produce a Renoir portrait of that period. It is staggering."

"It staggered me," agreed Blaise cheerfully.

"I hope," said Dr. Corum anxiously, "that you'll keep me advised of any further developments in that field."

"The drawing was the vital clue," said Blaise. "Without it I don't know if there is much or anything I can prove. I've put out some feelers here and in New York. If they scoop up anything interesting I'll let you know at once."

Staggering was the very word to describe the mood, Blaise reflected on his way out to the beach again. What was especially staggering was that the distinguished critic and expert should have referred to a still non-existent forgery specifically as a portrait.

15

"Operator X reporting," said Cassy briskly. "Stayed on post, did not fall asleep. Subject appeared in driveway over twenty minutes ago. Whistled Beethoven Ninth, switched to Schubert Unfinished, tried selections from Bach B-minor Mass. No sign of you, so followed subject up to house, trailing stealthily as taught in basic training with Brownies, Troop B, Santa Monica Patrol. Subject changed into dark-gray suit, copy of last year's Christian Dior model with flared waist and large pockets. Subject wore with this white, candy-striped blouse, shade too flashy in my opinion, but then am not subject's keeper. If was, would have clouted her one month ago. Subject then returned to gallery, made telephone call. Doors and windows closed, couldn't listen. Subject then left premises in own car, empty-handed. Roger. Over."

"Pretty fair report," said Blaise. He pulled her to her feet from her cross-legged position on the sand. "Want to go down in the cellar with me, little girl?"

"You're supposed to offer me candy."

"I'm the more frugal type of sex fiend. Keep down the overhead, that's the way to operate profitably." He left her at the gallery door, and borrowed the keys to the gallery and the vault from Lucas Edgerton, to whom he explained that he wanted to assemble the paintings they had listed for the proposed sale. He came back to the gallery, opened the door and turned on all the lights.

"When was this added?" he asked, and Cassy said, "About eight years ago, when the insurance premiums were threatening to eat Uncle Lucas out of house, home and collection. The appraisers had the value of the collection up to about ten million and the fire and flood insurance rates out here, with no city fire department around the corner, came to a big annual bite. So it was agreed to have two separate policies—one for the paintings kept in the house, which is old-fashioned wood and stucco, burns like driftwood, and another policy on the bulk of the paintings, stored here in air-conditioned, fireproof splendor. This is all steel and concrete.

"How does the burglar alarm work?"

"Right here." She pulled the curtains at the window nearest to the driveway door, revealing a black box with a protruding key or handle. "This is a signal to the office. The alarm goes on automatically at 6 P.M. and after that, even if the door is opened with a key, the alarm sounds at the patrol station in the city. Uncle Lucas wanders in and out of here all night long, so when the system was first installed the police were here almost every night. They finally worked out this method: within two minutes after the door is opened, a registration signal in code has to be flashed to the office. If they don't get it, they hot-foot it out here. If they do get it, they go back to the pinochle game."

"Very sound," said Blaise. "Do you know the code?" When she shook her head, he added, "I suppose that eliminates Simon, too."

"Miriam and Uncle Lucas are the only custodians. I've been wanting to ask," she continued soberly, "how Simon managed it?"

"He had his own methods," said Blaise. "The only mystery is how he learned enough about the system to out-guess it. You see, Cassy, the principle of the burglar alarm is to protect the premises against intruders from the outside. Each window is hooked into the alarm system. Once the window-fastening is closed, any attempt to open the catch or pry up the window sounds the tocsin. In this case, a thin staple depressed the alarm switch on one window, and when the lock was closed it slid right into place. However, when Simon opened the window, the staple held the signal button securely in place and the burglar alarm went right on clicking smoothly all the time he was going in and out."

"Simon thought of all that," she marveled.

"He may have had help," said Blaise drily. He led the way to the vault and opened the double door. On the gallery side these were of stained light walnut, but the inner lining was gleaming steel. The lock was a delicate cylinder device and the heavy doors were beautifully balanced to move smoothly and to close tight. A short flight of concrete steps led down into the vault. Fluorescent light bars flickered for a moment, then blazed up brightly, flooding the underground compartment from end to end. There were eight aisles made by triple-tiered stacks, all bulging with paintings. The canvases, most of them unframed, stood on end, and thin strands of steel separated them to give each its individual compartment. The only article of furniture in the vault was a cheap, battered desk and one wooden chair. A door behind the desk opened readily when Blaise tried it and he saw a bleak lavatory.

The compartments were numbered, corresponding to the index numbers, and there was a movable ladder in each row to give access to the upper tier of shelves.

"Glad you came?" asked Cassy drily.

"Not so far." He looked around the bare, ugly room. "Suppose you wanted to hide nine paintings in a hurry, Cassy?"

"I'm a small girl," she said apologetically. "It would be difficult."

"A simple way," he mused, "might be to put them in a portion of the vault in which the inventory had already been checked." He moved back to the steps and to the first row of shelves on the right, where the numbers began. He pulled out a canvas at random and saw that the number on the back corresponded with the number on the shelf. "Here we go, Cassy. You want the high road or the low road?"

"I'm not dressed for standing on ladders," she said delicately.

"I am," said Blaise. "Just crawl along down there on the bottom and see that the numbers on the paintings and the shelves agree."

In an hour of laborious climbing and stooping, they worked up and down row after row until Cassy finally announced, "I'm up to P, for Pissarro. Also," she added, with both hands in the small of her back, "for punchy."

"It was rather a good idea, don't you think?" said Blaise sheepishly from the ladder on which he was resting.

"On paper."

"I weave my web of dreams," he said loftily. "Let others do the humdrum, practical everyday sleuthing." He climbed down with some protest from aching, unaccustomed muscles. "Being a detective, I thought, would involve no more than coldly analytical thinking and, on the physical plane, occasionally belting a beautiful girl one in the beezer. Pride has dug a pitfall, Cassy, in which I now sprawl uncomfortably with my theory cut to ribbons."

"You'll have another idea," she consoled him.

"But I like the idea I had," was his wistful reply. "It was so tidy. It made such good sense."

"On paper," she repeated.

"I wish you'd stop saying that. It's one of your worst habits."

"Blaise!"

He turned to the steps at the sound of Edgerton's voice in this isolated, air-conditioned sub-cellar.

"Blaise—you down there?"

"Present," called Blaise, and then Lucas Edgerton came down the steps into the vault. He seemed surprised to see his niece in these surroundings.

"Cassy's helping me," explained Blaise.

The old man nodded. "Where are you putting the paintings?"

"The paintings?" echoed Blaise stupidly. Then, "Oh, yes, the paintings."

"The stuff you were in such a hurry to assemble," said Edgerton bitingly.

"Those paintings," said Cass sagely.

Edgerton didn't wait for an explanation. "Telegrams came for you," he said, handing Blaise two envelopes. "The hotel sent them over." He turned and stamped up the stairs heavily, looking back at the top for one more quizzical stare before he vanished into the gallery.

"Any uncle with a grain of decency," said Cass bitterly, "would have demanded to know your intentions on the spot."

Blaise was intent on the first of the two telegrams. It was from a customs agent he employed in New York, a go-between who handled the clearance of paintings and antiques for dealers and importers. It stated that some six months ago Jonas Astorg had imported a group of six paintings, "including two Renoirs, three-quarter portrait young girl in negligee, 1874, size 42 x 33 and landscape with figures, 1877, size 47 x 26, both unknown, new on market, consigned Astorg to Astorg." The last phrase referred to the details of the shipment, Astorg apparently having acquired the paintings abroad and shipping them to himself from a European address.

He tore open the second envelope. This was from his own secretary in New York: "Museum states Andrew Kullman, Hollywood, queried them on unknown Renoir, 1874."

Blaise stuffed both wires in his pocket. Cass was looking at him intently. "I'm getting to know that glazed look on your face. I'm about to be put back in my play-pen while you go whirling off on some brain wave."

"I must learn to mask my true feelings," said Blaise. "The fact is, Cassy, I think I am tottering on the brink of a good idea."

"Well, here we are in a nice, cool cellar."

"The idea," he went on firmly, "concerns significant revelations in the field of modern art."

"Oh, great!"

He lifted her to the second step on the stairs leading to the gallery, so that she was standing slightly above him. "A time for everything, Cassy. 'Time for you and time for me, and time yet for a hundred indecisions.' That's from T. S. Eliot."

"What's isn't?"

" 'There will be time to murder and create.' That's Eliot, too," said Blaise softly. "It recalls the urgent matters I must put straight into execution."

She put her hands on his shoulders, keeping him on the level below. "Take me with you."

"Not now, Cassy. Come to the Inn later, though, and I'll take you to dinner." He looked at his watch. "Give me about two hours start."

"Start running," said Cassy, as she stepped aside.

16

IT WAS almost seven o'clock when Blaise reached the Andrew Kullman studio, and the shabby, sprawling lot was all but deserted. The gateman directed him to the office and a weary secretary left the script she was typing to take him inside.

Kullman was a small, slender man, almost invisible behind the heaps of books and papers on his enormous desk. He took off his heavy reading glasses and blinked his relief as he led Blaise to the opposite end of the large room where more informal and comfortable furniture was arranged around a low, wide coffee-table. The inevitable piles of script were ranged here, too, but Kullman pushed them aside and in a few moments the secretary brought in a tray with coffee.

Blaise brought out the museum's letter about the Degas. Kullman glanced at it, then looked up at Blaise uncertainly.

"That was a long time ago," said Kullman. "I was a patron of the arts then. Things have changed."

"Forget it," said Blaise promptly.

"I meant it then," said Kullman. "I had a big year and fifty or sixty thousand didn't matter—came out of taxes mostly. This year it's been rough."

"Television?" asked Blaise.

Kullman nodded. "Television, drive-in theatres, mounting costs . . ." With a sad smile, he added, "And just between us, I made a couple of dreadful movies." He poured the coffee. "To tell you the truth, I forgot the offer to buy the painting months ago. When my secretary said you were working for Lucas Edgerton I thought it was about something else."

"What?"

"If you don't know," said Kullman, "then I was wrong."

"Anything I can do, or bring to Mr. Edgerton's attention?"

Kullman looked at him gravely for a moment, then

got up and went to an old break front secretary. He unlocked one of the tiny drawers with a key and came back to Blaise with some oblong slips of paper. They were I.O.U.'s, dated back some six months and the total of the four was thirty thousand dollars. They were made out to Andrew Kullman and signed Simon Edgerton.

Blaise handed them back. "Gambling?" he asked, and when Kullman nodded, he said, "Want me to give them to Edgerton?"

"Edgerton," said Kullman, "is a mean son-of-a-bitch, but he doesn't deserve that. Or, if he does, I won't do it to him." He tore the papers across, then gathered the pieces and tore them again. He dropped them on the table before Blaise. "You can give them to him now."

"You could have collected them," Blaise pointed out. "Still can. Whatever you think of Edgerton, and for whatever reason, he pays."

"I know," replied Kullman.

"It's a handy sum of money. This television fad might not blow over."

Kullman smiled thinly. "Maybe not." He spread the torn shreds of the I.O.U.'s with his fingertips. "Put it down to ego. Maybe it's worth the thirty thousand to feel that I did something nice. Just between us, the boy wasn't much good, but he was gay and there were lots of likable things about him."

Blaise looked down at the ragged bits of paper. "Was that a gambling debt?"

Kullman nodded. "A week-end in the mountains. The game went on all day and all night. Simon hit a bad losing streak and being that kind of a gambler, he stayed with it. I was a big winner," he said casually, "so it doesn't really matter. I tried to keep him out of the game—he didn't have a chance in it—but that wasn't a good tactic with Simon. He played like a man who didn't expect to pay, and then, like a chump, he paid."

"Any others he owed?" asked Blaise.

Kullman shook his head. "I was the big winner, so I took it all."

"When did he offer you the Renoir?" asked Blaise casually. When Kullman didn't immediately reply, he added, "Was it in payment, or was that a separate deal?"

"What line are you in?" asked Kullman. His voice was flat and thin, no warmth or cordiality left in it.

"I'm a dealer," said Blaise. "You know that, but I don't mind repeating it. I'm not out to track criminals, avenge anybody or anything, and I'm not running for any office, least of all sheriff. If I'm a busybody it's because I'm an art dealer and I want to remain one. I think the painting you were offered is a fake." At Kullman's sharp look of surprise, he added, "A great fake. So good that it becomes a threat to everybody that buys or collects paintings. What television is to you," he finished, with a grin, "that kind of a forgery is to me."

"I didn't buy it," said Kullman thoughtfully. "But by God, not because I thought it was a fake."

"You thought it was hot?"

"Of course. I knew Simon pretty well, and while I don't know the statistics on Edgerton's collection, he must be wallowing in Renoirs. I just took it for granted that it belonged to the old man. I remember how embarrassed I was when he showed it to me. I just looked at him sadly and shook my head, and he must have known what I was thinking because he laughed out loud."

"You were interested, though," Blaise pointed out. "You checked it with the museum."

"I'm a collector. It was an unusual offering. Besides,

I was curious to see if the kid had stolen it. I sent the museum a photo and the specifications. They didn't tell me a thing." He looked at Blaise, as if much intrigued. "I'm not the greatest expert in the world, but it certainly looked good to me. What makes you think it's a fake?"

"I've never laid eyes on the painting," confessed Blaise, and at Kullman's astonished look, he said, "I'm building up a theory the way they build up a dinosaur, just from the discovery of a tooth, or an inch of the tail."

"You know more than that," said Kullman. "I don't care, unless maybe there is a movie in it, but you know something."

"What made you decide not to buy it?" asked Blaise.

"I don't exactly know," said Kullman slowly. "It was too good. Too good for Simon to be handling, too good for him to be offering it to me. If this was the depression again, no buyers with cash, I could understand such an opportunity coming my way. Or, if the painting was only fair, or even just good, I could understand that, too. But this was great, rare—I had the impression that I was looking at a perfectly baited trap."

Blaise nodded. "I understand. I'll bet you've got a hell of a good collection."

"Sight unseen?"

"I like the way your mind works."

"Tell that to the exhibitors," said Kullman wistfully. "The current joke in town is that I ought to burn my pictures and release my paintings."

"Did Simon give you any history on the painting?" asked Blaise.

"Naturally. Even that was perfect. The owner was Roger Vernet, a refugee whose family once had a big artists' supply house in Paris. Vernet's grandfather supplied paint and materials to Renoir himself; that's how he was supposed to have acquired this painting. You wouldn't want a better, more respectable story on a canvas, and Vernet is on tap right here in Los Angeles to back it all up."

"It gets better and better," sighed Blaise. "In time, you know, the forgeries will probably be worth more than the Renoirs." He stood up, and Kullman rose with him.

"I'd like you to see my paintings," said his host. "After Edgerton's I don't expect you to be impressed, but some of them are worth a look. Come in tonight, if you can. I'm not on the waterfront, but Brentwood isn't much of a drive. I'll send a car for you."

"Thanks. I've got a car."

"Astorg is coming," said Kullman, as they walked to the door, "and a local man named Kenneth Lurie."

"Know them both," said Blaise.

"I thought you would. Since you're so keen on Renoir." Kullman's expression was innocently bland. He wrote an address on a slip of his notepaper and handed it to Blaise.

"What did Simon offer you—a portrait or a landscape?"

"A still life," was Kullman's reply. "Apples in a dish, a bottle of wine on a tray with two glasses. A table with a white cloth, painted slightly from above, a wall with flowered paper in the background." Blaise could not restrain the sudden, pained grimace. "What's the matter —bad news?"

"We're on virgin soil," murmured Blaise. "I knew there were portraits and landscapes. The still life is a surprise."

"Why not?" shrugged Kullman. "You could get one Renoir a week until you had a complete set. The way we used to give away dishes."

"That's a lovely thought," said Blaise sadly. "I'll be obliged if you'll keep it to yourself."

"Come in tonight," said Kullman in parting. "I'm a collector; I've got a stake in this. Perhaps I can help you with your second act."

17

THE TERRACE RESTAURANT, jutting into space from the ocean side of the hotel, had no walls or ceilings to tempt the decorators. It was, therefore, the handsomest part of the establishment. The lighting was soft and scattered, no more than the minimum candle-power specified by Los Angeles County law, and barely that in the back booth where Cass Edgerton and Blaise were finishing dinner.

"Did the laird object to your going out?" asked Blaise.

"He was delighted. Dr. Corum stayed on and they can talk happily about proofs, states, formulas and technical gibberish that makes my head spin."

"Mine, too."

"Yours? I should think you'd have the whole racket at your fingertips."

"When they get into proofs and states," Blaise told her, "that's etching talk. A special plane of fanaticism attained by only a few true believers. I've memorized some of the jargon, for emergencies, but I'd just as soon avoid being put to the test."

"Uncle Lucas sent you a message," laughed Cassy. "He said, and I quote, tell that soft-headed idiot I didn't bring him three thousand miles to make passes at my niece."

Blaise considered this. "Do you suppose he'd go for fifteen hundred? I might pay half the fare myself."

"Doctor Corum, on the other hand," she continued, "gave it as his opinion that you were an extremely able and intelligent young man."

"I hope he's right," murmured Blaise earnestly. "I think I'll know soon."

"The game's afoot, eh? And the hounds in full cry?"

"The 57th Street pack, Ellis Blaise, Master-of-the-Hounds," he said sadly, "is at the moment being badly outdistanced. The trouble is, Cassy, that I'm the only one who really believes my tall tale about the great Renoir forgeries, and I myself, at times, am inclined to take it with a grain of salt. Dr. Corum knows I'm right but he won't let himself believe it."

"Uncle Lucas trusts him," said Cassy. "That must mean something. He trusts darn few people."

"The experts always take a beating when some great forgery passes for the real thing. Corum probably feels his reputation is at stake." Blaise signed the check and pressed some money into the eager palm of the captain. "Ready, Cassy?"

"Ready. Why are we going to Andrew Kullman's house? He's made some terrible pictures, but none of them were forgeries."

"He asked me to drop in tonight. Do you mind?"

"Not at all," said Cassy. "I like him. He offered me a screen test."

"You'd be good in pictures," said Blaise. "Mother parts, or the kind elder sisters who keep heroines pure for the fade-out. How was the test? Did you pass?"

Cassy sighed. "For all my vast and compelling physical attractions, I knew that what he really wanted was a look at the collection. I invited him to lunch. That solved his problem and left me with my amateur standing."

"Doesn't Uncle Lucas do nip-ups when you invite the peasantry for a meal?"

"Oh, he had fits. He screamed about upstarts, interlopers, pants-manufacturers who spied on him—you know Uncle Lucas when he's wound up and winging. I simply told him that if I couldn't entertain my friends I would pack up and go somewhere else. That cooled him off. I can't say that he actually fawned on poor Mr. Kullman, but he grunted cordially a couple of times. You know the trick painting he has by Rouault?"

Blaise nodded. She was referring to an unusual canvas painted early in his career by the French artist, Georges Rouault. It was deceptively classical in conception and technique and only a few bits of vivid color gave any hint of the violent palette the artist was subsequently to employ. It was a favorite trap of Edgerton's to refer to it casually as a Manet, which it did indeed resemble. Blaise himself had accepted it and endured Edgerton's hoots and jeers for hours.

"Don't tell me Kullman spotted it?" When she nodded, he said, "Well, good for him."

"I tipped him off," said Cassy modestly. "I knew he'd have it sprung on him and it was worth all the trouble to see Uncle Lucas's jaw go slack and his eyes pop. Mr. Kullman just looked smug and self-satisfied, but he twinkled at me every chance he got and the next day he sent me about two hundred dollars' worth of flowers."

Blaise chuckled. "You little sneak. Why didn't you do as much for me?"

"You're an expert. It's your business to know these things."

"Altogether too much is expected of us experts," sighed Blaise. He led the way out through the lobby of the hotel and to his car, parked in the area provided by the management. "He lives in something called Brentwood," said Blaise.

"Drive on down the road a-piece," said Cassy. "I will direct you and point out the homes of movie stars and places of interest as we pass them by. On your left at this moment," she intoned, "is the refreshment stand where in 1908 Dr. Rupert Nutburger invented the delicacy which now bears his name. On your right, the Bayside Beach Club which provides outings at the seashore for rich, white American Protestants. On your left again," she said, more demurely this time, "a motorcycle cop who is about to give you a ticket for driving without lights."

18

ANDREW KULLMAN hated a quiet dinner. His working day was a long, taut struggle with other temperaments and the evening meal, coming close on the heels of this tension, bored him unless it maintained some equivalent level of excitement. Other hosts, faced with the same problem, fell back on after-dinner specialties that ran the gamut from chamber music to animal acts, but Kullman delighted in the subtle fanning of a feud. He conceded that this trait was mildly sadistic, though he never indulged in the practice of bringing together wives and mistresses and husbands and lovers, which delighted some jaded entertainers. But if he could invite the author of some recent book and the critic who had flayed it in last Sunday's paper, or a new idol of the screen and the executive who had advised him to give it all up and go back to the laundry, then Kullman was the ideal picador, shrewdly planting the barbs that brought the antagonists to fighting pitch. Then, being a man of some wit and much power, he would resolve it all, leaving the contestants, if they still felt like swinging, free to go on to Mocambo or some standard arena.

Tonight, with Jonas Astorg and Kenneth Lurie as his only dinner guests, Kullman had been anticipating only clinical chat about activities and trends in the world of art. Now he was intrigued by what Blaise had confided, and in a mood of high anticipation. He barely listened as Astorg analyzed a recent auction, explaining away the poor prices achieved by some excellent paintings.

"Utrillo," Astorg was saying, "has become the official painter of the decorators' union. It is true also to some extent of Vlaminck, Dufy, Derain and some others. But the Utrillo over the fireplace must be figured in the budget of a room like the sofas or the piano and the price has nothing to do with the value of the painting—it simply reflects conditions in the decorating business."

Kullman smiled faintly.

"Besides," put in Kenneth Lurie, "faking them is right now the fourth biggest industry in France. Here, too, for all I know."

"Ellis Blaise is coming in later," murmured Kullman. He looked straight down the table between his two guests, concentrating on the tall candelabra. He was rewarded by a moment of silence.

"I didn't know you knew Ellis," said Astorg.

"Nice chap," was Lurie's comment.

"Did he talk to you about the paintings Edgerton is going to sell?" asked Astorg.

Kullman considered this, and finally said, "No," leaving it up to them to wonder just what Blaise had talked about. He was enjoying himself already. He waited until the butler, who was passing the cigars, stepped away from Astorg, and then added, "I also asked Roger Vernet to stop in for a drink. Oh, by the way, Lurie, what you said about the faking of Utrillo reminded me of something." The match just then en route to the tip of Lurie's cigar stopped in mid-air.

"Yes?" asked Lurie quietly.

Kullman was already busy with the butler. "Coffee in the library," he was saying, "and put out enough for some extra guests."

"Yes, sir," murmured the butler, and withdrew.

Lurie was still waiting, but Kullman ignored him. "What were you saying?" the dealer asked finally.

"About what?" was the bland reply.

"Something I said about the faking of Utrillo reminded you of a story you wanted to tell me."

"Oh." Kullman looked blank. "Well, it couldn't have been very important." He pushed back his chair and led the way out of the dining room. He could sense the barometer falling and, without turning to look, could project for himself the glances exchanged behind his back.

"By the way, Lurie," said Kullman, "did you send your chauffeur in to have some dinner?"

"He drove into town. He'll be back to pick me up."

"He could have had his dinner here," protested the host. Then he sighed. "Perhaps it's just as well—he frightens my cook."

Lurie laughed. "Sully? He isn't exactly the English servant type, is he? To tell you the truth, in town he makes even me feel a little nervous. But on the road, when I've got pictures worth many thousands in the car, Sully radiates such confidence that even the insurance company is impressed."

The butler came in with the coffee, and while it was handed around, Blaise and Cass Edgerton arrived.

Astorg bowed low over her hand. "You were a little girl when I used to come to your uncle's home, Miss Edgerton."

"I remember. One Christmas you sent me a scooter."

"A slight expression of my regard," murmured Astorg.

"I meant to send you a thank-you note as soon as I learned to write. Still, better late than never. Thank you."

"It was my pleasure."

"Gold-digger," whispered Blaise. He left her at the coffee with the others and moved around the room, Kullman at his side, to see the paintings. Kullman's collection was small, but, as Blaise had anticipated, chosen with great care and taste.

Blaise stopped before a large, biting Daumier, a courtroom scene, the prisoner and the judge facing each other across the vast boundary of class which was this great French artist's special concern. "Nice, isn't it?" murmured Kullman. "That was the year I made a movie about an earthquake. I was always lucky with disasters. Typhoons, hurricanes, forest fires, floods, epidemics." He turned to point out a lush, rippling Monet canvas, a stand of poplars by a shimmering lake. "That came from a film I did on the plague that swept London."

"I've got a pretty Mary Cassatt painting you'd like," said Blaise, "and I also know a lot about Typhoid Mary. You can have a package deal."

"It sounds fine," said Kullman, then went into the hall to greet two new arrivals, Molly Dann in the company of a tall, good-looking foreigner whom Kullman introduced as Roger Vernet. Vernet was all charm and good manners, but Molly Dann was fairly seething with some inner conflict. She nodded to Blaise, and curtly acknowledged her introduction to Astorg, then whirled on Kenneth Lurie.

"Listen, Mister," she said angrily. "You'd better keep Paul Weldon under lock and key or he'll be taken away in a butterfly net."

Lurie shrugged, showing only what seemed to be honest surprise, and Molly continued angrily. "I had to chase him away from my house this afternoon, and tonight, damned if he didn't follow Roger and me to the Beachcomber and try to start a fight there."

"It was nothing," said Vernet, deprecatingly. "Believe me, Molly, I didn't mind in the least."

"I did," insisted Molly.

"I'm only his dealer," said Lurie, in an annoyed tone, "and not his doctor." He turned to explain to Kullman. "He's a young painter I handle—you've seen his work. I gave him a show last year and one the year before. He's crazy about Molly."

"Understandably," smiled Kullman. He handed Molly a large snifter glass, in the bottom of which was a coating of brandy. She tossed it off, while the others sat rolling their own glasses in the palms of their hands, inhaling the aroma delicately. She put the glass down on the copper sheathing of the bar and then, as she turned away, she saw Cass Edgerton for the first time.

"Hello, Molly," said Cass agreeably. "I wondered when you were going to notice me."

"I'm sorry," muttered Molly. She accepted mechanically the fresh glass Kullman handed her. "I shouldn't have come tearing in like that." She was groping for some expression of condolence or sympathy. "I'm sorry," she repeated.

"Thanks, Molly." Cassy reached for her purse. "I'm off to the boudoir. Shall we show them that girls know how to stick together?"

"Sure," said Molly.

The men rose as the two girls went out. Kullman's butler moved from cup to cup with fresh coffee and Roger Vernet exchanged some polite phrases in French with Jonas Astorg. The dealer inquired about his family and Vernet, thanking him a thousand times for the goodness of his concern, was happy to assure him that mother and father had resettled in the family apartment in Paris and that all went well.

"Oh, Lurie," said Kullman, when this interchange was over. He was leaning against the mantelpiece with Astorg and Vernet on his right, Lurie and Blaise at his left.

"Yes, Andrew?" the dealer queried politely.

"I remember now what it was I wanted to say when you were talking about the fake Utrillos. It was a story Blaise told me yesterday."

Lurie's eyes met Astorg's briefly, then fell away. He turned to Blaise. "Really?"

Blaise nodded. "The Renoir drawing I showed you yesterday was a forgery."

Lurie was obviously taken aback. "How can that be?

True, I only saw it for a minute, but it was marvelous—perfect." He looked across at Astorg. "Don't you agree, Jonas?"

Astorg said, "Go on, Blaise."

"Not much more to tell. Lurie's right. The drawing was perfect. With a microscope and an enlarger you might have found flaws, but maybe not even then. As far as what was on the paper, it was a Renoir. But the paper itself was the dead giveaway. Modern paper, made right here in Los Angeles."

There was a hush, broken by Kullman. "Here's to crime," he offered cheerfully.

"Well, then," said Lurie, "it exposes itself. No question that it is a forgery."

"Not to me," said Blaise. "Unfortunately, it is lost. After I checked the paper, I telephoned the police. Then I went to my hotel and someone was waiting for me. I was knocked out and relieved of the drawing."

"In his hotel, mind you," emphasized Kullman. "In the room right next to yours, Jonas."

Astorg was pale and even in the shadowy light Blaise thought he saw veins on his face and forehead that were visible for the first time.

"You've got the makings of a real thriller there," said Lurie.

"I thought so at the time. I'm not so sure it impressed the police."

The discussion was diverted as Molly and Cass came back into the room. A cozy powder-room chat had done a lot to restore Molly's hearty good nature, and she now spoke pleasantly to all.

"We're talking about forgery," said Kullman gaily. "What do you think, Astorg—is it confined to Renoir, or is it possible that everything we own is just as false?"

At the mention of Renoir, Molly turned to stare at Blaise. He smiled reassuringly, and after an instant she looked away.

"You, too, Roger," said Kullman to the young Frenchman. "You'd better have another look at that lovely Renoir still life. Chances are you'll find the canvas was made in Jersey City within the year."

"I doubt it," said Vernet, smiling coolly. "You see, the painting has been in my family for many years. Besides, paints and pigments are my own business. You would be surprised," he went on, twinkling, "at the number of forgeries I myself have exposed."

"I'm sure I would," replied Blaise.

Vernet was warming to a subject he obviously knew well. "Every great painter has had his own unique way of blending his colors. Those methods are known today."

Blaise nodded, interrupting. "Yes, deWild's Chronological Tables of Pigment. If you find zinc white in a Raphael, you just look in the book and it tells you that zinc white was not used until many years later."

"Maybe Raphael was ahead of his time," said Cassy.

Roger Vernet was a little annoyed, and Kullman fanned it by saying, "Is that your method of disclosing forgery, Roger?"

"Certainly not," snapped Vernet. "Naturally, forgers are skilled technicians. However, another means of identification is the age of the paint itself. It used to be that when a faked painting was being prepared the cracks would actually be drawn into the canvas with a sharp instrument. But that was clumsy, and comparatively easy to detect. Then the fakers learned how to cover the paint with a lacquer that would burn off under heat and crack the painting underneath just as naturally as years of exposure to light and atmosphere. Even that," and he smiled blandly, "can be proven false in the laboratory. Under the surface of the painting is the *gesso*, the plaster surface with which the artist prepared his canvas, and that is what finally determines the experts' opinion."

"Suppose the forger uses an old painting with an old, cracked *gesso?*" asked Blaise. "Then what finally determines the expert opinion?"

Vernet indulged himself in an impatient gesture. "Technically, such a forgery might present difficulties. There are still other devices available, however. One of them, or the sum of all, finally decides between the true and the false."

Blaise saw that Kullman was looking at him expectantly. "That's all very true," he said amiably to Vernet. "In the last analysis, it's the experts who decide."

Vernet accepted this as a victory. "Thank you," he said blandly.

Blaise smiled. "What's the rarest, most expensive painting a man might decide to buy, Mr. Vernet?"

The young Frenchman hesitated. "An authentic Giorgone," he said finally.

"No doubt about it," said Blaise. "How many such paintings exist today?"

Vernet shrugged. "Perhaps six in all."

"You may be right," said Blaise. "At any rate, it is an expert opinion, and a good one. However, some authorities, having examined all the disputed canvases, say there are forty. Another expert insists there are only fifteen. Another great critic puts the number at eight, and a truly distinguished expert maintains that only one of the paintings attributed to Giorgone was actually and entirely painted by him. All of these experts have access to the same information, scientific apparatus and history books."

"So much for expert opinion," said Kullman cheerfully.

"The thing to remember," said Blaise, "is that the books about how the masters mixed their paints and prepared their canvases are not sold only to experts. In New York, or any big city, anyone with a library card can find out just what made up Renoir's palette."

"You're wide of the mark," said Kullman delicately. "This started out as a discussion of Vernet's painting, something that's been in his family for many years. Probably acquired from Renoir himself."

"Perhaps," said Vernet pleasantly. The heat aroused in him by the discussion was giving way now to smooth, mannered charm. "Renoir mentions the painting—a large still life—in a letter to his dealer. By the way," he added, turning again to Blaise, "the letter is quite genuine."

Blaise laughed. "I'm sure of it."

"My grandfather," continued Vernet, "knew most of the Impressionists intimately. He acquired many examples of their work. This canvas was found by a member of my family in Grandfather's house in the country. He may have bought it at a time when Renoir had no reputation, and it was forgotten."

"You ought to show it to Blaise," urged Kullman. "He might pass it on to Lucas Edgerton."

Before Vernet could answer, Kenneth Lurie said, "Not if it's that early. Edgerton doesn't care for those."

"Who said it was early?" demanded Astorg.

Lurie hesitated, but only for a moment. "He just said, Jonas, that it was bought before Renoir had a reputation." He said this gently, as if to a backward child.

As Astorg subsided, Blaise said, "I'd like to see the painting."

"Of course," said Vernet. "At the moment a customer has it, but in a day or two I'll be delighted to show it to you."

"Count me in," said Astorg heavily. Then he turned to Blaise. "You say the police do not credit your story about the forgeries?"

"Forgery," said Blaise. "Singular. That's all I know so far." He smiled at Astorg, who received the correction with a nod of his head. "Lieutenant Ives is a smart man," Blaise continued, "but this must be a little out of his line. I don't think, for instance, that he can quite conceive of the profits such a forger might pile up. If he had the proper connections."

"Yes," said Astorg soberly. "That would be of the utmost importance."

"Don't sound so grim," said Lurie brightly. "It isn't threatening the foundations of art yet. I don't mean to belittle what you say, Blaise; I'm sure it's all true."

"I may be taking it too seriously," assented Blaise readily. He yielded at once to Kullman's proposal that he see the rest of the collection, and as the host went on ahead to light up, he found himself standing with Cass and Molly Dann.

Molly took the other girl's presence for granted. "The cop told me about the drawing. I figured there must be some reason why you didn't want to say you got it from me in there." She inclined her head, indicating the men in the other room.

"Just playing it safe. If somebody has to be conked I might as well be target for tonight."

"Thanks."

The others came drifting in. Kullman beckoned from

the hall, asking them to see a painting on the winding staircase, and Blaise hung back as he saw Astorg slow his steps to match.

"I brought in two early Renoirs this year," said Astorg in a low voice.

"I know."

"Both unknown, but mentioned in correspondence or history. From a very reliable source, Blaise—extremely reliable."

Blaise grinned. "Still think so?"

Kenneth Lurie turned in the doorway to wait for their lagging steps to bring them up to the group, and in Astorg's eyes, as he regarded his West Coast associate, was frigid, piercing hatred. "I was just mentioning to Blaise," he said in a flat, colorless undertone, "about my own Renoirs."

Lurie's smile was as meaningless as a mask held in an outstretched hand. "You picked the right man," he said. "Just the right man."

There were outstanding canvases hung along the sweep of the wide staircase and the upstairs hall, but Blaise found himself making casual, banal acknowledgments of them while he tried to digest the relationship between the two dealers, and, again, the role of the smooth Roger Vernet. Kullman seemed to understand his preoccupation, and as they wound their way downstairs again, he whispered an invitation to come back when there was less on his mind.

The arrangement of the paintings in Kullman's house was beautifully planned so that the guests finished the tour confronted by the front door and the butler standing in readiness at the coat closet. The house was only slightly set back from the quiet street and Blaise's car, with the others, was parked outside.

"I take it," said Cassy, as they went down the driveway to the street, "that the mumbo-jumbo about forgery was the principal business of the evening."

"Obvious, wasn't it?"

"Except for the fact that I didn't understand a word —yes."

Blaise helped her into the car. "The explanation will be forthcoming. Not only that, but one of the principals involved will supply it, and if I so stipulate, will bring it to me all written out on vellum, with hand-illuminated borders and in a rich binding. Thieves are about to fall out, Cassy. My job is to avoid being hit by a body." As he started the car, he added, "Present company excepted."

He edged away from the curb, and as he headed to the corner Cassy said, "These streets run around in circles. The one you want is Hillcliff Drive."

Blaise obediently turned on the spotlight, manipulating the beam to catch the narrow street-sign, and as he tilted the light it played across a man walking swiftly up the block toward the Kullman house. It was nobody he knew, but Cassy caught his arm.

"That's Paul Weldon," she said. "The fellow Molly said was making all that trouble tonight."

Blaise was half way across the intersection but he slammed on the brakes and leaned out to look back at the group of people still standing near their cars outside Kullman's house. He made the turn quickly and started back, jumping out of the car just as Weldon moved up out of the dark and clutched at Molly's arm. Weldon, a frail man, was so obviously drunk that he may have wanted only support to keep from falling, and Molly's reaction was more irritation than fright.

"For Christ's sake! How did you get out here?"

"Got to talk to you, Molly," said Weldon thickly, and as Vernet tried to pull him away he clung to the girl's arm. "None o' your business," he muttered. "Got to talk to Molly."

"Go on home," said Molly wearily. Vernet had succeeded in detaching Weldon now and held him off at arm's length. He was not a difficult target, or one likely to put up much fight, and Vernet's free hand was obviously cocked for the blow. "Don't hit him," said Molly. "He's too drunk to be any trouble."

Astorg was still standing in the driveway, near Lurie's car, alone now because the other dealer had moved up to the scene of conflict.

"Paul!" Lurie's voice snapped like a whip. He stepped up as Vernet reluctantly let go. Weldon slid a little but remained upright, peering at the newcomer in the uncertain light.

"Oh. Oh, it's you." Then aware of the others, he said plaintively, "What's the matter with everybody? I came to talk to Molly. Don't want to talk to anybody else."

Lurie's chauffeur had come down from the car and now approached the group with quick, light steps. "Wait a minute, Sully," said his employer. "We'll take Mr. Weldon home."

"No." Weldon ducked under Lurie's arm and made for Molly again. "Don't want to go with you. And don't anybody get tough with me because . . ."

That was as far as he got. Lurie swung him around easily and as he was still turning clipped him on the jaw so deftly that every movement could be followed at leisure like the slow-motion film of a fight. Weldon sagged and the chauffeur, Sully, caught him before he could fall.

"Very neat," said Blaise, admiringly. "Do you two work together?"

"Put him in the car," Lurie directed his man.

"Oh, hell," said Molly, in a troubled voice. "Why'd you have to do that?"

"You held me responsible for bothering you before," said Lurie, quite formally. "In any case, I barely touched him. He was just about ready to pass out." He turned to Astorg, who had come up as Sully retired the supine painter. "We'll take the boy home, Jonas. It just means a detour to drop him off."

"I'll go with Blaise," was Astorg's reply.

Lurie looked at him steadily for a moment, the fingers of his right hand opening and closing mechanically. "Very well," he said mildly.

It was for the most part a silent ride to the Ocean Inn. Astorg replied with a curt negative when Blaise asked him if he knew Paul Weldon at all and didn't seem interested when Cassy said that she had met him with Simon. At the door of the hotel he got out quickly, and after a vague and absent promise to call Blaise in the morning, trudged into the lobby still deep in thought.

When they were on the highway again, Cassy asked, "Do you still expect it all written out on vellum, in a rich binding?"

"More than ever."

"From Jonas Astorg?"

"In collaboration with a person or persons unknown." He reached down on the seat with his free hand, found Cassy's and covered it with his own. "A special providence watches over honest art dealers, Cassy."

"Oh, I don't know," was her modest reply. "I daresay I have faults like other girls."

"One of them," said Blaise, "is your brazen assumption that I'm referring to you." He pulled her closer to him on the seat and she slid across and put her head on his shoulder. "What all-seeing providence has decreed," he continued, "is that it takes quite a cast of characters to turn a great forgery into ready money. If it was a game that one or two could play, it could go on indefinitely. Not that I'm against games that two can play," he hastened to assure her, and she smiled up at him. "Not even if they go on indefinitely."

She nodded sleepily on his shoulder. "Check."

"Are you going to sleep, Cassy?"

She shook her head, though her eyes remained shut. "Just looking serene. It's one of my best looks."

"Very effective. Do you have to do it with your eyes closed?"

She nodded vigorously.

"I've never driven up here at night. I'm not sure I know where to turn off to get to the house."

A slow smile mingled with her serene look. "Drive on," she said softly.

19

CONSCIOUSNESS came filtering back to Paul Weldon, bits of detail leaping into focus so that he knew he was on the couch in his studio. His head ached, his mouth and jaw hurt and as he was groping for the cause of these assorted throbbings he saw the grim countence of Lurie's chauffeur, Sully.

"Hiya, boy?" was Sully's friendly greeting.

Weldon sat up, not without some groans as the excursion into a higher altitude set the pains dancing in his head. He licked his arid lips. "Did you beat me up?" he demanded.

Sully looked pained. "You call that gettin' beat up? Sure, I popped you one or two," he conceded, "but they were mercy punches. So you wouldn't hurt yourself bouncin' around. So you'd lay still, and take it easy."

"Thanks," was Weldon's bitter comment.

"Don't mention it."

Weldon swung his feet off the couch. Sully continued to watch him dispassionately from the window seat. As Weldon got to his feet the chauffeur seemed to stiffen a bit, as if for action, but when Weldon staggered toward the bathroom and bedroom he relaxed again. Weldon stood in the bedroom doorway for a moment, then uttered a shrill cry of alarm and dashed inside. Sully stood up, stretching luxuriously, and followed him.

Weldon was on his knees beside the circular night table. The lamp had been removed and the concealed compartment yawned. Weldon had both hands in the cylinder and was groping around, but his anguished contorted face revealed that the cupboard was bare.

"Mr. Lurie took the stuff you had there," said Sully quietly from the doorway.

Weldon turned, still on his knees. "Why?"

With a gesture of complete boredom, Sully drawled, "He said you wasn't trustworthy." Apologetically, he added, "You know me, kid—I don't mix in."

"I want to see him," said Weldon hotly.

"You'll see him. Believe me, you'll see him."

"He took my money. I don't care about the paints and the other stuff, but he took my money. I want it."

"Just relax," was Sully's amiable advice. For all the

friendship he exuded, however, he took pains to stand so that he filled the doorway.

Weldon was seething. It was as if the discovery of his loss had shocked him out of his hangover, and the attendant ills, and given him new strength and courage. He realized now that Sully's function was that of a guard, but he faced him staunchly.

"Get out of the way, Sully."

The chauffeur smiled. "Take it easy. If the boss took your dough there must be a good reason for it. He's probably keepin' it safe, or"—he chuckled delightedly—"maybe he fined you for disorderly conduct." He didn't even deign to move as Weldon swung at him but blocked the blow negligently with his forearm. He expressed only mild disapproval as Weldon lashed out again, once more ineffectually, and then with the cool detachment of a doctor administering an anesthetic, struck one blow that jolted Weldon's head back. The painter, his eyes glazed, took a series of funny little backward steps, then crumpled.

Sully picked him up easily, dropped him on the daybed and fished for a cigarette. By the time he lit it and had taken a few puffs Weldon's eyes were open and he was stirring uncertainly. Sully looked down at him sympathetically.

"Got the fight out of your system?"

Weldon nodded weakly.

"Good boy," Sully complimented him. "You ain't the fightin' type," he went on critically. "You'd only wind up with all your insides scrambled and you wouldn't even be givin' me a workout."

Weldon nodded again, conceding the truth of all this. He pulled himself to the side of the bed, sitting up with his feet on the floor.

"Here," said Sully, offering him the cigarette.

Weldon reached for it, muttering "Thanks." As he took the cigarette, it fell from his trembling fingers to the carpet and in his fuzzy state he didn't even seem to be aware of this.

"For Christ's sake!" muttered Sully. "You'll have the joint on fire." He dropped to his knees, his head down to look for the cigarette, and then Weldon's right foot lashed out, the heel of his heavy shoe catching Sully right on the temple. The chauffeur brought his head up, his expression one of intense pain at such a betrayal and Weldon kicked him again. Sully toppled over and lay still.

Weldon picked up the cigarette and took a puff he seemed to enjoy immensely.

20

Given something to go on, Lieutenant Ives was a very efficient and methodical man. The hunt for Hugh Norden had fanned out through all of California and the adjoining states and territories, and there was little he could do about this except to alert outlying officials at whatever points he could pick up a trace of the vanished dealer. Norden was alive and well, he knew that much, and probably prosperous. He was no longer wearing his heavy, prismatic glasses, which seemed incredible when the Lieutenant ran down Norden's doctor and saw the limits of vision which had to be corrected, but a flyer to neighboring towns revealed that Norden had been fitted for contact lenses within the year. He had secured these under another name, apparently realizing how handy they might be for masquerades and getaways. The Lieutenant also knew by now that Norden had shaved off his mustache and exactly what clothes and luggage he had bought up and down the coast to replace those abandoned in flight. He was able to bring the description up to date and to provide a new picture. Barring luck and accidents, he had to sit back and wait.

The nine paintings missing from the Edgerton collection were also tangibles, and armed with descriptions and specifications that included even the exact nature of the customs stamps, Lieutenant Ives was making certain that none of these had yet changed hands and that the art world had a guard mounted if they emerged.

His own aide, Sergeant Bonner, was methodically canvassing dealers and collectors in the Los Angeles area, phoning in from time to time to report and to ask instructions. This part of the investigation was nearly over. Like every other avenue Ives had traveled in the case, it was rapidly closing to a dead end, and the Lieutenant was now framing the patter he would employ in reporting to his chief.

When the phone rang, expecting the worst, Ives picked it up gingerly. "Lieutenant Ives," he admitted reluctantly.

"Bonner talking," said the Sergeant, and Ives knew at once that Bonner was not just reporting another succession of failures. "I'm down at Mazurin's. It's a little art gallery on Seventh Street. Nothing on the paintings, Lieutenant, but get this: Mazurin does framing for Paul Weldon—remember, Lieutenant, the painter?"

"Yes, of course," snapped Ives.

"Mazurin heard the news about Simon Edgerton on

one of the all-night radio programs, sometime between 4:30 and 5 in the morning. He got all excited and telephoned Weldon because Weldon and the Edgerton boy were friends, or knew each other. Weldon wasn't home. Mazurin says he tried him twice again, up to six in the morning—never got him."

Ives was standing up. "I'm on my way to Weldon's now, Bonner. Meet me there." He hung up, shouted for his car, and in a matter of minutes was racing across town to Hollywood.

The studio was deserted and Weldon's car was gone. While waiting for Bonner, Ives telephoned to Molly Dann, and after her denial of any knowledge of the painter's whereabouts, he listened thoughtfully while she reported the doings of the night before.

Bonner came in as he finished his talk with Molly and he left the Sergeant to put a man on guard at the studio and to supervise the details of getting a description of Weldon and his car on the police radio. He himself drove downtown to the Kenneth Lurie Gallery and was promptly taken inside.

"Molly embarrassed me last night," said the dealer slowly. "She made it appear that I was somehow responsible for Weldon's behavior." He shrugged his shoulders. "I was annoyed when he came to Kullman's house and tried to make another scene. First I tried to talk him into coming home but he had his heart set on sticking with Molly. I hit him, finally. Then my chauffeur and I got him into my car and took him home. After that"—with a helpless gesture—"I'm afraid I can't help you."

"Just how jealous would you say he could get?" asked Ives.

"You mean, could he get violent to some degree?"

Ives nodded. "Yes. With or without drink."

"He's an odd type," said Lurie reflectively, "and not easy to classify. Take the girl, Molly Dann, for instance. A big, loud, flashy beauty, and pretty much on the physical side. Weldon's not like that. But Molly is the only girl who ever got under his skin at all. Maybe that's why he needed her. Maybe she helped him fight off something else. Looking at it one way, I can't see Weldon caring much about any girl; looking at it another way, no telling what he might do. Last night, for instance, I thought he was crazy."

"Any idea where he might be?"

Lurie shook his head. "I don't actually know much about him."

"Your chauffeur about?" was Ives's next question, and Lurie promptly summoned his clerk, asking him to tell Sully to come in at once. The chauffeur appeared, in neat whipcord, cap in hand.

"Lieutenant Ives wants to ask you some questions about Mr. Weldon," Lurie told him, then turned to a stack of correspondence as if what was to follow had no interest for him. He didn't look up until Sully finished, having related that he drove the car with Messrs. Lurie and Weldon to the studio, then took Weldon upstairs while Mr. Lurie drove home in the car. Having seen the painter safely to bed, he then turned out the lights and departed, taking a taxi back to the house.

At the end of this recital Ives rose to go, and Sully, ever the well-trained servant, jumped up to hold the door open for him. Then he closed the door and turned to face his employer with considerably enhanced apprehension.

"You blundering ape," said Lurie caustically.

Sully hung his head, abject shame incongruous in his

scarred, ugly face. He was relieved when Lurie sat down. "Better watch the girl's place," said Lurie finally, in a patient voice. "Take your own car, and get out of that uniform."

Sully acknowledged this with a barely preceptible nod and eased himself gratefully out the door.

21

VICTOR GRANDI had stretched the Degas nude and the delicate application of some solvents to one corner had skillfully brought out the artist's original balance of color and light. He was pleased with the result, and now, alone in the gallery, was making certain that it was hung at precisely eye level.

Cassy strolled in the open door and came down into the gallery to watch him. "A little to the left," she said judicially. "Not so much." Then, "There, that's got it."

Grandi stepped away. "I'm glad I got it in place before your uncle took over. He'd hang half the paintings upside down if it amused him." He picked up some bits of wire severed in the operation of replacing the Degas, dropping them carefully in the basket at the desk. Cass followed him there, and as he seemed to be leaving, stopped him at the door.

"Victor, how much do you think of the great Renoir forgery tempest Ellis Blaise has whipped up in our teapot?"

"Why?" asked Grandi guardedly.

"It's interesting," she said casually. "It will be a sensation in the art business, won't it?"

"If it's true," said Grandi.

"Yes. If it's true."

The technician smiled suddenly. "Do you think our friend Blaise is risking his reputation?"

"It's his to risk, isn't it?" was her noncommittal reply.

"Cassy!" he said reproachfully. "My eyes are trained to observe. Not only canvas but what goes on around me."

A hint of a blush colored her cheeks. "Does it show on me, Victor?"

"It's very becoming."

"It's true," she murmured. "Imagine my falling for the first city slicker that came whistling down the pike." And then earnestly, "He isn't just making a fool of himself, is he, Victor? I don't want that to happen."

"He's a clever man," mused Grandi, "but he's honest. He may not be in the right business to capitalize on these attributes. In the matter of the Renoirs, however, I believe he will be vindicated."

She brightened. "I knew it. I just wanted an expert opinion." Then briskly, she went on, "Now show me some books dealing with art and fakes. If he does get into trouble I want to be able to defend him. What the hell, Portia did it, and she didn't even go to Vassar."

Grandi placed a ladder along the stack of books, pulling out a few titles so that they projected visibly. "Read these, pay attention, and you should be able to manufacture your own Rembrandts in a short time."

"Thanks, Victor." As he started out, she said, "I haven't announced anything yet. Not even," she put in reflectively, "to Blaise. I want to surprise Uncle Lucas."

"He will be overjoyed, I'm sure," said Grandi. He went out as Cassy settled herself at the desk with one of the bulky, extra-illustrated volumes he had chosen.

She was deep in a tortured maze of pigments, Roentgen tests, characteristics of brushwork, chemical analysis of paint and other such snappy subjects, her brow furrowed in the effort of word-by-word concentration on the text, when the telephone pulled her away. It was the gateman, asking if Ellis Blaise was there, and when she informed him that Blaise was expected soon, the man told her that Paul Weldon was at the gate.

"Send him up," said Cassy, after a moment's thought. "He can wait here."

Weldon seemed to be self-consciously aware of the assorted bruises and contusions that stood out on his vague, indeterminate features. He mumbled a greeting to Cassy and looked around the gallery with only a flicker of interest.

"You look awful," she said with her characteristic candor. "Did you go right on fighting last night?"

"I guess so. I'm not too sure." His bruised lips formed some equivalent of a grin. "I was drinking, you might say."

"Yes, you might. Want one now?"

He heaved a grateful affirmative. While she was pouring a drink at the cupboard, she said, "What do you want with Blaise?"

His expression grew somber again. "I've got something he can use."

"Paintings?"

"Maybe."

She handed him the glass. "Vague, aren't you?"

He drained the glass, a formidable drink, at one prolonged swallow. Then he glanced at his watch, moved restlessly to the curtained windows, staring intently out at the driveway.

"He'll be along," said Cassy. "Relax."

Weldon came back to the desk and sat down. He was still taut and tightly wound but he forced himself to some polite expressions. "I've never been here before. It's quite a place."

"Want to look around?"

"Not today. I'm too jumpy." He smiled ruefully. "Imagine passing up a chance to look at the Edgerton collection. When I was a student I pulled strings and wrote letters for years—never even got to the gate. Last year I asked Simon if he could get me in and he told me that even he was barred." He laughed mirthlessly, then quickly added, "I'm sorry." He was in such a state of turbulence as to seem to be all but foaming. He crossed and recrossed his legs and his thin, sensitive fingers tapped frantic, excited rhythms on the carved wooden edge of the chair. From time to time he licked his dry lips anxiously.

After a few moments of silence, Cassy said quietly, "It's about the Renoir, isn't it?"

Weldon was staring down at the floor and his head came up slowly. "Renoir? The painter?"

Cassy smiled. "No. Max Renoir, who runs a general store in Oxnard."

"In a way," said Weldon, "that is what I want to talk about with Mr. Blaise." Cautiously, placing one word after the other like a man fitting together a complicated mosaic, he said, "I heard that he was inquiring about some Renoirs. I've got a lot of friends and connections here and I picked up some news yesterday about something like that. It's second-hand information," he explained elaborately, "but it may be useful to him." He was fiddling with a pencil from the holder on the desk. "Naturally, if it helps him, he might be able to do something for me."

"Naturally," said Cass.

"I've been thinking," went on the painter, "that I'd like to go away somewhere. Just take it easy, paint a bit, forget about some things that have been fretting me."

"Good idea."

Weldon was making idle sketching movements on the pad near the telephone. They were semiautomatic, apparently aimless motions of the hand; he didn't do do more than glance down at the pad in a random, sightless way. "I'm too emotional," he volunteered. "People take advantage of me. I ought to go away somewhere and get it out of my system."

He dropped the pencil, looked anxiously at his watch and got up to peer out the windows again.

"You're sure he's coming?"

"He'll be along," promised Cassy. "I'll get you another drink." She picked up his glass and went past the desk to the cupboard. Quite accidentally she glanced down at the pad on which Weldon had been doodling and as she moved on her footsteps faltered and slowed. She turned to look again. The pad was covered with tiny, lovely drawings of the heads of women and children, and each was a perfect Renoir. She looked up at Weldon, who was still at the window but he was just turning. She looked away from the pad and went on to the cupboard. She poured the drink, trying to steady the trembling of her hand, then brought it back to Weldon, who had seated himself once more at the desk.

"Thanks," he said, taking the glass. He was staring down at the drawings before him, but completely unaware of them or of their significance. "Paris would be nice again," he mused. The pencil was in his hand again, the automatic sketching resumed. "I lived there for years. Must be changed now though. Probably full of Communists."

Cassy forced a smile. She was trying desperately to

avoid looking at the pad on which he was sketching. "I didn't see any last summer," she said. "Of course, they probably don't hang out at the Ritz and the Crillon or Maxim's." She cocked her head toward the window. "Is that a car?"

Weldon got up at once, striding to the window. In one swift motion, Cassy stepped to the desk, flicked off the top page of the pad and took her seat again, the paper stuffed in the pocket of her skirt.

Weldon turned from the window. "Nothing," he said in a disappointed voice.

"Sorry. Must have been a delivery in the back."

The painter sat down again, picked up his whiskey with one hand and instinctively reached for the pencil.

"Where did you live in Paris?" asked Cassy, intent on making conversation.

"I had a little house in Neuilly. Nice little place, with a pretty garden. I shared it with another painter who was studying there then." His hand had resumed the idle sketching motions on the clean page but while Cassy watched with her heart in her mouth, the movements slowed little by little and then stopped. Weldon's eyes searched the top of the desk. He lifted the pad, turned it over. She could see the muscles around his mouth twitching. His expression, when he looked up at her at last, was pained, almost reproachful.

"What's the matter?" asked Cassy, her voice faltering a bit.

"Now you know," said Weldon softly. He shook his head in a troubled, worried way. "So now you know," he said again, pushing his chair back as his right hand dropped into the pocket of his coat. "I always liked you," he said, in a dreamy, distant voice. "I said to Simon a couple of times how much I liked you." His hand came slowly out of the pocket and she saw the gleam of the gun. He extended his free hand, palm up. "Give me the paper."

"That won't solve anything," said Cass, but as he gestured impatiently with the gun, she produced the paper from her skirt. "Blaise knows all about you," she ventured.

"Does he?" said Weldon caustically, as he snatched at the piece of paper. "How?"

Cassy felt herself slipping. "Your confederate. Molly," she said tentatively.

A thin little smile curved across Weldon's bruised lips. He gestured to the gallery with the gun. "Get in there."

Cass backed slowly into the gallery, Weldon matching her little steps with his own. She kept her gaze fixed on the gun in his right hand. There was a cool, unhurried air about Weldon now, as if the flurry of violence had shocked him out of the jangled, hungover state in which he arrived.

"I won't say anything," pleaded Cassy. "I'll give you a chance to get away. I'll help you!"

Weldon moved her inflexibly to the open door of the vault. He circled her to look down into it and to examine the spring lock.

"Now, don't get Victorian," said Cassy. "You want me to stifle down there?"

"It's air-conditioned," said Weldon, indicating a knowledge of the premises at least equal to her own. He shifted the gun to his left hand, took up a section of wiring with his right, then braced himself in the narrow doorway. A solid yank freed the wiring, plunging the vault into darkness.

"Downstairs," said Weldon.

Cassy faced him defiantly. Weldon reversed the gun, holding it club-like by the barrel. "Downstairs," he said again. "I'm in a hurry." There was a flushed, raving quality to his actions and speech and Cassy moved reluctantly to the door.

"You can trust me," she said urgently, "I'll help you."

Weldon pushed the girl, who caught at the railing on the dark stairs to keep from falling. Then the door slammed shut and the lock clicked. She knew it was futile unless someone was in the gallery, that neither her cries for help nor the drumming of her fists on the door would penetrate the steel and concrete sufficiently to be heard more than a few feet away, but she couldn't help making the effort. Then exhausted and frightened, she groped timidly along the staircase, hoping to locate some sort of emergency switch or alarm. At the bottom step, having found nothing, she sank down on the rough cold stone and started to cry.

22

In the total, impenetrable dark of the vault, Cass sniffled away the last tear of the freshet launched by the initial shock of her imprisonment. She could detect the comforting whine of the air-conditioning system, making her feel that she was at least one up on Juliet in the tomb of the Capulets. She thought of going up the stairs again to renew her assault on the door, but she knew that only a few minutes had elapsed since Weldon put her in storage and that her best chance to be heard would be in an hour or two, after lunch, when Edgerton or Miriam would probably be working in the library.

Meanwhile, she sat up very straight on the bottom step which was her temporary H.Q., and with this as a focal point tried to project an image of the unfamiliar maze of stacks and shelving. It was not a wide room, there would hardly be more than seven or eight aisles between the picture bins, and at the other end was a desk in which there might conceivably be any number of useful articles.

She stood up and carefully groped to the beginning of the shelves, then held to the woodwork and moved cautiously through the aisle. She had one painful encounter with a ladder but reached the clear space at the other end with no other difficulty. She found the desk abruptly when she backed away from the shelves and into the sharp point. Rubbing herself gratefully she inched around it and into the chair. She groped over every inch of the middle drawer without coming on anything more useful than some scraps of paper and a stub of pencil. Her first thought, that she might scribble her last words and impressions like Scott of the Antarctic, she put firmly from her. The drawer on the right was bare of anything but a layer of dust, but her heart bumped as she tackled the one on the left with eager fingertips, and she heaved a sigh of thanksgiving as her hand closed on a crushed package of cigarettes, miraculously half full, and a little paper book of matches. She counted eight precious stems still attached, then put them on the desk and continued methodically through the remaining compartments. There was no further yield, and she sat back to think. She wanted a cigarette desperately, but it would involve striking a match and she determined to put it off until she could combine the treat with a planned look around.

She remembered a movie in which the hero, immured in something like her own cavern, had simply gathered paper and wood, set fire to the joint and in so doing touched off the sprinkler system and the fire alarm. In the vicinity of fine art, however, sprinklers were taboo, being capable of as much damage as the flame itself. But even here, reason prompted, some form of thermostatic switch must exist to warn the household and the brave fire laddies of sharply rising temperatures. It might be anywhere, she thought dolefully, but on the other hand, with some enthusiasm, it must be somewhere.

If I were a thermostatic switch, she asked herself, where would I be, and after some reflection she came to the conclusion that if she were a thermostatic switch with an ounce of intelligence—not one of those silly gadabout thermostatic switches—she would certainly be in close proximity to the paintings it was her sworn duty to protect. What better place than the bins themselves, and since maintenance of these sensitive devices would be a constant chore, they should be on the outside where a person could get at them.

She took a cigarette from the pack on the desk and with the matches in hand fumbled her way to the closest stack, then edged sideways until she was in approximately the middle. Then she struck the match and as it flared up, lit the cigarette in one quick inhalation, promptly holding the match aloft to scan the outside surface of the shelving. She held the match until it burned down almost to the nail polish, then dropped it and groped her way back to the desk. The cigarette made a bright incandescent beacon in the surrounding blackness. It was comforting and a source of much hope. She finished the cigarette slowly, then mindful that what she needed was not a roaring blaze, but a planned, orderly little fire, she crushed it carefully on the stone floor before resuming her examination of the vault.

Lucas Edgerton was in fine voice again. Ascending the staircase to his second-floor retreat, Blaise could hear the booming vibrations of Edgerton's tirade, and an occasional splutter as the luckless Lieutenant Ives raised a mild demurrer—ineffectually and in vain. It was the old Edgerton with a rich command of bullying invective, his vituperative powers enhanced, if anything, by the three-day lay-off.

". . . you're wallowing in taxpayers' money," Edgerton was raging. "Sitting back in your office, or joy-riding up and down the beach, waiting for the murderer to come in, confess, put on the handcuffs and march himself to the County Jail. You'll look pretty foolish, Lieutenant, if I have to send East for a detective. Stop hiding back of trees and billboards to catch speeders. I want action, or by God, I'll make such a stink in Sacramento that your whole staff will turn honest in the shock."

Blaise had the door open. Miriam Wayne was standing by the window, her back to the room, politely trying to pretend she wasn't present. Ives, red-faced and angry, was holding his own temper down with both hands.

With all stops available on the organ, Edgerton now switched to a gentle, withering sarcasm. "I realize, of course, Lieutenant, that you're busy with many other things. Desperate men and women who keep unlicensed spaniels and who have to be tracked down and punished; fiends in human form who park facing the wrong way on streets and highways; lawless scoundrels peddling Good Humors in restricted areas, and . . ."

"Just a minute," said Ives heavily. "I may not be handling this the way you like, but I'm handling it. You can bring in anybody you like, go over my head clear up to the Chief, or the Governor, or the Atomic Energy Commission. I don't care if you call out the National Guard—I'm still in charge of the investigation and I tell you I'm doing what I can. I know you hot-stove crusaders," he went on bitterly. "You'll holler 'uncle' and scramble to hush it up or buy me off the minute I step on one of your sensitive toes. All right. I'll give you action. But don't forget, that's what makes headlines and brings out the mob."

He stood up and snatched his hat off Edgerton's table.

"Attaboy," cheered Blaise.

Edgerton looked at him, a quick, searing glance, then turned back to Ives. He was already in retreat. "Now don't start jumping to conclusions, Lieutenant," he said soothingly. "After all, we're both out for the same thing." He stood up with Ives and shook the detective's reluctant hand energetically. "I'm an ornery old bastard," he confessed, "but I mean well."

Despite himself, Ives couldn't surpress the thaw he felt coming on. "Okay," he murmured.

"Soft soap," said Blaise gently, "turneth away wrath."

"Now what the hell do you want?" roared Edgerton. "My niece isn't here, so that winds up any interest you may have in what's going on."

"I just dropped in to borrow some poetry books," said Blaise. "Mighty handy in the moonlight."

"Blubberhead," muttered Edgerton, as he went out.

Miriam Wayne sighed her manifest relief. "I'm glad

you finally let him have it, Lieutenant Ives. He was becoming unbearable." Her nod of greeting to Blaise had been cool and devoid of any emotion or interest. "I'll be in the gallery," she said in leavetaking, "if you need me for anything at all."

Blaise stood aside to let her pass. "Nice girl," he said, when the door was closed.

"Is she?" was Ives's polite response.

Blaise shrugged. "Isn't she?"

"Nobody in this damned house levels with me," said Ives angrily. As Blaise looked at him in injured innocence, he demanded, "What made you start checking up on her?"

"Oh, that. No special reason. Just curious."

Ives replied with a skeptical grunt.

"If you found out about my inquiries," Blaise continued, "then you must have been working the same street. Any luck?" he asked politely.

"I've got more than that on my mind right now," said Ives impatiently, though Blaise felt that the subject was being changed arbitrarily. "Why was Paul Weldon so eager to see you today?"

"I don't know. I found a message at the hotel, but no number or any way to call him." He listened thoughtfully as Ives gave him a brief, trenchant outline of his new interest in the fugitive painter. "And it was you he was waiting for," finished Ives.

"I'm sorry," Blaise said honestly. "I've never spoken to Weldon, never saw him until last night. All I knew was what Molly Dann told me and I got the idea he was a sniveling sort of drunk without much backbone. What I saw last night just confirmed her diagnosis."

"A lot of liquor and a little gun gives some types plenty of backbone. He lied to set up an alibi." Ives seemed to be thinking hard. "There must be a reason why he wants to get to you. Want to help?"

"Sure."

"Go back to your hotel."

"Bait?" said Blaise plaintively. "Is that all I'm good for?" He nodded sadly. "All right. I take it you'll be somewhere around, ready to pounce?"

"I'll put somebody in the hotel, and a man in a car outside. If Weldon calls you and wants to meet somewhere make the date and my man will tail you."

"Suppose I have to give Weldon my word of honor that I'll come alone?"

"You'll manage," said Ives drily. "Get going."

"Favor for favor," said Blaise, "what did you find out about Miriam Wayne?"

"Not a hell of a lot," said Ives candidly. "She met Edgerton in the New York Library, in the Art Department, apparently by chance. When he offered her a job she told him all her experience had been as a free-lance artist, as a cataloguer and secretary, and a hitch as a researcher for Dr. Wesley Corum. That's all true, but she omitted some things. She'd worked for dealers in Paris and New York. Now she says that she wanted the job with Edgerton and she thought he'd be suspicious if he knew she had any background in the trade."

"That's perfectly true," said Blaise.

"I know," said Ives, "but I don't like it. There's very little about this affair that I do like. Corum vouched for her when she came to work. Now do you mean to say that he didn't know she'd worked for dealers? If he didn't, then she lied to him, too. Granted that she's got a first-class motive for not telling Edgerton, what's her reason for keeping her past from Corum?"

"A fair question," said Blaise. "I don't know the

answer, but I'll give you odds that our Miss Wayne will make it sound plausible." He started out, "I'll have a look on the beach for Cass, and then I'll stake myself out in my room at the hotel. I'll be delighted to lure Weldon out of hiding, but you seem to know how complicated the people and the motives are here. I doubt if Simon Edgerton died from anything as convenient as the jealous rage of a drunken painter."

The detective nodded absently. "The people are complicated," he agreed. "I've worked on a lot of murders. Solved quite a few, too. In the end, the motives are simple. Sex and money. That still covers a lot of territory," he conceded apologetically, "but it shows you that Paul Weldon, with or without backbone, could finally do something even he wouldn't believe he was capable of doing."

"Fair enough," said Blaise. "I'm on my way."

He was halfway down the stairs, in fact, when the shrill clamor of the alarm bell stopped him. As he looked around, Ives appeared on the landing, starting down swiftly, and Jennings, the houseman, came running in from backstairs in his shirt-sleeves.

"What the hell is that?" demanded Ives, as they ran downstairs.

"It's the fire-alarm, sir," said Jennings.

The entire household seemed to be racing for the gallery now and Blaise, with Ives at his side, fell in with them. The doors were open and Miriam Wayne was outside, looking up at the roof as if searching there for signs of the blaze.

Edgerton came puffing up in a robe and slippers, leading the way inside. He had his keys out and made directly for the vault. He flung the door wide, then stepped back as Cassy blinked at him in the sudden light.

"False alarm," she said, with a touch of hysterical laughter, "but I'm glad you came."

"I started past the desk to get him a drink," Cassy was saying. "Until then, I hadn't even been aware of his doodlings, but as I walked by, behind his chair, I looked down and there were all these Renoirs—more Renoirs than you could shake a stick at, a whole big page of little heads and figures."

She was lying on the chaise in her own room, the pallor of fright departed, flushed and animated as she recounted the adventure. Ives had firmly cleared the room of everyone but himself and Blaise. Edgerton, finally assured that Cassy had suffered nothing more than a scare, left reluctantly. Miriam Wayne, on the other hand, had not come up at all when Blaise carried Cassy upstairs. Nor had she betrayed any of the shocked surprise exhibited by the others in Cassy's first, immediate bulletin on Paul Weldon.

"I did my darnedest to avoid looking at what he was doing," continued Cass, "and he went on mumbling in a faraway voice about wanting to get away. Then"— she shrugged wistfully—"then I engineered my big bonehead play. I got him to the window by pretending I heard a car, and snatched the top page of the drawings while his back was turned. It worked like a charm, except that he sensed something the minute he sat down again, and before you could say 'Fantin-Latour' he was waving a nasty-looking gun and the jig was up."

"Would you know what kind of a gun, Miss Edgerton?"

Cass turned her head a trifle to look at Ives. "No. My hobbies are more ladylike."

Ives drew his own service revolver. "As big as this? Or larger, or smaller?" he urged.

Cassy shrank from the display of ordnance. "Not quite that formidable."

"Did Weldon say why he wanted to see me?" asked Blaise.

"No. After he'd been stewing for a few minutes I tried a hunch and mentioned Renoir. His head snapped right up, but then he got cautious. He had information, he said, and if it helped you he wanted you to help him." She turned to Ives. "I'm sorry, Lieutenant, but I'm afraid that's the whole story of how one brave little girl broke up this ring of desperados single-handed."

"You did fine, Cassy," said Blaise.

"You said before that Weldon locked you in the vault at ten-forty," said Ives. "Are you sure that was the exact time?"

She nodded. "When he backed me into the gallery, toward the vault, I knew instinctively what he was going to do. I remember seeing the clock while he was maneuvering me to the vault and thinking how long it might be before somebody came into the gallery. It was ten-forty," she said firmly. "On the nose."

"The gate-man checked Weldon out," said Ives with a troubled look, "at exactly eleven-five. He was on the place for twenty-five more minutes."

"That doesn't make any sense at all," said Blaise. "You'd think he would cut and run."

Ives stood up and beckoned to Blaise. "Come on. You're still the head snake-charmer."

"Who'll read to me in the long, slow days of my convalescence?" asked Cassy plaintively.

Blaise bent over the chaise and kissed her lightly on

the forehead while Lieutenant Ives moved delicately to the door.

"Stay put, Cassy," urged Blaise.

"You think they're out to get me?" she asked.

"I, for one, am."

"Oh, you. I can handle you."

Lieutenant Ives was shuffling his feet impatiently. When Blaise joined him and they went down together, he gave him a sidelong speculative glance. "Hit the jackpot, didn't you?"

"Don't be coarse, Lieutenant," said Blaise loftily.

"I have to live on fifty-six hundred a year," said Ives bitterly, "and if somebody downtown gives me a pound of tobacco on my birthday the reform element screams 'graft.' "

"You do a useful work. You'll retire some day with the plaudits of a grateful citizenry ringing in your ears."

"The ringing in my ears I'll guarantee," said Ives, in the same grudging manner. In the driveway, as Blaise was about to get into his car, the detective held him back. "How do you like my hunch on Weldon now?"

"Much better. Molly Dann is basically a good-natured girl. If Weldon killed every man she slept with, he'd be too busy to paint."

"Probably. But now he fits," said Ives.

"Does he? If he's capable of killing, why was he content to lock Cassy in the vault? He knew she'd be free in a couple of hours."

. "For one thing," said Ives, "he was sober today. All he wanted was time for a getaway."

"So he spends twenty-five minutes more on the place. Looking at pictures."

"We don't really know what he did. Maybe he waited for you to show up. He's on the run, I know that; now

I've got to know what's driving him. By the way," he added, "you were right all along about the forgeries, of course."

"You'll turn my head with such extravagant flattery," said Blaise, smiling. His triumphant look dissolved, however, as Ives went on.

"Located one," said the detective thoughtfully. "A San Francisco merchant named Nathan Ordmann bought one of the Renoirs your friend Astorg imported. I'll have it here tonight."

"Lieutenant, you astonish me," said Blaise weakly. "I thought you were convinced I was the village idiot. I didn't even think you were listening."

"I've been reading some books," Ives continued. "Can't say I understood a hell of a lot, but one thing juts out all over: a really slick job isn't just a matter of painting—it's a big technical operation."

"Just so," nodded Blaise.

"Well, it starts me thinking about technicians." He stepped away from the car. "My man Bonner has orders to stick to you and he knows how to rouse me out if Weldon does show up. I'm much obliged. If there's trouble, stay out of it."

Blaise watched him go down the driveway, turning in at Victor Grandi's little house. By the time he drove past, Grandi was in the doorway, greeting Ives with a wide, cordial smile, beckoning him in as a valued and honored guest.

23

JONAS ASTORG was looking somewhat the worse for wear. His clothes were wrinkled and his fine, normally spotless haberdashery showed a good day's wear. Unshaven, his face looked slack, and new lines of care seemed to have etched themselves around his prominent features.

"I'd leave town if I were you, Jonas," said Kenneth Lurie quite casually. "Why call attention to yourself?"

Astorg shook his head stubbornly.

"Well, then," said Lurie, "pull yourself together. You look as if you're about to burst into tears."

"You bastard!" said Astorg thickly. "You did this to me."

Lurie hunched his shoulders in a pained expression of helplessness. "How was I to know? The boy outsmarted us."

"I can imagine," said Astorg bitterly.

"Think what you like," said Lurie. "Do you want to blubber yourself to ruin or do you want to make a stand?"

Astorg looked down at the floor. "The police have been in touch with Nathan Ordmann. The Renoir is on its way," he said dully.

Lurie chuckled. "Their troubles are just beginning." He pulled up a chair and sat down facing Astorg so close that their knees all but touched. "Listen," he said sharply. When Astorg looked up at him, he said, "As far as anybody—yes, anybody," he repeated emphatically, "can say or prove, the painting you sold Ordmann is a

Renoir. They can take it apart inch by inch, analyze each blob of paint separately. Think, man," he went on urgently. "You accepted it as a Renoir, so did Wesley Corum, a great expert. Kullman damn near bought it, and he's got a good eye. Lucas Edgerton, one of the greatest authorities in the world, saw the painting and took it for granted that it was genuine."

"The eye is one thing; the laboratory another. I've been fooled, so has every dealer and expert in the world. The test comes when they turn the instruments on it."

Lurie nodded. "I know." He walked to the window of Astorg's bedroom and glanced out into the balcony. Then he carefully closed the windows and took his seat again facing the old dealer.

"Are we going to run this out together?" he demanded.

"Of course. What else can we do?"

"No whining, wailing or recriminations?"

"I'm not an idealist. I can't afford revenge."

"Good. I'm going to tell you exactly how the Renoirs were made. I handle Paul Weldon, you know."

With a bitter smile, Astorg said, "Yes, I know."

"Some rancor is quite understandable," Lurie said magnaminously. "At any rate, he is a talented man, in an extremely neurotic way. I got him a commission once to do a poster for a movie company—some foolish story along the lines of *Camille*, I think. He astonished me with a canvas amazingly like Renoir. His own work had overtones of Renoir, especially in the painting of flesh, but his drawing and composition is so fantastic, the affinity had not occurred to me."

"You junked the poster, of course," said Astorg.

"Of course. But first, however, I had him do some sketches—a few in oils—right before my eyes. He banged them out, one after another, like a stamping machine. It seems he lived in Paris and for a long time could not afford to study at any of the proper *ateliers*. He made up for it by copying all day, day after day, imitating the work of the great painters he loved. The one he loved the most, as it developed, was Auguste Renoir."

"That much," said Astorg irritably, "I could have filled in by guess-work. I still say, Lurie, that what you or I or Wesley Corum think means nothing. This painting is going to be subjected to every test in the laboratory."

Lurie's pleasure in the recital seemed undiminished. "You admit that on the surface it is foolproof?"

"Unquestionably."

"Then listen to what's underneath. The original canvas was a damaged still-life by Jean-Frederic Bazille." His smile widened. "You see, Jonas, we didn't stint on anything. We used a genuine Impressionist canvas. Not only that, we made sure it was one prepared just the way Renoir prepared his own. They can test until they run out of instruments—the canvas is 80 years old. Bazille prepared it in the last year of his life, and everything about it is consistent with Renoir in that period."

Astorg was sitting up straight now, and some of the glaze was peeling off his eyes.

"The Bazille painting was stripped away," continued Lurie, "but not the *gesso*—we left that intact, just as it had always been, in case the experts did get under the surface. Now, the painting. Weldon didn't merely mix the paints—they were ground by hand to match every chemical component of the original colors. Furthermore, I bought him a projector and he worked from enlargements of sections taken from ten different Renoirs of the same period so that the exact pattern of the brush-work and its overlaps could be determined. Let the laboratories have it!" His voice went up triumphantly. "Let the whole damn United States Bureau of Standards have it. Ellis Blaise isn't a fool. He isn't going to say the Renoir is a forgery unless he can prove it. He can be snowed under with suits for libel and damages. You can ruin him. When he sees the painting he's going to hem and haw, play it cagy, admit nothing."

"You smart son-of-a-bitch!" said Astorg, more in admiration than in anger. He was obviously invigorated by Lurie's recital.

"No recriminations," warned the other.

"The Paris background is perfect," mused Astorg. "If what you say is true . . ." his voice trailed off. "We're in great shape," he said, bitterly again. "Weldon is running around with God knows how many Renoir drawings, all probably done in Los Angeles high-school copy-books."

"I doubt it," said Lurie.

"Or else," sneered Astorg, "he can sit down any time and paint some more Renoirs just to show the police how they're done."

"You've put your big finger," said Lurie, "on the one undeniable soft spot in our little cabal. I do think, though," he added, "that if I can reach our talented friend before the police locate him, he can be persuaded to go away."

"For his health?" asked Astorg.

"For our health," said Lurie, with a smile. He picked up his hat from the side table. "But you see that the situation is not without its bright spots, don't you, Jonas?" Astorg didn't immediately reply, and Lurie went on softly. "It would be so wrong to fly into a panic," he said in his gently remonstrating voice. "An orgy of confession would serve no purpose at all."

"You have nothing to fear from me, Lurie. I don't say that as a friend, but I say it."

"I understand your resentment," said Lurie. "I have to be certain now that we will remain partners—to the very end." Astorg nodded patiently. "I would have preferred to operate alone," continued Lurie. "Personally, I don't mind the risks and all the profit is better than half. You were eager to participate, Jonas. I take the liberty of reminding you of that. You argued very convincingly that I didn't have the resources, reputation and standing to work alone on such an involved operation."

"You didn't tell me that the paintings were forgeries," said Astorg.

Lurie smiled. "Only that they were stolen. The exact degree of dishonesty is unimportant, I think."

"You also didn't tell me that the end of it would be a murder."

"The end of it?" repeated Lurie. He sighed. "How I wish that were true! By the way," he added delicately, "I don't like to pry, but what if you have to account for your presence on the Edgerton estate that fateful evening?"

"What about you?" demanded Astorg. His voice rose to a strident pitch. "I had a reason to go. I was suspicious of you. I was beginning to suspect the paintings. I wanted to talk to Simon alone. That's why I went to the house."

"By an odd coincidence," said Lurie, smiling broadly, "that is the exact explanation that I myself have prepared." He went on gently. "The police might believe one such story; two of them would be ridiculous. You see, Jonas, it would be pointless to try to shift the burden of guilt."

"Don't worry," said Astorg. "I don't know how."

Lurie laughed out loud. "I didn't think you did." He went out to his car and drove swiftly to Molly Dann's house. At the intersection he saw Sully in a parked car. He drove past slowly, giving the chauffeur a chance to notice him, then parked and walked back.

Sully's report was discouraging. "Not a sign of him. He ain't showed."

Submerged in thought, Lurie twisted a thin over-hanging branch from a tree and idly swished it against the trunk. "Chances are," he reflected, "that he's drunk by now, perhaps helpless in some saloon."

"I'd be glad to help him," said Sully.

"He's a creature of habit." Lurie was still apparently thinking out loud, but Sully's sharp little eyes were focused on him and the chauffeur was paying close attention. "He'll be cautious just until liquor relaxes him. Then he'll drift back into the usual pattern and start making the same old rounds."

"I know a few of the joints he likes," volunteered Sully.

Lurie nodded. "Don't ask questions," he warned. "Just drift around." He gestured toward Molly's house. "Is the girl still home?"

"Been in all day," said Sully. "I ambled by a little while ago. She was in the yard."

"I'll wait here for a while, then I'll go to the gallery," said Lurie. He walked back to his own car in the covering shadows of the houses and posted himself behind the wheel, slumped down in the seat so that he was barely visible. He saw Sully's car go past and watched the diminishing taillight until it disappeared.

24

IN THE BLEAK, shabby back room of the Santa Monica police station the painting was vastly incongruous. It stood on an easel improvised from two time-worn chairs, with powerful emergency searchlights focused on it, the elegance of the portrait somehow heightened by these lurid effects.

It was a three-quarter portrait of a young woman in a feathered negligee, the collar drawn up to frame the lovely, fragile face.

Lieutenant Ives stood off in one corner of the room, leaving the main target area free for Blaise, Lucas Edgerton and Wesley Corum. Edgerton, who looked completely baffled, was standing away from the portrait while Dr. Corum held a powerful magnifying glass to one section after another. Blaise, on his knees, was examining the back of the canvas. In another chair, from which the painting was not even visible, sat Victor Grandi. He looked very cheerful, as if enjoying the floundering perplexity of the others.

Edgerton was the first to speak. "I don't know about the rest of you," he said emphatically, "but that's a Renoir." As Blaise straightened up, shaking his head, Edgerton shouted, "God damn it, Blaise, I'll buy the painting just as it stands."

"That would be foolish," said Grandi quietly.

"Do you think it's a fake, Mr. Grandi?" asked Ives.

"A fake?" Grandi gave the painting a glance, then turned his imperturbable gaze back to the Lieutenant.

"In my opinion it is a great work of art. Unfortunately, such a work of art, if it is by Paul Weldon, is worth only a few hundred dollars; if by Auguste Renoir, many, many thousands."

"Well, which is it?" asked Ives wearily.

"In my opinion," replied Grandi, "this painting is a genuine Paul Weldon."

There was a grunt from Edgerton and the technician turned to him politely. "Yes?"

"What's wrong with it?" demanded Edgerton.

"Very little," said Grandi, with a smile. "It is perfect. Perhaps too perfect."

"You mean," said Edgerton scornfully, "that it's better than Renoir."

"In some ways," said Grandi. "However, I would not attack it as a forgery, because what I tell you is founded on instinct and such evidence, in a court of law, is not admissible."

"What do you think, Dr. Corum?" asked Ives.

"I agree with Grandi," said Corum slowly. "I wouldn't know how to prove it, but something about it is wrong."

"Perfect answer from an expert," said Edgerton insolently. "Turn it inside out, magnify it a thousand times and you still won't know what he really thinks."

"Is this the first time you've seen the painting, Dr. Corum?" asked Blaise suddenly.

Corum flushed. "What do you mean by that?"

"Just asking," said Blaise.

"I don't think that's any of your business," said the harassed critic.

He was about to turn away, when Ives stepped up. "In that event," he said harshly, "I'll ask the question."

Corum wavered, as if debating the nature of his reply, then said firmly, "I have never before seen that painting." He turned to say this directly to Blaise. Looking past him, Blaise could see the detective's curious stare.

"When we talked about the forgeries," said Blaise, "You marveled that there should be a painter around with skill enough to make a Renoir portrait. You definitely said 'portrait' though at that time none of us knew whether the forgeries were portraits, still lives, landscapes or murals."

"I knew of the painting," admitted Corum grudgingly. "I had not seen it, but I knew that it existed and that Nathan Ordmann was buying it."

"You didn't think it was worth mentioning?" asked Blaise.

"I did not," was Corum's reply.

Ives changed the subject abruptly. "Well, as it stands, there doesn't seem to be any way to prove just what that painting really represents."

"Not without Paul Weldon," said Blaise.

"I'm going home," said Lucas Edgerton. "If the rest of you want to chase your tails around in a circle, that's all right with me. I'm leaving. Come on, Corum," he said, almost in the manner of giving an order, and the critic nodded. "You coming, Victor?" he then asked Grandi.

"If these gentlemen have no further questions," said Grandi politely.

"I'd like you to make some analyses of the paint and canvas," Blaise started to say, but Edgerton cut him off at once.

"Victor is busy. He works for me and he's got my work to do." He looked steadily at Blaise. "So, if I'm not mistaken, have you. I'm not paying you, and paying your expenses, to play around with the police. Good night," he snapped, and slammed the door. The others followed more gracefully.

Ives turned off the lights focused on the painting. "Where are we?"

"Do you think I'm crazy?" asked Blaise.

"I'm not sure I care." The detective was staring at the door. "For a while," he said, "Edgerton was seething to run down the forgeries no matter whose reputation was splintered in the collision. Now he's running full speed astern. Is he always that unpredictable?"

"Stronger minds have buckled in trying to dope out Lucas Edgerton," said Blaise. "My guess is that he's had a chance to think. He owns more than a hundred Renoirs. The story of these forgeries could ruin the market."

"What about justice? Twenty-four hours ago he was bleating for action, vengeance, anything!"

"Those are intangibles," said Blaise. "Money is something else again. You can stack it up, bury it in vaults, get a lot of pleasure out of it."

The phone rang and Ives reached the desk in two steps. "Ives talking," he said, and then, "Yes, Bonner. Go on."

Blaise moved over to the desk. Ives's aide, Sergeant Bonner, had been left at the Ocean Inn to handle the incoming calls, since Weldon and Blaise did not know each other's voices. "Good work," said Ives. "Now stay in the room until Blaise gets there." He put the phone down. "Well, we're in business," he said to Blaise. "Weldon called. He wants you to meet him on the pier in Venice. He has two of the drawings and he'll give them to you, with an affidavit, for five thousand dollars."

"That's a fair, handsome offer. Do I pay it?"

"Just meet him," said Ives. "Leave the rest to me."

As they went out, Ives said, "I'll sneak you back into the hotel and you can make a proper start just in case Weldon is watching the place."

"You think of everything," said Blaise.

Blaise drove to the pier conspicuously alone, left his car in the lot and climbed back up to the garish boardwalk. The smell of popcorn and spun-sugar candy mingled with the odors of broiling frankfurters and stale beer. The clattering rides, the strident voices of barkers and pitchmen, and the sharp explosions from the shooting galleries all blended into shattering dissonance.

He didn't see Ives or his men, and, as instructed, didn't look for them, accepting Ives's assurance that they would be somewhere around keeping him steadily under surveillance. He took up a post near the entrance to the pier, flanked by a cheery individual who was guessing ladies' weights in a mildly lascivious fashion, and, on the right, a stout man in soiled surgical white, exhorting passers-by to visit his educational and thrilling demonstration of the horrors of dope on the human body and mind. A bored floozy in a wrapper, obviously Exhibit A or B, stood on a platform above him, helping out with encouraging smiles which proved that among the more unpredictable horrors of dope were very bad teeth. Across the way was Screamo, an amusement device consisting of two tiny cages attached to an enormous swinging and revolving pole. Eager adolescents crowded into this to subject themselves, at 25 cents a head, to experiments which if conducted in Germany under the Nazis would have put the operator into the dock at Nürnberg.

Of the fugitive painter there was no sign whatever. Without conspicuously searching for them, Blaise was able to pick out Lieutenant Ives among the bingo players opposite and one door down, and Sergeant Bonner was at the frankfurter stand nearby.

As the minutes crept by, Blaise found himself wondering if Weldon could have been somehow alerted by the substitution of Bonner for himself in their telephone conversation. He found comfort in Bonner's methodical honesty. The Sergeant had reported that Weldon was drunk, only intermittently coherent, and had accepted Bonner completely. At any rate, Weldon was only a few minutes past due. He saw Ives leave his chair in the bingo palace and stroll down to the entrance to the pier, where he walked a few steps to the right and left. Then he came back scanning the establishments on both sides of the Midway. He passed Blaise with no more than a glance, continuing toward the ocean end of the pier. He made the fruitless round trip and took up his vigil again, this time at a "Ham and Bacon" wheel, standing at the semicircular counter so that he faced the entrance.

It was the amusement center's peak hour. The rides, some of them nightmare contraptions, swooped, dived, rolled, and swayed, battering their patrons to an ecstatic pulp, and the Midway resounded with screams of excitement and terror.

It was Blaise who first saw the knot of people far out on the pier, huddled at the blank rail, peering down into the darkness below. It dawned on him gradually that there were no rides or games in this section and then suddenly he heard a scream that was not prompted by 30 cents' worth of mechanized excitement. This one was the real thing. A long shrieking, chilling sound. He was running at once, as was Ives, and all over the Midway others detached themselves from groups to race out.

Ives pushed through the crowd, Blaise following close. Fifteen feet below was a small car and beside it a boy in a flowered open shirt and a pretty, brassy girl in slacks and a sweater. "It's a dead man," she shrieked to those at the rail above. "It's a dead man! In there! He's dead!"

Ives acted swiftly. Shouting to his aides to follow, he swung himself over the rail and dropped to the soft sand. Blaise reluctantly made the same leap and as he ran to the car he heard the thud of other landings. Bonner held the two who had discovered the tragedy; another detective chased away the curiously morbid types who tried to descend. Ives looked into the car, then opened the door, using a handkerchief on the handle. Paul Weldon was slumped over the wheel, the right side of his head all but shot away. His hand, palm up, was grotesquely open and the fingers were curled around the butt of a revolver. What was left of his face, looking up from the broken pose over the wheel, was oddly peaceful and in repose.

"He was right on time," said Ives bitterly.

"Suicide?" asked Blaise.

"Looks like it, doesn't it?"

Blaise nodded. "Very much."

Ives sat down on the running-board. Bonner could be heard giving orders for the dispatch of all the necessary agencies dealing with violent death. "Sure looks like suicide," mused Ives. "Best-looking damn suicide I've seen in years."

In matters of death by shooting Lieutenant Ives had highly acute and sensitive critical faculties, tuned to detect the slightest deviation from absolute pitch. His first comment on the death of Paul Weldon was more than borne out by the technical evidence and by what was discovered on his person and in the car.

In the trunk, loosely wrapped in brown paper, were

the nine paintings missing from the Edgerton collection, and in Weldon's pockets, with the small change, keys fitting the locks of the gallery itself and the vault.

The gun in his hand, moreover, was a .38 Colt, consistent with that which killed Simon Edgerton.

Weldon had apparently driven onto the beach some two blocks from the pier, as established by the tire markings, parked up close in the shadows and shot himself in the head. In the general pandemonium, including the blasts from shooting galleries, the single shot had been completely obscured. The boy and girl who discovered the body had been in search of a quiet place to pet.

Ives announced these facts as they were brought to light with no apparent emotion. Blaise sat quietly in a corner of the Lieutenant's shabby office, ignored by Ives and the stream of technicians who came and went. Finally Bonner brought in an elderly, bespectacled man in dark pants and bedroom slippers, the Sergeant carrying a heavy black wooden box with brass handles.

Ives brightened at the sight of the newcomer. "Hi, Doc," he said. "Thanks for coming out."

"Don't mention it," said Dr. Vollmer testily. "This body-snatcher," he went on, indicating Sergeant Bonner, "dragged me away without even a chance to dress."

Bonner looked up from his kneeling position. "Sorry, Doctor," he muttered. He had the box open and carefully withdrew a large comparison microscope, a delicate and expensive masterpiece of the optician's art. It had two separate sets of focusing wheels, two metal trays under different sets of lenses and binocular eyepieces. Bonner put this on the desk and Dr. Vollmer took off his coat, revealing a wrinkled pajama top. He took a white cardboard box from his pants and from this an ugly conical slug of lead. He used tweezers to transfer the bullet from the box to one of the microscope trays. "Where's the baby's brother?" he asked Ives, and the Lieutenant handed him an envelope from which he similarly extracted another bullet. He shifted the desk light to suit himself, then took off his glasses and bent over the microscope. As he brought one side into focus he manipulated the tweezers with his left hand. Satisfied at last, Dr. Vollmer gave his attention to the other side, similarly manipulating the bullet and the microscope. His forehead was beaded with sweat when he finally straightened up.

"What's the score, Doc?" asked Ives.

"Dead heat," announced the doctor. "Have a look," he invited and Ives came around to peer through first one side, then the other, and finally both. Then he stood erect and beckoned to Blaise. "The one on the left," he said, indicating the microscope, "is the slug we took out of Simon Edgerton. The other is from Weldon."

Blaise bent over the microscope. It was a powerful device, magnifying the scarred, blasted surface of the bullets enormously. He followed the detective's procedure, examining first one and then the other. When he looked through both eyepieces, Dr. Vollmer slowly brought both bullets together until the view merged into one picture, then separated them. They were absolutely identical.

When he stood erect, Ives motioned to his aide. "Okay, Bonner." The Sergeant promptly started to pack the equipment and Dr. Vollmer struggled into his coat.

"Well, you solved yourself a murder," he said apathetically to Ives.

"Looks like it," said Ives.

"You've got the right idea," said the doctor. "Just lie down, take it easy, and wait for the criminal to shoot himself. It takes time, but it works." Bonner was at the door with the heavy box and Vollmer moved that way.

"Good night, Doc," said Ives. "Thanks for coming out."

Ives sat silently behind his desk when he was once more alone with Blaise. His normally calm intelligent features now seemed to reflect some difficult conflict.

"I don't like it," he said at last, flatly and decisively.

"Fake paintings, fake suicide," suggested Blaise. After another moment of silence, he said, "Weldon's suicide fits, doesn't it?"

"Custom-tailored. It fits all right; it wraps up everything. Still, I don't like it."

"Don't buy it."

"I've got to buy it. Who the hell am I not to like it? We run a business. An unsolved crime, that's a loss; one we wrap up, that's profit. End of the year if the losses outnumber the profits the boss starts looking for a new man to run the store. I go to my chief and I tell him all the evidence signifies that Paul Weldon killed Simon Edgerton for not just one very good motive, but two, then killed himself in a drunken riot of conscience. But then I tell him that evidence or no evidence, I don't think so. Instead of one solved crime, I've got two unsolved murders. And he asks me why I don't buy Paul Weldon's suicide and I have to give him a platter of mumbo-jumbo about hunches and instinct. I'd be lucky if I wound up downtown chasing phony fortune-tellers."

"Yours is an interesting dilemma," murmured Blaise. Ives nodded. "I like yours, too. How do you prove your stand on the Renoirs? Wait for Weldon to communicate with you from the spirit world?"

"I've been thinking of that. My neck is pretty far out, especially with Edgerton writing the minority decision on the forgeries. He's just about all the business I've got, and he's bounced other dealers for just misspelling a word, let alone a juicy boner like mine."

Ives smiled genially. "Welcome to the glue factory."

"I take it," said Blaise, "that the medical report on Weldon is suicide all the way."

"Everything. The wound, the burns, the time—the works."

"Any traces of a second party in the car?"

Ives shook his head. "That damn pair of juvenile delinquents trampled the sand all around the car. Inside, no traces yet of any prints but Weldon's. No prints but his on the gun. I've got a detail out with photos trying to establish where he spent the day and evening. There was one empty pint bottle in the car but he must have had a lot more than that to keep going for twelve hours." As Blaise was about to speak, he said, "Save your breath. The bottle had his fingerprints exclusively."

"Tell me something," said Blaise, eyeing the detective curiously. "It's right, it fits, it works—why won't you chime in with the others and wrap up the case?"

Ives smiled but his eyes were glacially cold. "Some smart son-of-a-bitch is home now, maybe sipping a drink, preening himself, ready for a good night's sleep. He's fooled the world, he has. He's riding high, nobody can touch him. Well, in a couple of months, maybe a couple of years, I'll be standing by a little plate-glass window looking into a little room no bigger than this, watching for the puff of smoke that comes when they explode the cylinder of gas."

Blaise shivered. "Don't ever let me cross you up, Lieutenant," he said softly. "I think I like it better on your side."

"Go on home," said Ives. "Get some sleep."

25

IN THE MORNING PAPERS, delivered to his room with the coffee by a waiter who looked at him with fresh respect, Blaise found that Lieutenant Ives was tentatively accepting Paul Weldon's suicide and guilt. He winced at the next paragraph which specifically handed him the credit for establishing the conspiracy to forge certain paintings by Auguste Renoir. Finding the same eulogy in almost the same words in the other paper, he discarded them both and also abandoned the coffee which until then had tasted very good indeed. He was dressing when Andrew Kullman phoned from downstairs, and Blaise invited him to come up.

The producer shook hands gravely. "Have some coffee," said Blaise. "It's good and it's hot. I lost my appetite reading the papers."

"Did you ever come right out and say the painting Nathan Ordmann bought from Astorg is a fake?" asked Kullman.

"Never," said Blaise. "I'm not that much of a fool, or maybe I am, but I didn't say it."

"The police commandeered the painting, you know," Kullman went on, "and according to Ordmann, because you said it was a fake."

"Ouch!"

"Ordmann is a good friend of mine. A nice man. He knows nothing about paintings. He's forming the collection as a gift for the museum up north. Since he knows nothing, he's very sensitive."

"I've an idea," said Blaise wistfully, "that this is not going to be one of my good days."

"I thought I'd tell you," said Kullman. "Ordmann came to my house last night. He was sizzling, naturally, and blowing most of the steam your way. I told him I thought you were a smart, honest man."

"Naturally," said Blaise, "that solved everything."

"He was all set to wake up his lawyers and file all kinds of suits then and there," Kullman went on to say, "but around midnight we got the news about Paul Weldon and I persuaded him to hold off." Blaise nodded. "So there you are," said Kullman, in conclusion.

"Just where would you say I am?" asked Blaise politely.

"You've seen the painting, haven't you?"

"Went all over it. Edgerton, Grandi, Wesley Corum and I. It's perfect. Today, Grandi is going to analyze some flecks of paint, check the age of the canvas and try some X-rays. I doubt if any of them make it seem less authentic. And the police are checking on how Astorg acquired it in France but that's bound to be impeccable. Quite candidly, Mr. Kullman, now that poor Weldon is out of the running, I don't think I've got a chance. The technical reports may help, but I doubt it. At any rate, even if I could convince a few people that the painting was a forgery, Astorg can bring dozens of experts to testify that it's genuine."

Kullman nodded sympathetically. "Have you got any money?"

"Some. Not much."

"For the time being, I'd put it in your wife's name."

"No wife," said Blaise.

"I'll speak to Ordmann again," promised Kullman.

"I tried to convince him that you were doing a great service for collectors, and that I believe in you."

"Thanks. Thanks a lot." He took Kullman to the door. The phone was ringing and he rushed back to answer it.

It was Cassy and the sound of her voice was suddenly an infinitely welcome and cheering note in the day's gathering pressures.

"I'm not allowed to see you or talk to you," she announced cheerfully, "and the butler and the gateman have orders to shoot to kill—on sight, that is."

"Uncle has the wind up, has he?"

"At breakfast, the nicest thing he called you was 'a trouble-making sneak.' Then he wanted to know how far things had gone with us. I told him I was with child and he almost bit through a Georgian candlestick worth several hundreds of dollars. Anyway, we have to meet secretly, in dark, secluded places."

"Well, that's something," said Blaise. "I think I may be in trouble, Cassy."

"I know," was her sober reply. "I'm sorry, Ellis."

"Want to help me?"

"Of course," she said indignantly. "I love you, you big clod!" There was no immediate reply, and she said plaintively, "Aren't you glad?"

"Very glad, Cassy. I didn't answer right away because I was so impressed."

She heaved a sigh of relief. "Good." Then, briskly, she went on, "Well, that's that. What do you want me to do?"

"I'm not quite sure. I have the beginnings of an idea, and if I can swing it, I'll need your help. You think I ought to stay away from Casa Edgerton today?"

"It would be prudent."

Blaise considered this. "To hell with prudence. I'll be out after lunch. If I'm turned away at the front door, I'll swim in from the ocean side."

"That's my boy," said Cass proudly. "I'll try to square you with Uncle meanwhile, but don't expect too much."

"Call waiting for you, Mr. Blaise," said the hotel operator. "I'll see you later," he said, and hung up. The phone rang again at once. It was Lieutenant Ives, calling from Paul Weldon's studio. Blaise dressed and retrieved the car, then drove down into Hollywood.

In the studio, two men in plain clothes were methodically taking the room apart. One of them straightened up from sounding of the moulding at the floor and indicated the open bedroom door. Molly Dann, her mouth set in a sullen, suspicious line, was sitting on the bed and Lieutenant Ives was staring thoughtfully at Weldon's secret cupboard in the night table which was yawning wide open now.

"I located this last night," Ives told him. "To play safe, I'm having the boys outside try for a dividend." He bent over the opening, sniffed and beckoned to Blaise to do likewise. "Paint, isn't it?" asked Ives.

"Sure. He had to use some extraordinary stuff and that's probably where he kept it."

"There was this, too," said Ives, exhibiting a narrow band of paper with the words "Inland Bank & Trust" poorly printed, and in a neat, clerical hand, "$1,000" written in pencil.

"The girl says he told her he had some money."

Blaise turned to Molly, and she nodded listlessly. "That's what he said. He wanted me to go away with him and he said he had money. More than I thought he had, that was what he said." She shrugged her smooth bare shoulders. "I didn't give a damn, but that's what he said." She looked at Blaise. "I guess you think I'm rough on boy friends." She laughed cynically. "A date with me is a short cut to Forest Lawn."

"I'm sorry, Molly," Blaise told her sincerely.

"He tells me"—she pointed to Ives—"that Paul left a will. I inherit all he had. How do you like that?"

"I'm glad," Blaise started to say, and then Ives cut in with, "Molly, did Weldon always work here in the studio?"

"Mostly. Sometimes he sketched up in the hills, but generally he worked here."

"Did he ever keep you away? Were there times when he was secretive about what he was doing?"

"I don't know," she said thoughtfully. "Once he told me he was going up to Carmel for a week, and not to count on posing, but later on somebody mentioned seeing him right here in town. I thought maybe he was having a fling he didn't want me to know about. I didn't care, so I never thought about it."

"You say he was frightened of Kenneth Lurie?" asked Ives. He look significantly across the girl at Blaise.

She nodded emphatically. "No doubt about it. Lurie had some kind of an Indian sign on Paul. And yesterday, twice I looked out in the afternoon and spotted that thug he uses for a driver. He was watching my house. I figured they must be hunting for Paul."

"Thanks," said Ives. "Thanks a lot, Molly."

She stood up, giving them a flash of her bare thighs, then tugged the dress down modestly. "Damn thing rides up on me," she muttered.

"It was a pleasure," said Blaise gallantly.

"Stop in," said Molly. "We'll talk about it." She went

out, both men looking after her provocative, rolling gait. She was wearing the comfortable Southern California minimum which heightened the effect.

"Any time you're ready," said Ives.

Blaise turned back to him sheepishly. "Sorry. Just daydreaming."

Ives sat down on the bed. "Hugh Norden should be about ready to creep out of hiding now. Weldon's death—whatever it was—probably puts him in the clear. He'll turn up now with some idiotic yarn—maybe even amnesia."

"He may be in the clear," said Blaise, "but he undoubtedly touched off the explosion when he gave Simon that fake drawing."

Ives nodded. "Probably. I figure now that he was blackmailing somebody. Maybe it was Simon, or maybe Lurie or Astorg. Which of them, by the way, do you think commissioned the forgeries?"

"My guess is Lurie. I think Astorg believed he was getting genuine Renoirs stolen from the Edgerton collection."

"It was a great break for them when Simon died. That eliminated one unreliable confederate. Now Weldon's suicide just makes it perfect. They're lucky. When people get that lucky—two in a row—I can't help thinking, maybe they're helping their luck along a little."

"Nicely put," said Blaise. "Is there anything you can do about it?"

"It's just an idea I had," said Ives.

There was a quiet moment, broken by Blaise. "Those keys you found on Weldon, Lieutenant—the gallery key and the one to the vault—what's become of them?"

Ives tapped his breast pocket. "Why?"

"If I had those keys," said Blaise softly, "I could try an idea of my own."

"You've got a hell of a nerve!" Ives looked at him searchingly. "You realize what you're saying?"

Blaise sighed. "I know. Want to hear my idea?"

"Edgerton's sore at you, isn't he?"

"Barred me from the premises," said Blaise candidly. "Not only that, your cop told Nathan Ordmann that it was I who branded his painting a fake, and he's going to sue me. I may be left high and dry. With nothing," he added temptingly, "but my idea."

"Must be one hell of an idea," muttered Ives. He seemed prepared to listen, though, and Blaise took advantage of it.

"I had the proof of the forgery in my hands once," said Blaise, "and because I was a fat-headed, big-mouthed idiot, I lost it and I'm in trouble. The drawing Molly Dann gave me was the key to the whole thing. If I had a few more of those drawings, I could put the firm of Lurie and Astorg through a wringer."

"Sure," said Ives promptly. "But you haven't got them."

"True. That's what makes mine such a good idea. If I had a few real drawings, not fakes but authentic drawings of the same period, our friends wouldn't know the difference. It's damn near impossible to tell them apart. They know I've had one of the forgeries, how would they be sure I didn't get others? The thing is," he went on carefully, "drawings like that are damn scarce. Edgerton has a few but it would take weeks to get them anywhere else."

"You think that somebody would go after the drawings?"

"I'm positive."

"You could get killed monkeying around with a crazy stunt like that," said Ives.

"In a way," said Blaise, "I'm fighting for my life."

Ives was thinking. "You couldn't put this up to Edgerton, could you?"

"Not a chance. Furthermore, the way it stands, I'm not sure I want to," he said bluntly.

Ives took a fresh package of cigarettes from an inside pocket and Blaise saw an envelope fall on the bed beside him. The contents gave off a metallic jingle but Ives ignored it elaborately. "Too damn risky," he said. "I could get broken right the hell off the force for something like that. And you'd be taking a big chance."

Blaise smiled. "You're right. Forget it."

Ives went to the door to consult the two men who were searching the studio, standing with his back turned. Blaise reached out for the envelope, saw the two keys, and put it in his pocket. Ives turned slowly. "Nothing doing so far," he said. "No reason for you to stick around."

"I've got some things to do," said Blaise. "I'll be in touch with you later on."

"Do that," said Ives sharply. "See that you do that."

26

THE FIRST HINT of his fall from grace came when Blaise nosed his car into the driveway only to have Edgerton's gateman bar the way. "Nothing doing, Mr. Blaise," said this functionary flatly. Even the dog at his side appeared to have been alerted. As Blaise leaned out the window of the car the animal growled and bared ugly teeth.

"Down, Rover," said Blaise, with little conviction. To the watchman he said, "I'm barred, eh?"

The gateman nodded, eyeing Blaise with admiration. "You must have really given the old man a hot-foot," he said. "He was all set to issue grenades and flame-throwers."

"Call him," said Blaise. "Tell him I'm here."

The man's eyes bulged. "After what he said?" He eyed the twenty-dollar bill in Blaise's hand with unmistakable longing.

"He hasn't heard my side of the story," said Blaise. "I'm entitled to a hearing. That's the American way." He spread the money in his hand so that not one but two twenties were visible.

The watchman wilted. "Hell, everybody ought to be entitled to a trial."

Blaise parted with the money, taking some comfort from the fact that this was still some of what Edgerton had issued for expenses. The gateman went to the phone in his hut. Blaise couldn't hear either end of the conversation, but he saw jerky convulsive motions of the watchman's head. Then he leaned out of the hut, jerking his thumb up toward the house. "He's waiting for you. Brother, is he waiting for you!"

Blaise threaded his way up the driveway to the house, parked in the space between the gallery and the residence, fixed a confident smile where he thought it would stay put, then went bravely into the gallery.

He emerged, in some twenty minutes, feeling like a man who has somehow survived an explosion that blasted him out of his clothes, leaving him naked to raging winds that blew hot and cold but seared at either extreme. He thought he knew what heights of execration this rancorous old man could attain but he had to admit, as he wobbled away from the library, that Edgerton had outdone himself. Not only were his revilements vicious and dazzling but they were larded with curses of Talmudic complexity and scope. To intensify Blaise's discomfort, Miriam Wayne was present throughout, standing by the desk with an idly open book in her slim fingers. She appeared—though he had little interest in the phenomenon—more beautiful than he had ever seen her look before. She was in black, as if she had robed herself for the execution. She wore a blouse cut boldly low and there was a new freedom in the shape and movement of her body.

It was Miriam who, at the last, handed him a check and efficiently asked for a statement of his expenses.

Blaise found Cassy on the beach, as arranged. "You look," she said, "like one of the more vivid illustrations in Foxe's *Book of Martyrs*. St. Sebastian, or one of those boys, complete with arrows."

He lowered himself gratefully to the sand. "I know. You haven't got a drink on you, have you, Cassy?"

"Where do you suppose it might be?" she asked, looking down at the few square inches of bright blue silk that covered her.

"I thought you might have a hollow tooth," said Blaise. He stood up and extending his hand pulled her up. "Let's go where we can get one."

Cassy tucked herself discreetly into a terrycloth robe and they went to his car in the driveway. "Farewell," said Blaise to the gateman as they rolled by. "Farewell! O scene of triumph, farewell!"

"Uncle tied a can to you, eh?"

Blaise nodded. "Not until, however, he had filled it with firecrackers. I was roasted to a turn, Cassy, and Miriam Wayne was right there to baste me whenever the juices threatened to overflow."

"You poor baby," was her motherly reply.

On the highway she guided him to a fish joint with a bar and a rickety terrace. After two doubles, Blaise recovered sufficiently to try the large stone crab, served cracked and cold.

"You said I could help," Cassy reminded him.

"I've got an idea," he said. "It's big trouble if it backfires." He told her about it while he explored remnants of shell for fugitive bits of crab. It enabled him to avoid looking at her face which grew small and anxious as he outlined his extravaganza.

"You could get the same results," she said, "by hanging a sign around your neck: 'Three Shots for a Quarter. Win a Prize.'"

"I'm stuck," said Blaise briefly. "It's all the idea I've got. Ives apparently thinks it might work," he said reassuringly. "That's how I got the keys."

"Ives," she pointed out, "will be home in bed, miles from the rattle of muskets."

"Not really. Getting the drawings should be a snap. From then on, Ives will cover me."

She was silent, looking at him quizzically. "Ellis, is this something you've got to do?"

"I think so," he answered gravely.

"Vanity?" He glanced up sharply, and she went on hastily. "I understand that. I'll do whatever you say, Ellis, and for whatever reason, or no reason at all."

He reached across the table to cover her hand with his. "I'm an art dealer, Cassy. It may seem like a silly thing to be, but there it is—I am. I sell important paintings to important people. I watch for new talent, too, and if I find an artist who's got something to say and technique enough to say it, I back him—against the world, if necessary. I see that he's got a place to live, enough to eat, and security to paint. Even if the critics belt my ears off and unsold canvases pile up like old newspapers. That's the good, the truly first-class part of being in my business. But to do it, or anything, I have to come back to the original premise: I sell important paintings to important people. Your uncle thinks he made that possible, and, as of now, he's absolutely right, but I think I would have realized it, sooner or later, on my own—as people began to have confidence in my judgment. That's my biggest asset. With it, if I tell a client a painting is a good buy at thirty, or forty, or fifty thousand dollars, a good chance exists that he'll concur, hang it proudly and defend his judgment and mine against sniping from other dealers and collectors. Without that atmosphere of confidence, I'm back in the bush league, selling Mother's Day cards and second-rate prints. My reputation is at stake. Your uncle fired me. That's bad enough, but luckily he's fired, at one time or another, every dealer on both sides of the Atlantic. What really worries me is the matter of the Renoirs. I'm going to be sued, that's certain. If I have to go into court with nothing but my hunch, I'll be cat meat when I come out."

Cassy looked up at him soberly, and he grinned. "That's the longest speech I made since I persuaded the president of two banks and three railroads to buy a Picasso with a hammer and sickle in the foreground."

"Thanks for the statement of policy," said Cassy softly.

"I laid it on thick," he said. "Actually, with a rich wife at my side, my fears are largely imaginary."

"What do I do?" asked Cass.

"A trifle," said Blaise, smiling. "Hide in the gallery, switch off the alarm, open the door and let me in."

Cassy considered this. "I don't think that's asking too much. After all, we're friends. I take it you're not actually going to steal anything from Uncle Lucas?"

"Just his niece."

Cassy's smile was torn in half. Blaise, alarmed at her sudden air of apprehension and dismay, instinctively started to turn, but she caught his arm in a frantic little gesture. "Don't turn around—you'll frighten him." She answered the unspoken question. "It's Hugh Norden. He looks funny without his glasses, but it's Hugh." As Blaise stiffened, she said, "I don't think he's seen us yet. He's inside. He's ordering. Turn around slowly now."

Blaise shifted himself slowly, Cassy's voice guiding him. "At the counter . . . next to the wall . . . in the light-blue suit." It took Blaise a moment to allow for the lack of spectacles and mustache, but it was Norden. He was neatly dressed and clean-shaven, but he sagged over the counter like a man about to drop from exhaustion. "Ives said he was heading this way," said Blaise. "He predicted we'd be hearing from him."

"You haven't heard yet," warned Cassy. "He's mean. Be careful."

Blaise moved along the strip of terrace which circled the building so that he could come in on Norden from the street. He sat down on one of the adjoining stools and was treated to a quick white-hot flash of panic as Norden recognized him.

"You've run a long way," said Blaise. "How are things on the road?"

"Stay away from me," said Norden, in a hoarse, anxious voice.

"I'm having a beer on the terrace with Cass Edgerton," said Blaise. "Come and join us." Norden was gripping the counter with both hands, steadying himself, it seemed, for some as yet undetermined move. "Be smart," urged Blaise. "I can show you how to get out of this jam all in one piece. Sooner or later, you've got to square yourself, Norden."

Norden's grip on the projecting counter relaxed slightly. "You won't yell for the cops?"

Blaise smiled. "The cops are inevitable—you know that. Your problem is how to face them. That's what I'm prepared to solve." He moved away a step. "Coming?"

Norden stood up and started the way Blaise indicated to the terrace. "He's with me," Blaise explained to the counterman.

27

THE AUTO-COURT MOTEL, a tourist facility in most areas, is that and more in Southern California. Some are establishments renting their cramped quarters by the month or year to families trapped in the housing shortage, but others specialize in the quick turn-over, leasing by the hour, or, in emergencies, by the minute. These are as much a part of the mating habits of the citizenry as sport-coats and convertibles, and it was in such a caravansary that Blaise found a lodging for Hugh Norden. For still another few hours it was important to keep Norden free, and the motel was ideal. The landlady, once recovered from her chagrin that the cabin was rented for the entire night, gave the register barely a glance, and Blaise was positive that had Norden signed

"Martin Luther" or "Shirley Temple" it would have been all the same to the management.

The cabin was mildewed and dreary, but Norden had a quart of whiskey to enliven the decor. "Don't worry," he said when Blaise gave the bottle a perturbed look. "I'm not a drinker. I need this. My nerves are shot." As he poured himself a drink he asked Blaise to draw the curtains, and when this was done, he delicately slipped the contact lenses from his eyes, replacing them with the familiar thick horn-rimmed glasses he normally wore. "I hate the God-damn things," he muttered, carefully putting the fragile lenses away.

"For an innocent man," said Blaise, "you went to a hell of a lot of trouble."

"On paper," said Norden, "you can make it come out the way you want it. In the clutch, when the pressure suddenly comes on, clear thinking doesn't come so easily." He sipped his drink, medicinally, Blaise was glad to see, and it seemed to be working for him. "There I was," went on Norden, "a trespasser on the place, with my record, and with what I knew damn well was going on. You'd spotted me with Simon, and for all I knew then—or now," he added significantly, "you were with the cops. That's a beautiful spot for me, with no alibi."

"I take it," said Blaise, "that you've got one for last night."

Norden nodded, showing his large teeth in a delighted grin.

"Will it stand up?" asked Blaise.

"I think so. I was in jail." At Blaise's startled look, he said solemnly, "So help me! Guy gave me a lift, and something was wrong with his registration. The cops in some rube town up north held us until after midnight."

"And they let you go?" marveled Blaise.

"There was a picture of me hanging in the squad room," said Norden. "I saw it when I went to the can. If the cops were all like that," said Norden, "it would be a pleasure. A man could steal and sleep nights. The one that scares me," he finished ruefully, "is that Ives."

"You're in the clear now," Blaise pointed out.

"I know. Ives may not be able to hold me, but the chances are I won't feel like walking out when he's through with me. He'll hang something on me just for putting him to all this trouble."

"When you ordered those contact lenses—the way you did it, under an assumed name—wasn't that for a getaway?"

Norden nodded. "That's true. The funny thing is I never meant to use them to hide from the police." As Blaise's eyebrows went up politely, he insisted, "That's true. I'd made up my mind to get myself into the Renoir business. I was broke, and this looked like my chance for that one big score. But I was scared of what Kenneth Lurie might do to me. That's why I had a gun that night. I'm no rootin'-tootin' shoot-'em-up. I've never fired a gun in my life, but I thought I might have to if I was going to crowd in with Lurie."

"How much were you charging Simon for the drawing?"

"Ten thousand," said Norden candidly. "I figured he'd get it from Lurie."

"Or else?"

"I would tell Astorg. I knew that would galvanize Lurie, even if it didn't impress Simon. But he surprised me. He told me he'd give me the money that very night, and that's why I went to the house."

"And you let him keep the drawing, on the strength of his promise?"

"Oh, sure. I could still spill everything to Astorg,

drawing or no drawing. You see," he said, with his shrewd, wolfish smile, "your problem is convincing an honest judge and an honest jury against the weight of the evidence. My problem was only to convince one crook that a couple of other crooks robbed him. Astorg bought the paintings on sight because they came from the Edgerton collection. I could prove that was a lie. Simon understood that. I don't know why he wanted the drawing so badly that night, but I was glad to let him have it."

"I think I'm beginning to," said Blaise thoughtfully. "Stay out of sight," he warned Norden in farewell. "I'll look in on you later."

"Okay. Leave me some cigarettes."

Blaise left him a full pack and went out to his car in the courtyard.

Her part in the adventure, Cassy realized as seven o'clock rolled around that evening, was going to demand cunning and nerve; furthermore, at a level on which she had not operated since boarding-school. In those carefree days, to be sure, she had developed a flair for distracting watchmen, climbing fences and shinnying up trees that had enabled her to enjoy the late, smart showings of all the new pictures. This was different, and for all the unconcerned innocence with which she sauntered into the gallery, her heart was bumping and she knew that some of the color had drained out of her face.

Edgerton was standing with one foot on a chair, sorting some documents spread on the desk. He looked up at her casually, muttered, "Hello, Cassy" in a distracted tone, then went back to his papers. Then he looked up at her again, sharply this time. "What's the matter with you?"

"Nothing. Why?"

"You look all washed out."

"Me?" She made a great show of peering in a mirror, pushing up her lip and sticking out her tongue. "I've got it," she announced resignedly. "Edgerton's Disease, the dread scourge of Highway 101. The symptoms are painful swelling of the ego, choleric rages, heavy deposits of money around the heart."

Edgerton looked surprised at her outburst, then, as if remembering something, said, "Oh! Blaise, huh? Well, in decency, I suppose you have to do a certain amount of fatuous mooning over him, so go right ahead. I'm surprised at you, Cassy!" he added reproachfully. "Hell, Blaise must be old enough to be your father."

"He's thirty-one," she said. "I'm twenty-five. Is that December and May?"

"Thirty-one!" snorted Edgerton. Then he seemed to think about it. "Well, age doesn't mean a thing. He's an irritating, driveling loudmouth, and doesn't know his backside from a Tintoretto."

"I suppose that's why for nearly two years you've been telling everyone how smart he is."

"Me?" hooted Edgerton. Then in a pained, hurt voice, he said, "Well, he took me in."

He was relieved not to have to pursue this with Cass, who had turned away and after a few moments he was happily absorbed in his studies once more. From the nearest row of shelves, Cass watched him out of the corner of her eye. It would be difficult to stay behind if he finished for the day. Her only hope was a diversion that might enable her plausibly to stow away. It came in the welcome shape of Victor Grandi and a spirited argument about the carving of a frame, a dispute that took both men down into the vault. Cassy slipped into the coat closet in the front of the gallery and pulled the door all but shut, leaving herself an infinitesimal slit for peeping. Edgerton, on returning to the gallery, would take it for granted that she had gone back to the house or out to the beach, and since she was not expected to dine with him and his guests, barring the unexpected, she should be in the clear.

She heard their voices again after only a few minutes in the closet.

"I made some tests today for Lieutenant Ives," Grandi was saying, while Edgerton checked the doors and windows. "I'm afraid the Lieutenant was quite disappointed. There is absolutely nothing on this canvas to betray the forgery. The others, I'm certain, are as finely made."

"Who says they're forgeries?" demanded Edgerton.

"You know they are," said Grandi quietly.

Cassy, risking detection, pushed her door open another fraction of an inch. She knew the challenging glare with which her uncle was now facing Grandi, measuring his opponent. Remarkably, she saw the flicker of defeat in the way his chin slumped.

"You saw the drawing," Grandi went on coolly, "and Cassy saw the forger at work in this very room."

"You didn't see the drawing, Victor, and you didn't see the forger practicing. What makes you so certain Blaise is right?"

Cassy could see the old handyman in three-quarter profile. There was always some mockery in his humility around Edgerton and now it was openly derisive. "For your information," he was saying, "Lieutenant Ives now suspects that I may be the alchemist who helped poor Weldon grind his colors. His suspicions were aroused when he found some significant ingredients in my workshop. Fortunately, I was able to tell him that they were imported to enable me to do some retouching for you. I am greatly in your debt," he added formally, "for confirming this story. Especially, since there was not one word of truth in it."

Edgerton's fists were clenched and his eyes bright with anger. Grandi, in his old, paint-flecked clothes, faced him like an inquisitor, turning the screws one at a time.

"I confirmed what you told Ives," said Edgerton finally, "because you're always bringing in some smelly paints and chemicals. I took it for granted that this was just another batch."

"I think not," said Grandi politely. "Your main concern now is that the great name of Edgerton should not be connected with these forgeries. Not even through a lowly employee like myself. I know what you think of your collection; what you're capable of doing to defend it."

"Gibberish," said Edgerton hotly. "Jealous, spiteful gibberish."

"In Paris many years ago," continued Grandi imperturbably, "when a dealer sold you a forged Sisley, you went to his office and made him give back your money at the point of a revolver. An interesting characteristic."

"I'm locking up," said Edgerton. "Get out."

"Yes, sir," was Grandi's meek reply.

In the closet, Cass leaned weakly against the wall. The lights went out, one after another, and then she heard the sound of the door opening and closing after Edgerton. She had a lighter this time and, masking its flame with her right hand, looked at the time. It was nearly eight o'clock and, as planned, Blaise would not appear until 9:30, when dinner would be in full swing and the chances of detection at a minimum. She was glad to have the interval in which to think, and she now had plenty to think about. Abandoning the closet, she moved quietly down into the farthest corner of the gallery, well away from the uncurtained windows, and here she lit a cigarette and sat down cross-legged on one of the thick scatter rugs. It was a bright, clear night, and she wondered if Blaise would be able to elude the two watchmen who now roamed the ocean side of the estate. She had been heart and soul for his success, but now, after the scene between Edgerton and Victor Grandi, she was assailed by all manner of conflicting loyalties and fears. She knew that Grandi was capable of biting, bitter cynicism and that Lucas Edgerton evoked this characteristic freely. But she was afraid to let her mind stray to the bitterness between Lucas Edgerton and his son, or to recall the wild rage in which Simon had been ordered out of the library the night he was killed. She tried to gather and focus the puzzling, elusive thoughts into some channel that would make sense. She was still gathering and focusing when she heard an imperative tapping at one of the windows, and, scuttling to it rapidly, saw Blaise crouching in the shrubbery. He grinned, gestured to the door, and she hurried to admit him. She set the switches rendering the alarm useless and silent, then opened the door.

Blaise kissed her, holding her tight. He could feel the tremor that coursed through her body. "You're the best little confederate a second-story man ever had, Cassy."

"I'm scared," she said, clinging to him.

"So am I. Leave me alone now, Cassy, so I can shiver in private." He took her by the shoulders, propelling her to the door. "Your job is lookout. Here."

Cassy gasped as he slipped something cold and shiny

into her hand, and closed her fingers around the butt of a gun. "I got this for you on my way up here," he whispered hoarsely. "Don't use it unless you must, but then shoot straight and save the last bullet for yourself." She gulped weakly and looked down. She was holding a glass gun full of jelly beans, but before she could talk, Blaise had the door open and eased her outside. She moved around to the side, from which point she could watch the house and the approaches to the gallery. Through the window she could see Blaise as he worked with a small electric torch in one hand, riffling through the large flat boxes in which the drawings, prints and etchings were stored. He worked neatly, replacing each drawer as he finished with it. Without access to the catalogue, which would have placed each item, he had to trust to time and luck.

He had been alone inside for nearly an hour when Cassy saw Miriam Wayne emerge from the driveway door of the main house and, after looking around from the step, start for the gallery. She rapped desperately on the glass and, as Blaise's head turned, pointed frantically to the door.

He nodded, swiftly pushed back into place the drawer he was working on, then slid around to the other side of the cabinets. Cassy's relief was instantly flooded by a new terror. If Miriam came into the gallery she would have to give the all-clear code signal on the burglar alarm immediately. Finding the alarm shut off, she would suspect an intruder and sound battle-stations at once. At the last moment, as Miriam had her key in the lock, Cassy threw her head back and screamed. It was a shattering, strident sound. She had her heart in it, and all the power of her healthy young lungs. The result was something suitable for air-raids and major fires. It froze

Miriam Wayne at the door and it brought Blaise, heedless of the risk of exposure, out of hiding and over to the window. He could see Cassy, apparently alive and unharmed, then Miriam approaching warily from one side while a watchman came running from the other.

"There was someone here," sobbed Cassy. "A man. He was looking in the window. He ran off that way." She pointed to the beach, and as the others looked that way, Blaise saw her gesture to him. It was an unmistakable signal to depart. He had three drawings, exactly suited to his purpose, and with these rolled up and tucked away, he eased himself out and circled the gallery to the beach. The watchman was supporting Cassy's limp body now, which was her contribution toward stalling the manhunt, and Blaise blew her a kiss as he edged into the comforting obscurity of the dunes.

28

BLAISE was stretched luxuriously on the couch in his living room. He had a drink in his hand and, as Cassy saw him from the doorway, seemed to be disgustingly at ease.

"How can you be so calm?" she asked, as she closed the door and came in. "I'm still weak in the knees."

Blaise jumped up, put his arm around her waist and steered her to the couch.

"By the time I was pretending to faint," she said feebly, "it was darn near the real thing." She sat down, leaned back and closed her eyes for a moment. Blaise patted her hand. "You were swell, Cassy. Pluckiest little girl I ever saw." He kissed her gently.

"Shot and shell fell all around," she pointed out, "but I never flinched."

"Not once." He kissed her again.

She smiled up at him. "Now you know the kind of a scream I can unleash in an emergency. I had to do something," she went on earnestly. "Miriam would have noticed that the alarm was turned off. You would have been cornered."

"I figured that out while I was running," said Blaise, "and I'm much obliged. I'm thinking about just how to reward you."

"Think hard," said Cassy. Then her smile faded, and she sat up on the couch. Soberly and in detail, she described the scene between Edgerton and Victor Grandi in the gallery before his arrival.

Blaise studied her as she finished this recital. "You feel disloyal, isn't that it, Cassy?"

"Who wouldn't? Here I am, helping you set traps as if it was open season in the beaver country, and for all I know the prize catch may turn out to be my uncle. I know how you feel, and I don't blame you, but I'm scared."

Blaise nodded. "I understand. The drawings are on the table, Cassy. Take them with you. I'll try to think of something else."

She leaned against him, turning up her troubled face. "That's no solution. You're the one I started out to help."

"I don't think," Blaise said carefully, "that your uncle is interested in anything more criminal than the desire to have this investigation wrapped up just where it stands. When the smoke is all cleared away—if and when it is—I think he'll regret it, but right now all he sees is a succession of scandals, to no purpose as far as his welfare is concerned, with the sacred name of Edgerton looming up in all of them. He's not the most public-spirited man alive and I don't think he cares much who gets trimmed, provided he doesn't."

"That sounds like Uncle Lucas. You don't think his doings are any darker than that?" she asked anxiously.

"This time tomorrow," said Blaise grandly, "your uncle will be bringing me my slippers, mixing me a drink, and offering to up your dowry by some splendid sum."

"Tomorrow night, eh? Do we have to wait until the check clears? If we don't," she rambled on contentedly, "we can have a police-station wedding, the kind every girl dreams about from childhood, with an arch formed by crossed night-sticks . . ."

The telephone rang and Blaise jumped for it so eagerly that she knew it was something prearranged and expected. Blaise said, "Yes, Ives." Then, after an instant, "Right away." He put down the phone, smiling again, and said, "Sorry I interrupted your orange-blossom reverie, Cassy."

"You're on your way?"

"Ives is waiting for me."

"All right," she said resignedly. "This is your last night for helling around in prowl cars, friend. Make the most of it. You'll be a better art dealer if you stay home nights and study." At the door, though, she clung to him apprehensively.

"Be careful, Blaise," she said softly. "Please be careful."

He tapped her under the chin with the rolled-up drawings in his right hand, and she tilted it obediently. "I'll be right up on deck tomorrow," he told her.

"Nothing can stop me." He kissed her and Cassy's arms came up to hold him tight. He disengaged himself reluctantly. "Ives is waiting for me, Cassy."

"Let him wait. I'm a taxpayer." But she let go and they went out together. Blaise went off alone, heading north to the motel where he had put Hugh Norden earlier in the day. The headlights of a car parked in the dark road nearby winked on and off, and Blaise pulled up behind it and got out. Ives was walking to meet him.

"What's in here?" asked the detective curiously, indicating the motel.

"Your friend and mine—Hugh Norden."

"The hell you say!" It was the first time Blaise had seen the Lieutenant actually startled. He told Ives briefly how they had spotted the fugitive at lunch and of his anxiety to square himself.

"I'll square him," muttered Ives. "I'll put corners on him while I'm about it. And he damn well better still be here," he added darkly.

"He's here," said Blaise. He could see the lights burning back of the shades in Norden's cubicle. "I located a couple of those drawings I mentioned," he said casually. "With those, and if Norden really wants to be of some help, I think we can go places."

Ives took only a moment for reflection. "Let's go inside," he said. On the way, Blaise noticed that he unbuttoned his coat and reached under it to adjust the holster he was wearing.

At the sight of Lieutenant Ives, Norden's eyes all but revolved in their sockets. The detective pushed him back in roughly, then came in with Blaise and closed the door. A moment later, the landlady who was listening outside, heard a thump followed by a curious whimpering sound. Then there was conversation in an undertone which didn't carry to her and she abandoned this in favor of the adjoining cabin, where a dapper old man and a flashy little blonde had registered as father and daughter.

29

JONAS ASTORG was resting, lying almost at full length on a couch in Kenneth Lurie's chic drawing room. His eyes were closed, not in sleep but because all the lamps were brightly lit. Lurie was showing some pictures in the next room, an oval study, and Astorg half listened to the patter, the clichés of buyer and seller which followed each other like tracer bullets. He was in a strangely supine state. Having accepted the leadership of Kenneth Lurie, it was if he had relinquished responsibility and initiative. He was afraid of Lurie now. He knew that and it rendered him helpless. He was afraid to leave, afraid to stay, and, most of all, afraid to ask questions.

He sat up on the couch as the voices came clearer and saw Lurie with his customer, a rawboned lady on whom all the arts of Nieman-Marcus had been lavished in vain. Astorg, scanning the bracelets on her arm, established the age and extent of her fortune as a forestry expert might establish the age and quality of a tree from the rings girdling its trunk.

Lurie's exquisite Regency house, stocked with modern treasure from the gallery, was not a home but an annex. It was in the smartest residential area of the state, just west of Beverly Hills. It was as if the planners, having shown in Beverly the best that free enterprise could produce, now went one step beyond. Here the lawns and shrubbery were cut and trimmed with the care and devotion a devout Moslem might lavish on the Beard of the Prophet. Tennis courts, swiming pools and even a private golf course dotted the landscape. It was a monument to block booking, capital gains and the generous deductions allowed oilmen for the depletion of capital assets.

Lurie brought his customer into the drawing room. "Jonas!" he cried. "You'll never guess what this wicked, wicked woman has done. She's taking away our Sisley!"

Astorg clasped his hands in horror. "No!" he cried in shattered disbelief. "She can't!" The Sisley was a shabby landscape, probably a sketch for a painting, reluctantly accepted in trade. It had been kept, literally, in dead storage since neither partner was willing to exhibit it. Astorg now turned a look of piteous reproach on the triumphant customer. "I wanted that for my personal collection."

"So did I," said Lurie mournfully. "She went straight to it," he told Astorg. "Ignored all the things I wanted to sell. But," he went on resignedly, "it's going into a happy collection. Mrs. Parnell," he informed Astorg solemnly, "has the largest collection of Marie Laurencin in Texas."

"I know," said Astorg, while Mrs. Parnell twinkled with pleasure.

Lurie was ready to take her away and Astorg bowed low over her hard, rugged hand. Her car was waiting in the street and Lurie took her to it, promising immediate delivery of the Sisley. His careful, fitted smile stayed on until she drove away, still waving back roguishly, then he allowed himself the luxury of a sneer and started back into the house.

"Lurie!"

The dealer stopped, turning slowly. Hugh Norden had materialized in the trees blocked by his customer's car. He was about ten yards away, his right hand in the pocket of his loose gabardine coat.

"Oh, it's you," said Lurie, after a repugnant stare. "What do you want?"

"I'd like to talk to you," said Norden politely.

"What about?"

"I'd like to show you a Renoir drawing," was the reply. "An early one, about 1875." As Lurie seemed to consider this, he added, "Like the one I gave Simon Edgerton."

Lurie nodded his head, as if this was altogether an unexpected development. "I'll take you somewhere else, where we can talk. I'm not alone . . ."

"Astorg," said Norden, interrupting him. "I know. It's all right with me, if it's all right with you."

"Come in," said Lurie quietly. Norden waited for him to go ahead, and with a puzzled shrug, Lurie led the way. On the doorstep, Norden said, "I've got a gun." He said it quite simply and Lurie accepted it with an understanding nod. "This isn't a stickup—you know that." Lurie nodded again. "I just wanted you to know."

"Come on in," the dealer said. "We'll talk about it."

Norden followed him down the short hall, into the drawing room. "This is Hugh Norden, Jonas," said Lurie, with an air of utter resignation. "He'd like to show us an early Renoir drawing." When Astorg bounced upright on the couch, Lurie added, "By the way, he's got a gun."

Norden said, "Pleased to meet you, Mr. Astorg." Keeping his right hand in his pocket he reached under the baggy coat with his left. He drew out a sheet of paper rolled into a tube and tossed this to Astorg.

Astorg's fingers trembled as he unrolled the paper, but Lurie was steady and calm, not even troubling as yet to glance at the drawing.

"*The* Renoir?" asked Lurie.

"Or thereabouts," replied Norden.

Lurie moved around to look down over his colleague's shoulder. "Close enough," he said sadly. "How much?"

"Ten thousand."

"For one drawing?" Lurie's eyebrows went up.

"For three."

Astorg spoke for the first time. "How many have you got?"

"Three," said Norden, with a smile, and at Astorg's skeptical glance, added, "That's the lot."

"I know this man," said Lurie. "He's honest. I vouch for him."

Norden made him a little bow. "Likewise, I'm sure."

"You've brought the other two?" asked Lurie hopefully.

"They're handy," was the reply. After a moment, Norden asked, "How handy is the ten thousand?"

Lurie looked at Astorg. "What do you think, Jonas?"

Astorg pushed himself up, as if this took a lot of his strength. He stared at Norden, his eyes wide, his mouth a little slack. "Blackmailing devil," he muttered suddenly and launched himself at Norden, his fingers curved into claws raking at the other man. Norden fell back quickly, his right hand whipping out with a gun. Lurie caught the old man's shoulder, spun him around and pushed him back so that he staggered into the couch and sat down abruptly. Norden, watching as he sagged, slowly let his hand fall back into the pocket.

Lurie smiled apologetically. "He's not used to these transactions." Astorg was sitting up stiffly on the edge of

222

the sofa. "I'll handle this for both of us," went on Lurie quietly. "All right, Jonas?"

The other nodded. He was back again in the oddly detached, semipresent mood, listening to the other two voices as if they were coming in faintly from far away.

"You've got three drawings—that's all?"

"Three," repeated Norden firmly.

"I take it you don't plan to spend the money right here in Southern California."

"I want to get away. A friend of mine is on a ship going out of San Pedro tomorrow morning. He'll sign me on and that's the end of me up here."

Lurie seemed to give grave assent to the wisdom of these proposals. Then, while Norden stiffened, he reached slowly into his breast pocket. A thin sheaf of currency was held flat in a black wallet. He ran his fingers over the edges of the bills and tossed them beside the drawing on the table. "There's a couple of thousand. How do you want the rest?"

"No checks." Norden picked up the money. "Tonight, any time you say."

"Midnight?"

"Fine. I'm at the Far West. It's a motel out on the Highway. About eight miles down from the Edgerton place."

"I'll find it," said Lurie simply. As Norden started to edge out, he said, "By the way, you got these from poor Weldon, didn't you?"

"I picked him up one night about a month ago," recited Norden calmly. "He was pretty far gone and I helped him home. After he was asleep I couldn't resist taking a look around. Amazing!" he marveled. "There were the five drawings . . ." At Lurie's sharp look, he added, "I only took four—and locked away in a closet a

223

half-finished Renoir. Believe me," he finished with his wolfish grin, "I had a new respect for Paul Weldon."

"An extraordinary talent," murmured Lurie. "A very able man. A month ago, eh?"

"More or less."

"Why did you wait?"

"What would be the point of exposing Weldon? I had to know what was involved, who was involved, and how much. I watched Weldon and that way I picked up the connection to Simon Edgerton. That damn near drove me crazy. I couldn't figure his place in the set-up at all." His eyes wavered to Astorg, still on the couch.

"Go on," said Astorg. "I might as well hear it all now."

Norden looked at Lurie quizzically, as if asking permission. When he saw no sign of protest, he said, "Maybe it's just knowing how certain minds work—anyway, I knew you wouldn't need Simon if you were dealing with a collector. It would mean admitting the paintings were hot. But Simon was obviously a key man and that could only mean that he was needed to make the paintings authentic. When I found out that Mr. Astorg had these great new Renoirs"—he smiled modestly—"from there it was easy. It was a great idea," he said respectfully to Lurie. "I wish I'd thought of it when I had Simon on my side. I knew an artist then who could knock out Pissarro and Monet with his eyes shut."

"You're quite right," said Astorg stiffly. "I was the gull." He turned his bitter stare on Lurie. "My partner! My friend!"

"Don't be a fool," said Lurie. "Am I in business to make friends? Are you?"

Astorg nodded sullenly. "Thank you."

"Anyway," said Norden brightly, "once I knew the

program, all I had to do was pick the weakest spot and start tunneling in that way. I thought it would be Simon," he finished thoughtfully. "As it turned out, that may have been a mistake. You knew the truth by then, didn't you?" he asked Astorg.

The old dealer shook his head. "I'm rather more dense than you think."

"Oh. I thought you did because. . . ." His voice trailed off. "It doesn't matter," he added lamely.

"He means," said Lurie delicately, "because he saw you at the Edgerton place that night."

"Before or after you arrived?" demanded Astorg.

"Before," said Norden, after a moment's pause.

Astorg laughed brutally. "Then I think we can take it for granted that Simon was still alive."

"I think we ought to change the subject," said Lurie, "before we raise the price of the other two drawings."

Norden chuckled. "I was just thinking about that. I'll say good night," he said politely. "I'm sure you must have a lot to talk about."

Lurie went out into the hall with the departing guest, then Astorg heard the opening and closing of the door and the rattle of the bolt. Lurie came back with a humidor from which he selected a large cigar. "Want one?"

Astorg shook his head. "Bad for my heart," he said drily.

"You must be careful," said Lurie gravely. He took a minute or two for the perforation and even lighting of the cigar. Then he closed the humidor, carefully moved it so that it was in the center of the long library table, and after cocking an eye was dissatisfied with the effect. There was a small, gracefully executed bronze, a nude in bas-relief on a roughly finished plaque, and he placed

225

this on the humidor. "Maillol," he told Astorg. "Not to my mind a first-class artist, but I've had this for many years. It was in the first good collection I ever handled. I sold everything in it but this plaque and at last decided to keep it for luck."

"The story of your life, when you get around to it," said Astorg bitingly, "should be very interesting. Let me know if you need a finish."

Lurie laughed. "I'm glad you're showing some spirit, Jonas. You were beginning to depress me. I'm ashamed of what happened here. That a sniveling little thief like Norden should have the gall to come here and demand money!"

"Is that why you gave it to him so readily?"

Lurie spread his hands helplessly. "I'm not a fool. It would be sheer, egotistical folly to deny that Norden stands to make a lot of trouble. But," he finished with satisfaction, "we've been lucky so far."

"What are you going to do?"

Lurie tapped the ash gently from his cigar. "Would you really like to know, Jonas?"

"No!"

The other man smiled. "That's what I thought." The smile receded. "I'll do," he said gravely, "what I have to do. Neither more nor less. Something like this has been inevitable. In the back of my mind, I think I knew that and subconsciously prepared myself. I was never content with running just a business, Jonas—not even when it was very successful. Were you?" he asked abruptly.

"I know what you mean," was Astorg's low, hesitant reply.

"I'm sure you do. My earliest admiration for you was touched off years ago when I saw some things you sold an auto magnate in Detroit. A quarter of a million dollars' worth of great, authentic paintings, but you couldn't resist sneaking in a few worthless pre-Columbian vessels made right here in Los Angeles. That gave me great pleasure. I knew then that we were destined to be partners."

"Why did you have to fool me?" demanded Astorg. "Of all people, why me?"

Lurie shrugged. "Challenge, or ego, or arrogance, I suppose. Most collectors and dealers bore me. I am frequently honest in my dealings with them only because they're so gullible that fleecing them is like shooting a sitting duck. But with you, Jonas," he said affectionately, "my faculties had to be at their very keenest." He put down the cigar and stretched, arching his long arms gracefully. "I'm going to the beach," he said. "Shall I drop you, or will you wait for me here?"

"I'll go home," said Astorg quietly.

In the same chatty, confiding manner, Lurie said, "It's a little early to call on our friend Norden, but he won't mind."

Astorg paused in the hall. "Have you got the money?"

Lurie nodded. "Oh, yes."

Astorg caught his arm and his partner turned in wide-eyed surprise. "Give him the money," said Astorg, in a tone of voice that was almost a plea. "You can count on me for my share—all of it, if necessary."

"That's very generous."

"Do you hear, Lurie?" said Astorg insistently. "Don't get a crazy notion of pride or revenge now. Give him the money."

"Of course," said Lurie mildly. He turned off the lamps in the hall, facing the other man in the fitfully scattered light from the salon. "I rather dislike putting myself in the clutches of such a blackmailing scoundrel.

Who knows," he went on piously, "what unreasonable demands he may make in the future?"

"That we can think about later on. I want those drawings tonight, and I want to be sure Norden isn't going to trouble us."

Lurie smiled. "I give you my word. My word of honor." Astorg seemed about to speak, then subsided. "What is it you want to say?" he asked politely.

"Nothing. Nothing at all," muttered Astorg. He took his coat from the chair on which it was folded, then silently followed Lurie to the big black car in the driveway.

30

AT THE FAR WEST the motel business was booming. Ives had requisitioned the two bungalows adjoining Norden's original space, and another facing this layout on the other side of the court. The hag who managed the inn had delightedly evicted the tenants in these accommodations, giving them barely time to dress, shooing them into the night with raucous and obscene suggestions of sanctuary.

Norden rendered a faithful account of his interview, after which Ives relieved him of the two thousand and the gun. Sergeant Bonner took charge of both, settling himself in a well-lit corner with the currency and several sheets of closely typed onion-skin paper.

"If it's all the same to you, Lieutenant," said Norden respectfully, "I'd just as soon meet Lurie in a tank or an armored car."

"Sit down, scum," said Ives coldly, and Norden obediently sat down. "I'm using you," continued Ives, "but don't crowd your luck. I use stool-pigeons, even drug addicts when I have to. If you're useful, I may let you plead to something easy. If you're not, you'll wish Lurie had stuffed you with cement."

"Yes, sir," said Norden uneasily.

"The Lieutenant really likes you," said Blaise. 'His manner is gruff but underneath beats a heart like. . . ." He never finished the simile. The normally well-controlled Sergeant Bonner jumped up from his researches. "Here it is. The whole two thousand is part of what Weldon drew out of the bank."

Ives grinned suddenly. "Well, what do you know!" he said gently. "What do you know!"

Blaise, not quite so poised, was excitely looking down at the pages Bonner extended, the Sergeant showing him how the bank kept track of its currency. "We don't know exactly what bills the bank issued to Weldon," the Sergeant explained, "but we know that on the day he made this withdrawal they issued twenties, fifties and hundreds with serial numbers somewhere in this range. And here they are."

"How much did Weldon have?" asked Blaise.

"He got six thousand in this batch," Ives told him. "We may get more of it later."

In a pained, fearful voice, Norden said, "Jesus, Lieutenant, you don't really think Lurie is coming here to give me that money, do you?"

"Shut up."

When Norden subsided, Ives condescended to add, "Of course, he'll give you the money. He's got to have the drawings. His best bet is to kill you," he said thoughtfully, as if he were trying to guess his opponent's strategy in a game of chess, "but not until he has the drawings, and definitely not here."

"I'm glad," said Norden, licking his dry lips nervously.

"Is there any way I can meet Lurie?" asked Blaise, and at Ives's curious look, he added, "It was my idea."

"You've got an honest face. Lurie would never believe you were blackmailing him. Besides, if anything happened to you there'd be an awful stink. This one"—he jerked his thumb at Norden—"he's expendable."

"I'd like a drink," said Norden.

Ives nodded. "Give it to him, Bonner."

Sergeant Bonner, whose duties were varied, took a bottle from a cupboard and poured a stiff drink into a tumbler, watching his superior for orders to suspend pouring. Norden swallowed it desperately then lit a cigarette with trembling fingers. "All I need now," he said bitterly, "is a blindfold."

It was eleven-thirty now, and though Ives had lookouts posted to warn of an untimely appearance by Lurie, he thought it best to clear for action. A tape-recorder, its spool wound for two hours' running-time, was planted in a cupboard and the invaluable Bonner had substituted for one of the motel's lamps an undistinguished fixture the bulbs of which were lighted by a battery so that the dangling wire actually connected to the recorder. The shade housed a sensitive directional microphone. Sergeant Bonner started the device, checking for noise or vibration, and it was left running.

Norden looked like a horse with a broken leg who knew he was about to be abandoned to die.

"You're doing fine," Blaise told him reassuringly on the way out.

Bonner stayed on the dark side of Norden's bungalow, his own gun loose in its holster, crouched at a window where the shade had been adjusted to give him a meager slice of light. The Lieutenant and Blaise went into the adjoining bungalow. A thin, nervous crackling issued from a loudspeaker on the floor, over which they heard the heavy sound of Norden's footsteps, the noise rising and receding as he paced the room. Then the footsteps stopped and there was a creaking sound, followed an instant later by a gurgling splash.

"He's at the whiskey," said Ives in a matter-of-fact tone. "Well, he can use it."

"Think he'll be all right?" asked Blaise.

Ives nodded confidently. "Do you suppose I'd risk it if I didn't think so? It's a hundred to one Lurie won't try anything here, and if he should, Bonner is the best shot in the Department. My main concern is whether or not he talks."

"I think he will," said Blaise. "He won't just take Norden's word that these are all the drawings. He'll try to . . ."

Ives gripped his wrist as Lurie's voice came over the speaker. "I'm a few minutes early," he was saying in his grave, deliberate voice. "I'm pleased to find you at home."

They heard Norden fiddling with the bolts. "I don't think the streets in this neighborhood are safe at night," he said.

Ives seemed to relax. "He'll be all right," he whispered to Blaise.

"Let me see the three drawings," Lurie said casually.

"Two drawings. I gave you one at the house."

"So you did." There was a momentary pause, then Lurie said, "I myself am not a suspicious type but my colleague is inclined to think that you may be holding back a few things as security for your old age."

"I'm not. I had four of Weldon's drawings originally. I gave one to Simon Edgerton, left you another tonight, I've got two more and that's all."

"I hope so. Even an impoverished old age is better than none. I'm giving you a great deal of money, you know."

"Because you've got a hell of a lot at stake." Blaise was gratified to hear Norden take a line he had suggested. "You've got at least three more fakes and with me out of the way there's nothing to stop you from unloading them."

"I'm well aware of that," said Lurie calmly. "However, the proceeds from our pleasant little counterfeits do not represent a bottomless pit of money. Frankly, I was inclined to think we had too many partners to begin with. To be sure, the ranks have thinned out somewhat. You might speculate for a moment on the hazards of the career you are embracing. Would you care to know what actuarial tables predict as the life-span of the average blackmailer? No? Well, perhaps the subject is a depressing one." In a brisk, businesslike manner, he said, "I've brought the money." There was a pause, probably for its exhibition, then, "Let me see the drawings."

Ives, still listening and waiting, had nevertheless moved to the door. The microphone next door picked up and transported the rustle of papers, then there was only the faint buzz of the apparatus.

"Nice," said Lurie. "Oh, very nice! How frustrating it must have been for Weldon to have this marvelous talent locked up in him!"

Something strained and taut in Lurie's voice made Blaise throw a warning glance at Ives.

"These are good enough to fool anyone," Lurie was saying. "Actually, for all I know these might be genuine

Renoirs. This one on top has even once been mounted, as if it had been exhibited somewhere. There are marks of tape in the corners."

"I wanted—I tried to sell it when I was ducking the police," muttered Norden in a frightened, quavering voice.

"You lying stool-pigeon!" bellowed Lurie. "What kind of drawings are these?"

Ives yanked the door open, and gun in hand jumped from the top step. Blaise followed him, just as two shots were fired almost simultaneously. Sergeant Bonner, also with his automatic ready, reached the front of the bungalow from his post as Ives rushed up, then the door banged open silhouetting Lurie as in a frame. He was clutching his shattered, bloody right wrist, his face twisted with pain, but when he saw the police and Blaise he dropped both arms and forced the muscles of his face into some part of their accustomed composure. Hugh Norden, unharmed but green with fright, leaned weakly against the cupboard in the background.

"This way out," said Ives quietly, and Lurie obediently descended, following the two detectives to the waiting car.

31

THOUGH A MAN of erratic and inconstant personal habit and taste, in some minute particulars Lucas Edgerton followed a rigid and inflexible pattern. One of these was his breakfast, served to him alone every morning at seven-thirty in the huge dining room. He might appear in a ragged burnoose and a fez, but the butler and houseman were in impeccable livery; his breakfast might consist of one bite of toast and a cup of coffee, but the sideboard was crowded with silver dishes and covers offering an enormous variety of foods.

The hour itself generally afforded privacy. Beyond that, it was a rare being who would face the ruling Edgerton on an empty stomach. He betrayed no surprise, however, when Cassy padded in, her slippers scuffing the thick rug. She was wearing a housecoat, some inches of nightgown protruding at the hem.

"Damn it, Cassy," said Edgerton, who was wearing a blue blazer with brass buttons over his pajama coat, "can't you get decently dressed for breakfast?"

Cassy ignored him. "I want," she said dreamily to the startled houseman, "caviar, blini with sour cream, and a pint of champagne." Edgerton's coffee cup banged the saucer in his astonishment, and she turned to him. "Do not unquiet yourself," she said loftily. "I have odd whims, but I'm not pregnant."

"Fine talk," muttered Edgerton. Then he looked up at Jennings. "You heard Miss Cassandra," he roared. "Get a move on."

"Yes, sir."

Cassy smiled. "Orange juice, toast and coffee, Jennings," she said meekly.

"Yes, Miss," sighed the butler.

Edgerton ate his scrambled eggs, concentrating on each fragment as if he were determining its molecular weight.

"I talked to Blaise," said Cassy.

Edgerton nodded. "God-damn G-man," he muttered. "Seen too many movies. Damn things have sapped his brain."

234

"He's coming out," she continued imperturbably.

Edgerton shrugged. "Don't suppose I could stop him. I remember," he added bitterly, "when this place used to be private property. Nothing but a lousy public picnic ground now."

"You need more contact with the outside world," said Cassy severely. "This gilded hermitage has made you grumpy, arbitrary, pig-headed and vain. However, Blaise and I are going to live with you for the first few years. The house will be filled with the laughter of young people, and, who knows, perhaps the patter of little feet."

"Can I keep my room," asked Edgerton bitterly, "or will you be needing it?"

Jennings materialized with her breakfast and cleared Edgerton's place before retiring into the pantry again.

"Are you joking—about Blaise?" asked Edgerton in a subdued tone.

She shook her head gravely. "No, I'm not. We're getting married." There was still a note of defiance in her voice.

"Right away?"

"Today. 'Act—act in the living present,' " she quoted to bolster this announcement.

Edgerton said nothing at once but after tentative advances and withdrawals reached out and patted her hand awkwardly. "All right, Cassy," he murmured gently.

At this sudden and warm surrender Cassy broke into tears. Pained by this development, Edgerton inched his chair around. "It's all right, Cassy," he repeated uncomfortably, and then, in more predictable tones, "Goddamn it, Cassy, stop crying! It's all right, I say."

"You don't mind?" she blubbered.

"What the hell—I suppose you've got to marry somebody."

"I do. I'm all matured and everything." She took the handkerchief he extended and mopped up daintily. "By the way, you've never told me about the birds and the bees and stuff like that. This is just about your last chance."

"I'll buy you a book. Incidentally, in your girlish enthusiasm I don't suppose you managed to suppress the facts about your income, did you?"

"He knew," said Cassy proudly. "He checked up right away. He's really awfully smart."

"You were able to overcome his manly opposition to living on your money?"

"The facts are, as you darn well know, that Blaise is very successful." She shut off his attempted interruption. "Oh, don't give me that old story about your being his only client. Today you need him more than he needs you. He was right about the forgeries, and you were as wrong as Christmas in July. If he isn't working for you today and from now on, people are going to be asking themselves why he was fired and probably coming to the conclusion that he got canned because he was too smart and too honest to have access to the great Edgerton Collection. Mix that," she concluded with great satisfaction, "in your brown umber, add a touch of zinc white, and smoke it."

"He's thought of all that, has he?"

"I've thought of it, and I'm not the type to keep secrets from my husband."

Edgerton pushed back his chair. "You'll make a great wife for an art dealer, Cassy."

"That's my plan," she answered firmly. "Bear it in mind if you still want to fire Blaise."

"Fire him?" Edgerton looked shocked. "I want to buy a piece of the business."

32

THE MORNING PAPERS were scattered all over the desk and table in the library, glaring headlines and smudged half-tones telling the story of last night's exploits. Blaise figured prominently in these, and his first act on entering the library was to gather them and drop the bundle in the fireplace.

"They shot my bad profile," he complained, looking at the subdued group around Edgerton. Wesley Corum, as usual dressed as for an autopsy, rewarded him with a weak smile, but neither Victor Grandi nor Miriam Wayne, both of whom were present, ventured any comment.

"You're a red-hot celebrity," sneered Edgerton. "I'm hoping you'll give me your autograph."

"I've already been invited to appear," Blaise informed him, "on 'Meet the People' and I think I can arrange a booking for you on 'It Pays to Be Ignorant.'"

For a moment it seemed that Edgerton was about to shoot up like a rocket, but he subsided at last. "I guess I had that coming to me," he said, with some difficulty.

"I think we have all underestimated Mr. Blaise," Grandi interposed smoothly. "I, for one, wish to express my complete admiration."

Dr. Corum nodded soberly. "And I."

"You know how I feel," said Miriam Wayne, and Blaise smiled. "Yes, I think I do."

He handed Edgerton the three rolled-up drawings. "Anyway, you earned an assist."

"I'll be damned!" said Edgerton softly, when he

smoothed out the drawings. He looked up at Miriam sharply. "Did you give him these?"

"No," she answered thoughtfully, "but I think I understand your niece's fainting spell last night."

"Right," said Blaise. "I was collecting these in the gallery. It isn't easy," he added, "to find three early Renoir drawings in a hurry, and Lurie and Astorg had to be convinced that proof of the forgery still existed. You can still have me jugged for breaking and entering. I confess freely."

Edgerton laughed out loud suddenly. "They thought these were forgeries? What muggs!" he chortled happily. "Do they know how they hung themselves?"

"There were some bitter reproaches," said Blaise. "In the heat of recrimination between the partners a good deal of the background of the conspiracy was exposed." His gaze swept the group and there was a momentary silence. It was broken when Dr. Corum cleared his throat nervously.

"My God!" said Edgerton, in an awed voice. "Don't tell me he was in on it?"

A word at a time, like a faltering schoolboy, Dr. Corum said, "I authenticated the painting that was sold to Nathan Ordmann."

"That's no disgrace. I saw it. I was fooled. Anybody would be."

"I vouched for the history of the painting," said Corum, in the same low, hang-dog voice. He tried to meet Edgerton's stare but failed. "I corroborated the background Astorg made up." In what was almost a wail, he continued, "The painting was perfect. I would have taken an oath it was genuine. The rest of it—well, I didn't think that mattered. I needed the fee," he finished miserably.

"It was all very plausible," said Blaise. "Roger Vernet was right here to swear the paintings had been in his family for years. That would carry a lot of weight in itself. By the way, Vernet had no idea the paintings were forged. The story they told him was that they had been bought from Nazis who were in hiding in South America. He didn't object to that despite the fact that both his brothers were murdered by the Germans in Auschwitz."

"Oh, nice," said Edgerton admiringly. "It's quite a cast of characters. Sit down," he said sharply as Corum got unsteadily to his feet. "Don't start slinking out into the night like an unmarried mother in a melodrama." He turned to Blaise. "What else?"

"I believe the floor is mine," said Victor Grandi promptly. With no apparent embarrassment whatever, he went on, "Lieutenant Ives has already notified me that I am to await questioning. You see, our poor Paul Weldon, while undoubtedly an enormously skillful painter, was a poor student and only a fair chemist. Quite a long time ago he started coming to me with questions about the composition of colors and it was soon obvious that he was attempting to build his palette in imitation of Renoir. The poor chap—his first attempts were ludicrously bad."

"You helped him?" demanded Edgerton.

"Certainly."

"Why?"

Grandi smiled. "Why not? I knew that whatever forgeries he made would be sold to sophisticated, opulent dealers and collectors. My work has not filled me with boundless respect for this manifestation of our culture."

"Meaning me, I suppose," said Edgerton dourly.

"I was delighted to give Weldon all the assistance in

my power," said Grandi coolly. "I did not, however, except for the pleasure it gave me, receive a fee. You may ascribe my participation to a labor of love."

"Get out," said Edgerton harshly.

"Gladly." Grandi paused on his way to the door, addressing Blaise directly. "I did not know that Simon Edgerton was involved in any way with Weldon, Lurie or the forgeries." He said this simply and directly, and then, with a little bow, added, "I will await Lieutenant Ives in my cottage."

"Don't do anything rash," advised Blaise. "When I left Lieutenant Ives he was trying to figure out what laws you'd broken and he hadn't found one."

Grandi smiled. "I think far too much of myself even to consider self-destruction, Mr. Blaise." He bowed again, and was gone.

"Which the hell side are you on?" asked Edgerton irritably.

"I like him," said Blaise candidly. "He told the truth about what he did for Weldon. More than that, he practically pushed me into action on the forgeries when everyone else was steering me wrong or blowing dust in my face."

"I want to make it plain," said Dr. Corum hoarsely, "that I was no part of any plot. I did a foolish and greedy thing, Lucas, but on my word of honor, I knew nothing of what was involved, or that Simon . . ."

"Oh, be quiet, Wesley. Nobody suspects you of being anything more than a fathead and I've known that for thirty years. If you were strapped and needed a fee, you should have come to me . . ." As Corum, pale with shock, rocked unsteadily, Edgerton jumped to his side. "Easy now. Easy, Wes." He supported the wilting critic with his arm. "Come on into the house. You need a rest."

"Good idea," said Blaise. He stepped up to help, but Edgerton waved him away. He watched the faltering departure of the two men, Edgerton maintaining a running commentary of sympathy and warmth. Then he turned to look at Miriam Wayne. She was leaning back against a low cabinet. "Amazing what odd reactions an act of violence churns up. I thought the old man's heart was set in a hand-carved frame, shellacked and lacquered against the elements."

"Perhaps you bring out the best in people," the girl said mildly. "We are all very much in your debt," she added in a formal tone that was belied by her look of amusement.

"I did only what any real, red-blooded American boy would have done," said Blaise. "Besides, until a few petty details are filled in—the identity of the murderer, for instance—it doesn't really amount to very much."

"I thought"—her low voice was barely audible in the huge room—"we all thought it was Lurie."

"So did I. Another of my cockeyed ideas."

"Oh, well," said Miriam, with more composure now, "I'm sure you'll have another theory before long."

"I've got it." Blaise sat down on the edge of the long paper-strewn table. The girl was still in her position against the cabinet, but her hands now gripped the edge so that her knuckles showed as dead white bulges. "Walk out that door," said Blaise quietly, "and you'll find out what it is."

She looked at him steadily, then let go of the cabinet edge, removing her hands slowly, first one and then the other. She walked to the library door, her head held high, and as she threw the door open wide, Sergeant Bonner stepped up to fill the doorway.

"Will you wait, please, Miss?" he said politely. He

reached in for the knob, the girl taking two short backward steps to let him close the door. She did not turn to face Blaise and there was an oppressive silence broken by the rasping of a match as he lit a cigarette.

"That was Sergeant Bonner, Miriam. I believe you talked to him on the phone."

She swung around. "That's not true!" she cried.

"Take it easy," cautioned Blaise. "Why be so vehement about that? Before you know it," he went on gently, "you'll be giving yourself away."

She looked up. Her dark eyes were luminous. "I see that Lurie has talked some nonsense." She hesitated. "I did supply the books and drawings Weldon worked from. That much is true. I didn't want to, but Lurie threatened me."

"What else is true?" asked Blaise. "Were you in love with Simon, or did it just seem like an advantageous marriage?"

"I loved Simon." Her voice was low, a little shaky. "And he was in love with me."

"The day I arrived," said Blaise, "Simon was in a state of pure terror. It was obvious when I'd been here an hour that he was stealing from the collection and was terrified of exposure. But later on, the same night, when I accused him of that he laughed at me. I know now what happened in the interim."

"I don't care," said Miriam sharply. "I've admitted my own part in this. Do what you like."

"Simon didn't know the paintings were forgeries, did he, Miriam? He thought he was stealing them from the collection, and that you were covering up for him. That was your hold on him."

"That's a lie!" Her voice came explosively. "Don't

you see that Lurie and Astorg are trying to distract you from themselves?"

"Oddly enough," he told her, "this is all my idea. Lurie did say that you insisted on handling Simon yourself, keeping him in the dark about the forgeries. He thinks your plan was to force Simon to marry you. If Simon tried to shake you, you could expose him to his father."

"A pack of lies," she said contemptuously. "Lurie is jealous, always has been."

"The night he was killed," said Blaise steadily, "Simon learned from Hugh Norden that the Renoirs were forgeries. He came home, woke you up, if you were asleep, and told you he was out from under the whip-hand. You knew then that you'd lost him forever. Then he went to the gallery to return the cards he'd stolen from me. That gave you a few minutes to think beautiful thoughts. When he emerged, you were waiting for him. You could get up close, maybe to plead for another chance—it had to be someone he knew pretty well to fire at point-blank range like that."

"You're mad! You're talking absolute nonsense."

"Don't listen," suggested Blaise. "Read an improving book, write a letter, or—if your thoughts turn in that direction—make your will."

"You heartless son-of-a-bitch!"

"I suppose I should be sorry for you," said Blaise. "But then I think of Simon, and I think of Paul Weldon, off his neurotic perch with anxiety and drink, not even a real threat to your safety, but you saw a chance to pin everything on him. It only meant one more killing, an easy one, considering the shape he was in. Am I boring you?" he asked politely.

243

She struck at him suddenly, a round-house slap, then cried out in pain as Blaise caught her wrist an inch from his face. He held her like this while her free hand lashed out impotently.

"I see that I'm not boring you. I'm glad. You jumped too soon and too high when I said you had talked to Sergeant Bonner on the phone. As a matter of fact, that's when Lieutenant Ives began to measure you for this part. Weldon was drunk, incoherent and rambling; anyone might have imitated speech like that, even a woman provided her voice was naturally low. But it had to be someone who knew that I was out, and that Bonner, who had never heard Weldon's voice—or yours—was in my room waiting for the call. That narrowed it down to someone in this household and Corum and Edgerton were both with me. Weldon was desperate for money because we know now that Lurie had taken what he had hidden in the studio. He was washed up, frantic to get away. Despite that he spent twenty-five minutes here *after* he locked Cassy in the vault. He spent that time with you, Miriam, pleading for help. Needless to say, he got it."

He was still holding her wrist but her thrashings had stopped. When he relaxed his grip she staggered back and slumped into a chair. Her eyes were boring into his, as if searching for an avenue of escape. "You can't prove that," she said hoarsely. "Not a word of it."

"Ives can," said Blaise, "and he will. Everything in your apartment has been carted downtown and Ives is up in your room in the house. Did you burn everything you wore in that last scene with Simon Edgerton, or when you snuggled up to Paul Weldon in the car? Are you counting on Kenneth Lurie to save your pretty neck if it means risking his own?"

She buried her face in both hands suddenly and a

shudder rocked her slim body. There was a choking sound, as though she were gasping for breath, then great, anguished sobs.

Blaise watched her for a moment and then turned away when he heard the door open quietly. It was Lieutenant Ives, grim and hollow-eyed in his rumpled clothes. He was holding the door open.

A little wind was whipping in from the sea as Blaise came out, and he was grateful for the clean, stinging breeze. He walked across the lawn to the beach and he saw Cassy far out on the rocks jutting into the surf. She was waving to him, scrambling back in, and he stood at the base of the jetty until she appeared overhead. He raised his arms, bracing himself in the loose sand, and she jumped.